HOPELESSLY

Wild

LEESA BOW

ISBN: 978-0-6456871-1-8

Editing by Swish Design & Editing
Proofing by Swish Design & Editing
Editing by Lauren at Creating Ink
Cover design by Letitia at RBA Designs
Photography by Rafa G Catala
Cover Model is Alejandro Caracuel
Cover Image Copyright 2022

Please join my mailing list to be notified of Leesa's latest releases.

You can learn more about me on my website.

If you're on Facebook, I haver a reader group where I chat about books, offer giveaways, and sneak peeks of upcoming books.

You can join here.

To Jamie-Lee,
My eldest, beautiful daughter.
A woman with a heart equally wild, devoted, and grounded.
You remind me of Eden.
Adventurous at heart.
Yet you adapt effortlessly to be who you need to be—for those you love.

A NOTE FOR THE READER

This book's heroine is Australian, and, as such, some euphemisms and slang words that form part of the UK/Australian spoken word are included for authenticity.

Please remember that the words are not misspelled or incorrect.

If you would like further explanation or to discuss the translation or meaning of a particular word, please do not hesitate to contact the author. For your convenience, contact details have been provided at the end of this book. Also provided below is a limited dictionary of explanations for your convenience.

DICTIONARY

Bloody – British slang meaning 'very' but can also be used as an expletive.

Dickhead – Idiot or jerk.

Footy – Football. Australian rules for football.

Stuff up – British and Australian slang for a big mistake.

Mum – Australian for Mom.
Tepui – Flat-top mountain found in Venezuela

1

EDEN

The rainforest is dying.

A scent not born from fire—instead, it's a distinct stench of death like decaying meat.

Wet and musty.

Rotten wood.

Mold.

A smell I can't escape since it's rained nonstop every day for the past two weeks.

When I arrived in mid-September, we had sunshine and occasional drizzly rain.

"You brought the sunshine with you," Samuel had told me. "At least you missed the worst of the rainy season."

What the hell is this?

Never have I seen so much rain.

A blanket of water falls from the sky every minute, and I can barely see ten feet in front of me. I'm a prisoner in the hut, only venturing out to visit the jungle toilet, and I hold off as long as possible. My soaked, muddy shoes remain near the hut entrance. I shifted my belongings away from the open windows, even though there's barely a puff of wind to blow the rain anywhere except directly downward. The grass-thatched roof overhangs the structure, directing rain runoff to form a waterfall imprisoning us in a fluid fence. The overspill creates small rivers throughout the village. A moat-like trench surrounds Samuel's hut, and the past few days has seen the water lap at the entrance, concealing the two wooden steps below the doorway.

Everything smells damp. There's no escaping the mildewy aroma. Only the raucous insects distract your thoughts, and I wish they would shut up.

During the day, I'm left to go stir-crazy while Samuel attempts to save some of the precious herbs. He pots the plants and lugs the clay pots into the long house. Many of the plants thrive, being acclimatized to this weather. Only the shaman is afraid of losing the rare ones, and considering we've had around twenty inches of rain in a short period, the water isn't draining away fast enough, and the plants sink in a deluge of muddy water.

Fungus is a threat, and after Samuel's story of how fungus can grow inside an ant until it bursts out of its thorax, I know the jungle has the power to control every living species that lives in her womb. No single species will dominate, and the balance can be horrific.

It's why I need to protect the one that grows in my womb from the unseen dangers lurking in the green cavern on the edge of the village.

Opening my sack, I retrieve the plastic bag from the bottom and unwind the tightly wrapped package. It's the one thing I have avoided for months. Only today, I'm unsettled and need to divert my thoughts from the miserable weather and the fact I may as well be in a prison cell.

I push on the tiny brass button before yanking at the flap binding the diary to the lock.

Shit.

Scurrying through some instruments on Samuel's workbench, I find a small steel-pointy object he has used on wounds and poke it at the lock. It doesn't fit. I rustle through his bag, and at the bottom, I find a random paperclip. Pulling the sharp end away, I jab the lock and twist several times, using more force than necessary.

"Give me a break," I yell and toss the book against the wall. Reflecting my patience, the flap snaps on impact and lands open on the ground. I let out a gasp and scoop it up, brushing dust from the pages and cover. I slide into the hammock, curl into a lazy C-shape, and open Gran's diary at the beginning.

To My Darling Ivy on your 18th birthday.
All my love,
Albert xx

I suck in a breath and turn to the first page.

18th January 1956

My first entry in my new diary from Albert.
He surprised me, and I think he understands me better than I understand myself.

I didn't expect us to last since I plan to move away from him

3

for at least three years while I live at the hospital. Albert claims to understand, but three years is a long time apart.

It's the start of my new life after working at the local delicatessen since finishing school two years ago.

Two years. And I've been with Albert for almost a year. Tonight, I'm heading to his house because his parents are out playing cards with his relatives. He said the card games can continue into the early hours of the morning. I know what he's implying.

I'm not afraid. In fact, I'm excited knowing we will be alone.

I turn the page back and forth, but that entry doesn't continue. Hell, was that my grandparents' first time? My breath catches, and guilt fills me knowing I'm reading my grandmother's private notes, only I can't look away.

19th January 1956

Last night wasn't as bad as I'd thought it was going to be—not after the stories I'd heard from the other girls. Maybe it's because we have come close on other occasions. This time he was prepared. The latex hurt a little, so I need to find an alternative, and I'm not sure who to ask. I'm not telling anyone I have lost my virginity because I don't want them to judge me. And they will judge.

Last night, Albert accepted my decision about nursing.

6th February 1956

Do they really expect us to wear these starched uniforms? Matron has a ruler and measured the length of my tunic. After one day, I can predict we will not get along. But I want this more than anything, so I will have to abide by the rules. At least my room in the nurses' quarters is near Brenda's room.

"Hey."

I drop the diary and scramble out of the hammock.

Samuel runs his fingers along the netting covering the doorway and adheres the mosquito net to the edges. Leaning forward, he shakes water from his hair as though he has just stepped out of a shower.

"How are you feeling?" He wipes his hands over his face and flicks water from his fingers before checking the net remains secure on our open windows.

"Good. I'm..." I hesitate. His gaze lands on the diary in the hammock. "I have Gran's diary, and up to now, I was too afraid to read it. The jammed lock didn't help, but I picked it. I found a paperclip in your bag, and I think it loosened the clasp." I fail to mention the impact of the diary landing on the wall resulted from my frustration of acting like a caged animal. He wouldn't know it now, for in the short time reading Gran's words, it feels as though I'm embarking on a journey with her. I'm in her time warp, and it's almost serene.

He raises a solitary brow. "My only paperclip?"

Is he seriously concerned about one paperclip?

"So you're not concerned about the fact I foraged through your stuff or that I'm learning about my grandmother?" I fold my arms over my chest and release them with a sudden ache. Every week my boobs are growing and becoming more uncomfortable.

"You're reading about her past. Something we can't change. So, no, it doesn't concern me. The only thing that matters to me is you. It's the first thing I asked when I stepped inside." He takes me in his wet arms and rubs his hands up and down my back. The moisture left on his skin gives some relief to the muggy heat, so I rest my cheek on his chest, hoping to cool my face. "So, how are you?"

I turn to hide my face in his hard chest. "Hormonal," I murmur. "I'm sorry if I've been narky these past few days, but I am going stir-crazy. I mean, if you were here with me then—"

He takes my shoulders and pries me off him. "I'm here. I told the shaman I need to focus on you. I can't do much more until the rain settles."

"Which is when? I can't believe how much I miss the weather app or the news. I mean, even if I could play my Spotify list, it would help. There's nothing to do." A mischievous smile tweaks my lips. "I thought about reading your notebooks, but when I picked up one of them, I didn't even get through the first page of not understanding half of it. The medical terminology? I'm not even pretending to know what you're talking about." I throw my arms in the air. "So, I decided today was the day I faced my fear and open Gran's diary."

His lips curl into a smile. "Face your fear." A light chuckle bursts from him. "You're in the jungle. You traveled here alone, and your fear is in a small book with words of the past?"

"You wouldn't understand." I turn and scoop water

from the bowl in the corner and cover it again with weaved twine.

"I think I'd understand, considering my past. You're lucky I have all day for you to tell me what spooks you most." He comes over, bundles me in his arms, and carries me to the hammock. He curses when he lays me down and swats at the buzzing above his head. A small clay dish on the bench holds the balm he uses to protect us from the mosquitoes. Samuel grabs it and stops the hammock from swaying before lathering it over my face, arms, and legs. I could do it, only it's like a relaxation massage by the one person whose touch I crave. Flicking my hair from my shoulders, I expose my breasts. I close my eyes, relishing the way his hands make circles over my skin, over my stomach, around my breasts, to my shoulders, and my neck. Warm fingers glide down to my breasts again, the action slower with a gentle squeeze. I open my eyes and meet the fire in his blue hues.

"Did you say you had all day?" I rasp between moans.

"I do." He places the tub of balm on the ground. "I'll do your back after."

"After?"

He leans in, lowering his lips to mine. I sigh into his mouth, and it's enough for him to lift a leg onto the hammock. A giggle passes my lips when the hammock sways.

"You're losing your touch."

He lifts his head and frowns at me.

"Your balance. Not your touch with me." Do I have to explain everything to him? I know my Aussie lingo confuses him at times, but Samuel has been away from society so long that he misses the joke.

"Just kiss me already," I say. Wrapping my hand around the back of his neck, I guide his lips to mine.

The hammock rocks a little more when his entire weight is beside me. He lifts my knee, and since I'm only wearing a grass skirt, he arouses me with ease. "Have you been thinking about me?" he whispers.

"Yes." Our kiss intensifies, our tongues entwine, and my body craves him inside of me. "I'm always ready for you." My hormones have me wanting him all the time. Every hour if I could.

He climbs over me with the balance of a cat, hovers until the sway of the hammock is minimal.

"How are you going to cope when we're back in society, and I wear underwear?" I smile before my hand guides him to my entrance. The look he gives me is a touch unsettling, as though he hasn't contemplated us both returning any time soon. I don't have time to dwell. His mouth covers my lips, his tongue seeks mine and he tastes me as though he has been starved for weeks. The butterfly sensation of fluttering in my stomach transforms to the wings of a hummingbird hovering. Lust streams through every part of me. Samuel loves me slowly, intimately, the hammock barely rocks. His thrusts are deep, and I feel all of him. He builds slowly, the hammock moving with him. A gentle sway while making love is my new favorite thing. A romantic motion and I'll take it as there are no red roses or romantic private restaurant dinner dates. His hands glide smoothly over my oiled skin. His fingers caress one breast, my nipples harden and then he finds the other. Eyes closed, I savor his touch, moan his name as my orgasm builds. Samuel thrusts faster, and faster until the bliss overwhelms everything else, and I sigh his name, exhausted with pleasure. Exhausted as my labia remain swollen from last night. Not a complaint, I'm happy to have an orgasm more than once a day. My hormones demand it. Yet we remain discreet about our sex life not wanting to offend the Ularans which is why our special times are when no-one else is around. The last thing I want is to be sent away.

So, I'll take every opportunity to love him, blind to what tomorrow brings. My limited time is like a bomb ticking away inside my heart.

2

EDEN

Sun blooms over the treetops—an invitation to a new day. The raw light streams into the hut and onto the empty hammock beside me. Absent of any breeze, the choking heat makes me crazy in my dreams, and last night was no exception.

Beyond our hut, life pulses with new vitality. The squawk of insects and screeching monkeys echo from the thriving jungle. I stumble out of my hammock to peer out the netted doorway and sense the jungle has crept closer to the village overnight.

Steam rises from the leaves of the low-lying vines, threatening to strangle everything in its path. My shoulders fall with every sharp breath of thick air. It's early morning, and yet the layer of sweat covering my bare chest glistens in the filtered light.

Samuel said he'd be back by lunch. Many hours remain to amuse myself, and although the rain has eased, I'm not enticed to leave the hut until some of the mud hardens. When I have to relieve myself, the mosquitoes circling above my head sound like a swarm. The horror stories of all the mosquito-transmitted diseases spook me enough to be mindful.

I swat at one buzzing near my ear. In defeat, I fasten the protective net and retrieve the balm to cover my face and limbs. During the long, lonely hours while Samuel works, I question my sanity in being here, risking my and my baby's life for him.

A banana and a basket of berries sit on the bench near a bowl of clean water—my breakfast. I eat the fruit as slow as possible to pass the time until more light filters in. Today, I have a date with my grandmother.

I retrieve her diary and the family photographs from my backpack. I take my favorite one of Gran and slide it inside the diary's cover. Clambering into the hammock, I'm ready to be transported to 1956.

4th June 1956

Last night Brenda and I snuck out of the nurses' quarters window when the matron's bedroom light went out. Mary kept watch, ensuring the window remained open around midnight for when we returned.

We giggled as we ran across the wet path, holding each other's hand so we didn't slip over. My other hand was supporting my bra where I hid the sheath. Mary put me on to it, and I know she won't tell. It felt weird against my skin, a jellyfish texture. Brenda was more concerned about the rain flattening her curls. She wanted to impress Jonathon far more than I did Albert. She told me she knew Jonathon was the one for her. It made me a little envious how she knew what her heart desired before getting to know a man properly. A quick wedding, a baby straight away, and to give up nursing? I couldn't fathom not nursing. Women stop working when they marry or fall pregnant. Here, it's enforced without a choice. I've worked hard, and I'll not give it up because it's expected all women want is to be married and have children.

The idea of helping others gives me much more happiness.

My mother had told me happiness is all that matters.

Every time I think about traveling and discovering new places, I get a tingling along my spine. It's the rush I thrive on, and it's why I want to work in the emergency department.

Like tonight. The rush of sneaking out to meet Albert was half the fun. He makes me laugh, but I wonder if it's enough? Sure, he's tall, dark, and handsome. He's got eyes the color of whiskey and a heart so kind. How could I say no to him? Ever? Not even in the back of a car.

It's kind of fun.

Brenda wants to wait until they're married.

It's why she wants to rush into a wedding, especially after I told her how good it feels. The secrecy doesn't bother me. I know he loves me. I guess I love him too. But I'm not sure if I want to marry him... yet. There's so much more I want to do. Travel.

Nurse overseas.

Live!

One page and it tells me so much about my grandmother. I turn the page as though I'm reading a great book. Only the next few entries are about my grandfather and her private times, so I skip those.

I'm surprised by the time lapse between her entries. There's no mention of special times like birthdays or her parents.

17th December 1956

Today I met a doctor who told me all about his travels. It wasn't the discovering unknown places or staying in luxury hotels that impressed me, but his time volunteering in Africa and South America.
It sounded so exciting, and listening to him, I know, in my heart, it's what I want to do. Ethiopia is where I want to travel. Africa, the mother country. The large animals, well, I wish I had enough money saved so I could leave now. I'm having lunch with him in the cafeteria tomorrow.
I have many questions I want to ask. First, I need to set a plan for my savings. Not only to get there but how much I'll need to live on if I'm away for twelve months or more.

I take a moment to absorb my grandmother's words. No mention of Christmas. Only her dreams and not a word about my grandfather. Is she still with him? I flip the page and realize she is because the next few lines are about intimate times. More private times follow on several pages, but on skimming the words, not once do I find mention of the word *love*.

13th September 1957

Matron hates me.
I wonder if she knows I've been sneaking out at night?
Maybe she likes Dr. Anderson? That could be it since she didn't stop staring at me when I sat with him at lunch. When I giggled—well, laughed loudly—at his story, she came over to

the table and stood over me and said, "Nurse, isn't it time you went back to the ward? Your lunch break is over."
She didn't like that I had a reply and told her I was on the afternoon shift.
"Then keep it down," she said like I was a child. "You're disturbing the other staff."
She is so prim. I bet she's frigid too.

Shit. My gran is a bad ass.

I'm not ready to stop reading so I turn the page.

18th December 1957

Albert's grandparents died last month. As sad as it was, his cousin inherited money since they were the next generation of first-born males. The concept angered me, knowing the daughters of his uncles got nothing. Albert is an only child, so there were no siblings to feel sorry for because I'd be speaking up if I were his sister.
Family. I'm glad I'm not close to my parents. But there are days I'd be grateful for some support because I worry about where I'm going to live when I finish nursing. Without even asking, I know what my dad would say. "Marry Albert."
Albert is always thinking of our future even though I never bring it up with him. How can I when the unknown scares me?
He has a surprise for me for Christmas.
I'm nervous because I hope it's not a proposal.

My poor Pop. Even reading between the lines, I can tell how much he loves Gran.

2nd January 1958

*Albert has bought a motel complex. Three levels on the
esplanade at Glenelg. He said we could run it together, have a
family, and set up a future for them. On paper, it makes sense.
He purchased it at a bargain price because the building needs
repair. Only I never envisaged this as my future. He didn't
even ask me if it's what I wanted.*
*It's 'my' Christmas present, and now I feel bad for being
ungrateful.*
I'm so confused.
He hasn't spoken to me in a week.

Shit. I can imagine them fighting. I turn the diary and
look at the cover as though it's more valuable than any
diamond. I'm glad to be on this journey with them. To
think this is the beginning of my family's business. Monte
Hotel's birth. At some point in time, my parents changed
it from motel to hotel.

19th January 1958

Albert is talking to me again.
I knew it wouldn't last because he can't keep his hands off me.

I stop reading and flick the page, then double-check the
dates. It's been more than a year since her last entry.
What happened during that time?

18th February 1959

I intend to undertake a further year of study and do the
Heidelberg Infectious Disease Course at Heidelberg Hospital.
It's the only place that offers the course, and it's in Melbourne.
I don't know how to break the news to Albert.
Brenda wants to study midwifery because she wants a family
and feels like it would help her. If Jonathon proposes
beforehand, then she's quitting.
Eight more weeks, and I'll be a qualified nurse.
My father said I'd never finish.
I can't wait to wave my certificate in his face if I see him.
They haven't visited in over a year, so I won't hold my breath.
The last thing he told me was just to be a good girl and marry
Albert.

My guess? That's the worst thing her father could've said.

29th April 1959

Mary smuggled in bottles of beer for Brenda and me to
celebrate our graduation. We were so drunk that she had to
keep coming to our rooms and shushing us as she could hear us
all the way down the corridor.
Mary is mentoring Brenda because Mary has almost finished
her midwifery course.
Brenda keeps crying about me leaving. She said it won't be the
same without me. Giving in to emotion, I allowed myself to cry
because she's more like a sister to me than a friend. I'll miss her
more than anyone.
Albert has finally come around to accepting I'm leaving. He
admitted it might be for the best as he spends most of his time
at the motel, getting it up and running again. In a way, it has
been perfect for him. He finished his plumbing trade and can

fix any of those issues in the building. We've barely seen each other with my studies and Albert working two jobs, so it won't make a world of difference by my being in Melbourne. We'll work out special times when he can catch the bus and visit on weekends, and his parents can manage the motel. His parents spend most of their days helping him, anyway.

I guess I'm a little jealous of the support of his parents. I know he's doing it for us. I'm just not ready to commit to him. Some days I see him as the one. But when he becomes frustrated by my ambition to have a career, I wonder if he's the right person for me.

Yet, I can't imagine myself with anyone else.

Or anyone at all.

I close the diary and take a deep breath. I know how this story ends, and yet I'm nervous to read on. Pushing up, I find the bottle of folic acid tablets and down one with water. My bladder is ready to burst. I slip on my shoes and trudge through the muddy soil in slow, exaggerated steps. I want to bathe. Hopefully, I can get down to the stream with most of the flood water filtering in the opposite direction toward the river.

Scanning in all directions before I squat, I let out a sigh because this baby has me peeing far more frequently than I want to.

Something rustles in the undergrowth nearby, so I rush back to the hut, kicking my shoes off, and doing my best to reseal the netting around the doorway. Mud flecks dot my calves, and I don't care because I need to know what happens next.

11th November 1959

One of the few weekends I returned to Adelaide, Albert proposed, surprising me with a ring and flowers. He got down on one knee and asked me like you would ask someone if they wanted a cup of tea.

I saw it coming because he keeps asking me what I'm going to do when I finish. Where will I work?

On his last trip to Melbourne, I cried, saying how confused I was and didn't know where I was going to live.

He told me I didn't have to worry as we had the motel.

I guess he misunderstood.

My career is in nursing, not running a motel.

He had set the whole thing up with Brenda and Jonathon, so they were waiting at the pub for us. Brenda and I drank champagne until our cheeks hurt from giggling.

I can't stop staring at the diamond on my finger.

Only I can't wear it in Melbourne. You're not allowed while you're studying, so it will remain locked in my safe.

I'm still in shock, yet somehow, I know I made the right decision.

He loves me.

It's a weird feeling because it's like I'm lowering a wall and agreeing to let him take care of me. He didn't say those words, but marriage is confusing. I'm scared I'm going to lose who I am to be with someone who loves me.

I also love him, but I'd never ask him to give up anything for me. Yet it's expected, as a woman, my dreams and life are now ones I share with a future husband.

I'm making a promise to myself—my happiness will not be compromised by marriage.

I take a moment to absorb my grandmother's words. I didn't get to know my grandfather like I did my gran since he died when I was a child. My heart is torn. I'm reading a love story and vying for the couple only to know the sadness in how it ends.

The next few pages show how much she loves him because it's only an account of each night they get to share because my grandfather took a week's holiday to visit Gran in Melbourne. So, she snuck out of the nurses' quarters every night for a week.

Dad was born in 1961. So I can safely read on knowing my grandparents were still happy.

29th November 1959

I never believed a nursing subject would excite me like microbiology and pharmacology. I'm excited to be living in the 1950s. I'm spending many hours reading textbooks in my room. It distracts me from getting angry when I think about Albert's parents. They told Albert I couldn't move into the motel until we're married. As if they have a right to tell me what to do.
Albert spoke up for me, and his plan is to have separate rooms until then. The nights they don't stay over, they'll never know if we're sleeping together. All I can think about is sleeping in a double bed with Albert and not in this hard single bed. It will feel strange in a good way.

2nd December 1959

Dr. Anderson visited the hospital to give a talk on mosquito-borne diseases.

I was so excited to speak to him after the lecture. He informed me he's leaving for England in a couple of weeks, so I asked him to send me his address and direct it to Albert's motel. I told him I was still interested in volunteer work. If he has any contacts to please send me their address so I can apply.

The look he gave me made the hairs stand up on the back of my neck.

"But you'll be married by then," he said.

"Are you telling me they won't take me as a volunteer because I'm married? God forbid a woman leave her husband to help the poor. Why am I studying bacteria and diseases if I'm not able to use my skills?"

He smiled and patted my shoulder and told me, "You'll do just fine."

I close the book and smile because I know where I inherited my determination and maybe some of my stubbornness too.

🌴

My eyes flicker open to a soft touch on my hair and forehead.

Squinting and only half awake, my vision clears. It's Kaikare, my beautiful aunt, not Samuel touching me. She smiles, resting her hand on my shoulder.

"I'm okay," I tell her. I take the diary and put it on my other side, away from her. Ridiculous when she can't read it. Yet I'm filled with guilt reading words about her mother when she's entitled to the truth more so than me. When I finish reading Gran's diary, I'll ask Samuel to translate parts for Kaikare. A filtered version, depending on how the story pans out.

She points to the bowl of water. Her hand goes to her mouth as though she's scooping water from the river to drink. She makes me smile, and even though we have been apart for days, something has passed between us. She's my family, and while our societies and communities have raised us in different ways, an understanding that we're of the same blood subconsciously makes us closer. Even when I first came to the village, we both connected quickly. Maybe the universe was telling me something.

I scramble out of the hammock. The last thing I need is for her to report back to her father that I'm tired, weak, or not coping.

Is it why she's here?

Samuel said he'd be back by lunch. Maybe he sent her?

I walk over to the water bowl and scoop myself a glass of fresh water. When I turn around, I find the manual sphygmomanometer on Samuel's bench.

Surely, a week hasn't passed since I had my blood pressure taken. Days pass slowly when trapped in a hut, but when I think of how much time has already passed, I want to panic, knowing every hour is one closer to the day I have to leave.

When I turn, Kaikare is by the hammock looking at the diary. She picks it up and flicks over the pages, studies the leather cover, opens the pages again, and the photograph of Gran falls into her hands. She studies it a moment, then her eyes meet mine. Placing my cup on the bench, I go to her.

All I can do is nod and offer a gentle smile. I lower my gaze to where my hand rests over hers, holding her mother's—my grandmother's—life in words. I wish she could also read it. Although I'm not sure she could or would understand our lifestyle.

A privileged life.

I open my mouth and look her in the eye, ready to say something. Anything. Only words catch in my throat when a single tear cascades down her cheek. Not knowing what else to do, I throw my arms around her and squeeze. With trapped arms by her side, she lays her forehead on my shoulder.

"I'm sorry," I croak.

Sorry for not being able to communicate with you about what your mother was like.

Sorry for upsetting you because as an Ularan, I'm sure she shouldn't be feeling emotions as strong as sadness or anger.

Sorry because I came into your world uninvited and turned your life as you know it upside down.

"What's going on?" Samuel asks from behind us.

I release Kaikare and spin to him. He's covered in mud up to his thigh. With one hand, he leans on the doorway for support, and the way his shoulders slump, I want to ask him if he needs a hand?

Kaikare nods to him, then tosses the diary onto the hammock before rushing past him and out the door.

"What did you do?"

"Nothing. She came in here and saw the diary. She knows it's about Gran because she saw the photograph and shed a tear," I say, exasperated. "You should go after her."

He pushes through the mosquito net, and it floats like a parachute back to the doorway.

It feels like I'm in trouble, yet he can't blame me for Kaikare feeling all this new emotion. It all comes back to secrets.

Kaikare deserves to know about her mother.

3

EDEN

Clueless to time, I pace the room for what seems like hours before the netting separates like a curtain to reveal Samuel's presence.

"Is she okay?" I blurt out before he has both feet inside the hut.

"Yes. Put on your runners. We'll take a walk to the stream." He holds the net wide for me to pass through the doorway to sit on the step and slip on my shoes.

The water is slowly seeping into the earth or making its way to the river systems. In the wet season, new tributaries are temporarily formed. The ground is now muddy with decaying leaves dumped everywhere, along with puddles of water that have nowhere to go. These puddles can also breed more mosquitoes. I turn to the plant I notice out of the corner of my eye. It's a vine in a pot near the doorway and the window. There's another placed on the other side of the doorway, and it reminds me of home—decorative pots of plants strategically placed to make a house more appealing. Only these will not be for decorative reasons.

"These are new."

"The vine is to deter mosquitoes." He walks away, so I plod along after him, consciously lifting my feet with every stride.

"What did you say to Kaikare?" I swat insects away from my face. Macaws shriek from above as if they find my words offensive. If the bloody monkeys can just shut up for five minutes, then I might clear my head.

"Mind this puddle." He points to a shallow pool of water. "It's deeper than it appears." He waits a few seconds before answering as though he's assessing what's ahead. "I told her you only started reading words about her mother's life, and when you understand the words, you'll tell her about it. We chatted about her emotions and how she is feeling things she has never felt before. She's confused as to why she's feeling sad about a woman she never knew."

"I understand."

"It's not about your grandmother. It's not their way. Kaikare is feeling like she doesn't belong in some way, and those feelings of trust and sadness are confusing her as the elders have taught her not to succumb to those emotions. She's feeling not like a failure but almost an intruder. It's like another personality is coming out in her."

"She has our genes." I give an empathetic sigh as I step over tree roots and concentrate not to slip on the decaying leaves and bark forming a layer over the earth.

"No. She has her father's genes, and environmental influences are what she has learned here. You and I..." he motions his finger between us, "... we need to be invisible and not bring our ways to confuse the Ularans. All you know isn't to be revealed here."

I second-guess what I wanted to achieve by coming here. Obviously, I wanted to inform Samuel I was pregnant with his baby. I also wanted the joy of being with him wherever that was because I love him. He loves me too, yet I can't shake the feeling he has no plans to leave Ulara soon.

"I'm still learning, and if we're honest, I'm the intruder. Our baby is due in a matter of weeks. I have to go home soon. I can't keep living day to day waiting for you to say I'm coming home with you, and we live happily ever after."

He stops walking and takes both of my hands in his. "You're no longer an intruder. You're doing great learning their ways, but it will take time." He leans in and kisses my forehead before brushing wayward strands from my eyes. "You can leave at any time. I'd never make you stay. I can't leave until my contract is finished and—"

"What?"

He looks into the jungle as though it holds the answers he seeks. "There's enough evidence the flower from the tepui is a success in cancer treatment."

"One flower. They'll need more than one."

When he nods, my thoughts become thick like fog. "You'll need to make another trip?"

He takes my hand, and we keep walking. "I don't want to assume anything. They can search for other tepuis by helicopter. While I'm here, I'll continue to learn from the shaman and help the community where I can."

"The Ularans mean more to you than a community, right?"

"I know you find it hard to understand, but they are my family now." He hesitates. "Until I met you, they were all I had."

It's an opening for me to say something about his parents, but I decide to focus on us. "So if they find the flower on other tepuis, your contract will end quicker, and you'll be free to leave with me?"

"I intend to be with you and our child. I can't give you a date or time frame until I hear more about the research findings."

"So, we wait?"

He squeezes my hand and smiles at me. God, he doesn't need to say another word because his smile does all sorts of things to my insides.

"Yes, my love, we wait. Like we're waiting for that beautiful baby to grow inside of you, some things can't be rushed."

My hand lifts to rest on the swell of my stomach. "I don't want to have this baby alone. I want you there."

He turns and pulls me into his arms and kisses me. "I love you," he murmurs against my lips. "I want to be there with you too. Please understand I'll do everything in my power to make sure you're both safe."

I wrap my arms around him and rest my cheek against his firm chest. "Thank you."

Samuel drapes an arm over my shoulder, and we walk the remainder of the way at a slower pace.

We arrive at the stream, and small beams of broken sunlight stream through the trees. Everything seems quieter here in our special place.

Samuel kicks off his shoes, then drops to his knees to assist me to slide mine off. I lean both hands on his shoulders, grateful not to bend over because my stomach is already getting in the way. He unties his skirt, and I do the same with mine.

Inspecting his back and long legs, I can tell they are

thinner than when we first met. When he turns, his eyes lower to my naked body, and he holds out a hand for me to use as support. I step to him, and now closer, I see the fire burning in his eyes.

"I love you," I tell him. "Everything I do is because I love you."

"I know," he rasps out. "I love you too."

The moment our bodies submerge in the water, I wrap my legs around his hips, my arms around his neck, and I kiss him, knowing it's the one way to simplify everything between us.

His lips meet mine in need. I still feel like an intruder despite Samuel's words. The only way I could explain to the shaman and the chief my being here is like being a drug addict, and Samuel is the euphoria. They wouldn't understand, but they may understand him as my ayahuasca. He heals me, takes me to a better place where our hearts are one.

🌴

The cuff of the sphygmomanometer tightens around my arm. Samuel listens through the stethoscope, then releases the valve and smiles. "All well."

"I expect it to be. There's no past medical history to think otherwise, and I eat healthily," I say to minimize his concern. "Those watches and modern devices? Well, if I had one, I could check it myself."

He writes the results on a notepad and closes it. "This is reliable. It only needs to be calibrated every five years. And I'm not relying on batteries or other energy devices for it to work."

"Right."

He stacks the notepad and the sphygmomanometer in a corner. "I want us to take a visit to Ciudad Guayana. You need to have an ultrasound and have some blood taken."

"I had an ultrasound before I came. And blood. Everything is fine. I made sure of it first." He gives me a look that says not to argue with him, but when he slips into doctor mode with me, I want to do just that—argue. "I have a good doctor. Or is it me you don't trust?"

His eyes meet mine, and today he's failing to hide his frustration even though only hours ago we made love. "I'm safeguarding *our* baby."

"What do the women do here?" I know the answer and want to hear him say it.

"You're not Ularan." He folds his arms over his chest. "They are used to giving birth with no medical intervention."

"I'm here with you. I know you'll look after me. I don't want to waste time leaving for a few tests, then having to go through your self-enforced quarantine out there." I point to the jungle where we hide out for days anytime we return to the camp. "That scares me. It's unhealthy."

His eyes widen. I should take his blood pressure.

"And you think your being here isn't a risk to our baby? To you?"

"Maybe, but here women do it all the time, so I'm staying with the man I love," I say with emphasis, almost desperate.

Samuel runs a hand over his cheek. "Your being here concerns me. I'm distracted, and so is shaman by Kaikare's emotions that have stirred since you've arrived."

I slide off the table and stand before him, so he has to

look me square in the eye. "Fine. Blame me. Do you want me to leave?"

"No," he says the word so I barely hear him. "No, because I need you here more than I realize. I have purpose and feel like a person again." He leans his forehead against mine. "I'm sorry. I didn't intend for my words to sound like you're a problem. Only I'm surprised by how stressed I am about you and our baby's well-being. I'm afraid if something goes wrong, I'll be incapable of helping you. And the idea of failing you both will destroy me."

I wrap my arms around his middle and rest my cheek on his hard chest. I let out a sigh when his arms snake around my back, pulling me closer to him. "I didn't come here for you to protect me. I came here because it was the right thing to do. I need to be with you and will adapt and do whatever it takes to stay."

For how long, I'm unsure. All I know is I want to be with Samuel as I'm a stronger person when I'm with him. Today, I'm brave, and I'm ready to take steps to remain in Ulara and have my baby here just like my grandmother. I blow out air slowly.

Shit. Is that a commitment I'm ready to make?

"Are we having dinner in the long house tonight?" I ask, ready to change the subject.

Samuel kisses the top of my head. "We are. The shaman will tell a story about a Kanaima spirit and why some crops were lost."

"Well, they can't blame me for the weather."

When Samuel says nothing to reassure me, I squeeze my arms tighter. Maybe there's more to his concern than he's letting on. Maybe I look to him to protect me.

"Please stop," I whisper to Samuel.

I didn't want Samuel to translate the story further. It began in a roundabout way with the mountain spirit of the dead being unhappy, and the rain resulted from his unhappiness. I sit between Samuel's legs with my head resting on his chest. I look around the gathering of Ularans, all eyes on the shaman, the star attraction wearing his red-feathered headdress like a king would a crown. They believe every word that comes from his mouth. He's a healer, so they have no reason to doubt his word when, as Samuel has told me, he has performed miracles beyond what Samuel can medically explain.

Tonight, the shaman's voice is louder than his calm, talking voice yet not theatrical. His tone has picked up an octave but not in emotion. He's always cool-tempered. I don't know if it's the herbs because I seriously don't understand how these people can be so calm all the time.

Acceptance.

This is how it is, and they accept it.

I feel sorry for the pregnant women and teenagers with raging hormones. Glancing around the semi-circle, I find the young girl who I saw with a boy beyond the field all those months ago. I assume it's her because she's staring at the boy sitting across from her in the circle.

The shaman lifts both arms and looks to the heavens after finishing his tale about a Kanaima. "A-pantoní-pe nichii." *May you take advantage of this story.*

People stand from a seated cross-legged position. The families regroup and file toward their huts. I watch the teenage girl head off alone. The boy watches her as well.

"I need to pee," I tell Samuel.

"Do you want me to come with you?"

"No. I'm okay."

She walks in, and I follow a few steps and stop, afraid to venture further. Unlike the Ularans, my night vision sucks.

Rustles shift the leaves ahead of me.

Their moans are so quiet anyone further away wouldn't hear it over the jungle squawks and clicking insects.

I remain deathly still, listening for any sign of—

What am I listening for? The sound of lovers having sex? Because it's none of my business. It's against the rules, and like me, this couple is taking a risk to be together in a forbidden love affair. What I guess I'm listening for is if he's forcing her to have sex with him because she doesn't look much older than fifteen. Maybe both are underage by Western society standards, but not here. They accept love when it's done the right way. And I'm sure his hammock isn't hanging in this young girl's family hut.

I guess it proves that not all Ularans agree with the rules set by the shaman and chief. It mightn't be my business, but if they are caught, I *care* about the consequences inflicted upon them.

4

EDEN

Today I didn't wake up in a film of sweat.

A small win.

It's late October, and the rainy season is hopefully over, and to think Christmas is only eight weeks away.

Christmas.

My mind works around the date out of habit as it's the hotel's busiest period. Only I had planned on staying here for Christmas with Samuel and leaving immediately after, only days before I was thirty-six weeks pregnant. There's an underlying urgency in booking a return flight as my travel requires permission from authorities after that date. Unless I have special permission from an obstetrician to certify I'm low risk.

There's no indication of a complicated pregnancy, and I intend to stay as long as possible. I miss home, but leaving Samuel isn't something I want to think about, so I open Gran's diary and read the words of her past. She taught me to be grateful for small things, and right now, her words connect me to home.

30th January 1960

It has to be one of the hottest months ever. I can't think straight in my room. No air conditioning. No breeze. No wonder people have died in this heatwave. The thought of wearing that stiff uniform to work this afternoon makes me want to say I'm sick. Only it's more comfortable on the hospital ward than in my room.
I have one more month before I'm heading home to Adelaide to be with Albert.

15th May 1960

Today is the best day of my life, apparently, and yet here I am vomiting up my guts. My fault since I wasn't careful when I first arrived home in Adelaide.
Brenda is by my side to help me get through the day. I need her to tell me I'm doing the right thing.
I know I'm doing the 'right thing' for everyone else and my reputation, only is it what I truly want?
Brenda told me not to panic because everyone gets cold feet.

Shit. Was that my gran's wedding day? Her *reputation*. I inhale hot air and allow myself a moment to absorb her words.

She was pregnant.

It seems she writes in the diary when she's troubled or unsure. It's not an account of happier times except for the times she and Pop made out. Only I want to see those happier times. I want to know my grandparents were happy together, at least for some of their lives. If not, I'm unsure if I want to keep reading.

16th December 1960

Our baby is due next month. I can barely walk from the kitchen chair to the bedroom, and all Albert is worried about is the fact the Aussies drew with the West Indies in a test match in Brisbane.
When he was yelling at the television, I wanted to cry. Why can't he be that supportive of me?

I let out a sob, understanding her frustration. "Oh, Gran," I murmur and rest my hand on the swell of my stomach. If only I could hug her one more time.

11th April 1961

I barely sleep.
Winston cries all the time.
I've tried everything for colic, and nothing works.
Winston and I sleep in the same room since we know Albert is tired from working the motel and needs to be up at five every morning.
I've never felt more alone, even more than on my first day arriving in Melbourne and knowing no one. This is much worse, and I feel like no one cares.

If only I could tell her that Pop cared. They didn't expect men in those times to help around the house, but he did love her.

I can't read anymore today. Placing the diary in my sack, I slip on my runners. There's been no rain for three days, and I want to go for a walk, maybe to the fields, even though Samuel insisted I stay in the long house and help prep the vegetables. At twenty-eight weeks, I'm still capable of helping some, although the rate my baby is growing has surprised me. I smile and run my hand over the swell of my stomach. I'm not short, and Samuel is more than six feet, so our baby won't be small.

Kaikare stands when I reach the long house. She says something to the lady squatting beside her stirring a pot of water before coming to my side. She takes my hand, and we walk to the other end of the village. The lack of communication is getting to me—an annoying barrier between us.

Does the shaman prefer it that way?

I know he loves Kaikare, and in the community, love is important.

No matter the curiosity eating at her about her mother, she grew up loved and in a safe environment. It's more than some of my affluent friends.

It dawns on me it could be why Samuel has spoken little about his parents and his life in LA. I know they are wealthy, yet he refuses to talk about them.

He deflects all his energy to Ulara and is in denial about his previous life. Before now, I didn't question it, I abided by the rules, and my reward was to stay longer. Only now, I have a ticking time bomb inside me.

Why is he scared to leave?

What happened for him to come here and hide away?

I'm not accepting that he's a workaholic or career-minded or that it's his contract, and he wants to find a cure for some disease. Something happened for him to be like this, and I'm so mad at myself for not seeing it sooner.

I let out a little sigh with the realization.

Kaikare stops walking and lands a gentle hand on my shoulder with a questioning look on her face.

"I'm fine," I say quickly, even though she doesn't understand. So, I smile and keep walking, despite not knowing where she's taking me.

We reach the village edge, and she leads me into the jungle. Vines choke the trees that are so tall they almost touch the heavens. We pass a tree crawling with bullet ants before she leads me into a garden of orchids and other brightly colored flowers.

I've been here before.

We continue along a narrow path where the vines reach out like fingers as though trying to touch us. Then I hear the shaman's song. His voice thrills me with the sensation of life. It's a sound that wraps you in a secure blanket, and you feel safe, relaxed, and euphoric. We continue until we find him and Samuel in a herb garden. I walk past strategically placed wooden signs, all an arm's length long with identifiable names painted on the wood.

"Eden." Samuel comes to me. He smiles from ear to ear. "How are you feeling?"

"I'm fine. If there's something wrong, I'll tell you." I squeeze his hand. "Please stop worrying about me." I point to the garden. "Did you make the signs?"

"Yes." He takes my hand, and we walk a few steps to the first sign.

Banisteriiopsis Caapi
Ayahuasca vine

Next is

Psychotria Viridis
Chacruna DMT

I smile at him. "This is where you grow your plants for the special tea?"

"Some, yes." He takes my hand and leads me to a deep purple flower growing on top of stones with minimal soil. "This is the flower I picked from the tepui when I left you..." he stalls on the last word. "I sent samples away and kept some. Despite the rain, it has survived. It's a breakthrough." His gaze is fixed on the plant as though it's a million dollars left on the ground for someone to find.

The shaman continues to sing from behind us, and I turn to see Kaikare picking the vine. "Another ceremony?"

"The warriors are heading out on a hunt. They haven't eaten meat in weeks."

"Will more boys be initiated?"

"Not tonight."

"Good. I don't have the stomach to sit through that kind of ceremony," I murmur.

"Are you nauseous?" His beautiful eyes study my face.

"No more than I was back home in the first trimester." My hand lifts to my stomach and rubs gently as though to calm my child. Samuel's gaze lowers and lands where my hand rests.

"Have you thought any more about taking a visit to Ciudad Guayana?"

"We can chat about it tonight among other things."

"About a hospital visit?"

"No." I steel myself, ready for his reaction. "About your family."

His eyes meet mine, and there's a fury there I've never seen before. "I told you before my family isn't up for discussion."

"And since our child has your family's blood pumping through his or her veins, it's up for discussion. I don't want to skirt around this anymore."

I follow Samuel's gaze over my shoulder. Only now do I realize the shaman has stopped singing.

"Here isn't the place," he says in a softer tone. "We'll talk later."

"Yes, you will." I give him a look that my father used to give me when I needed pulling into line.

Kaikare walks over and takes my hand. A smile is on her face. I know she smiles a lot. Is it because I'm standing up to the men?

🌴

I'm in the hammock, clutching my grandmother's diary when Samuel enters the hut. He creeps around, seemingly unaware my eyes are open and watching him. His blond hair is ruffled like I have run my fingers through it, and I imagine him doing just that as he concentrates or right before he decides on something. I'll never tire of simply looking at him. Admiring him. Even the way the muscles in his back contract when he moves those glorious arms. His long legs, muscular but lean thighs and calves like a marathon runner—they are so lickable.

It would be an effort to get back up when I'm on the ground, but still, it would be worth it.

Samuel rearranges objects on the bench before turning, creeping a few steps, and freezes. "I'm sorry, did I wake you?"

"I wasn't asleep. Only resting before I help with dinner. I was appreciating the view."

"Are you up to it?"

I raise my eyebrows. He misunderstood the view as meaning beyond the hut to the jungle.

"You don't have to help if you're tired."

"I do what I'm allowed to prepare." Which isn't a hell of a lot since I'm still earning their trust. "Come here." I pat the hammock where I lie. "I want to ask you something."

"Does it affect you and me?"

"It could in the future." My gaze travels down his sun-kissed body from his hard pecs to his washboard abs where his grass skirt sits low on his hips and the indented 'V' points below the band of the skirt.

"If you keep looking at me..." he clears his throat, "... we won't be talking."

"No. We talk first." I lift my arm to motion for him to come beside me. "Lay with me."

His expression is apprehensive, yet he comes to me and slides into the hammock with it barely swaying.

"Tell me about your life."

"My life?" he rasps on the last word. "Why?"

"Because I want to get to know the father of my baby."

His brow pulls tight. "You already do, more so than anyone else alive."

"I only know Samuel, who gives everything he has to make others happy. The man who has dedicated his life to work in a primitive community whose inhabitants don't know the world beyond the jungle."

"This is who I am... now." He kisses my cheek and snuggles into my shoulder as though he needs to rest. "You don't need to know anything else."

But I do.

"What if I ask a question, and you answer it the best way you can? If it's too hard, then you say pass. That way, you don't have to start any conversation."

He grumbles something, and I swear it's a curse in another language. "I'll make a deal. You get to ask questions if I can take you to Ciudad Guayana."

"Fine," I say, even though I have no intention of leaving here unless it's absolutely necessary. I take a deep breath and then start with something easy—something I know will get him talking.

"Who were your best friends in college?"

It must have hit a chord because he remains quiet for a moment before answering, "Carter. Brant. And you already met Michael, Sean, and Harrison."

I want to groan at the sound of Michael's name. We haven't discussed him since I have returned, and I want to remind him he's barely a friend after the stunt he pulled in Peru. "First girlfriend in high school or college?"

"In high school, it was Sienna. I didn't have girlfriends in college." He stiffens beside me.

"No dates, or did you just have friends with benefits?"

He remains quiet for a moment.

"It's okay. We've all done things we regret."

He gives me a dark look, one that implies I wouldn't understand. "What mistakes did you make?"

41

"You know about Ethan." I stare up at the bamboo beams supporting the thatched grass. "And my trust issues. Coming here to be with you was a big step for me." I pause for a moment and swallow the lump at the back of my throat that grows with the memory of when Ethan killed my faith in guys. A part of me died that day. "But I trust you." I swivel so I can see his eyes. His eyes tell me what he's thinking, so I need to see how he reacts when I say the next sentence. "It was one of the most challenging things I've had to do. I took a risk, hurt others, yet in my gut, and even though I was scared of so much going wrong, I knew I had to take a giant leap and be with you."

His eyes hold mine, and in those bright baby blue hues, appreciation swirls. Only I can sense he's holding back.

"You were always a good person, Eden. No matter what shit went down or how hurt you were, you were the good person."

"Well, yeah—"

"I wasn't," he says it bluntly as though I wouldn't understand. "I was the guy you'd hate."

"I doubt it."

He brushes my cheek with the back of his hand. "If you attended the same college as me, then we wouldn't be together. I'd probably be doing my damnedest to hit on you because back then, all I did was fuck girls."

My breath hitches at his harsh tone. Only I don't react because he's waiting for me to do just that. Show the shock on my face. "I was familiar with fucking," I whisper. It's a white lie as I've only been with a couple of guys.

He chuckles lightly as though he knows it's not true.

"You weren't familiar with my type. If you were, then you'd have run far away from the likes of me."

"But many didn't..."

"No. Many didn't," he says in a strangled voice.

His eyes become distant as though he's recalling a memory.

"Did you have any feelings for some of them? Want it to be more?"

He squints with a hint of humor in his eyes. "Feelings? Only the sexual kind where I'd fuck them again. I recall Michael and I having a limit. Ten times with a certain girl, and then no matter how good she was in bed, ten was a hard limit. Then, with no explanation, I'd stop talking to her."

"That's rough." I tilt up and search his face for a sign of remorse. Only he's a closed book, wearing the mask he wore when I first met him in Brazil all those months ago.

"I was more than rough," he says in almost a growl. "And I never *slept* with any of them. Trust me when I tell you, you don't want to know the younger version of me."

He pushes up, throws his leg over the edge of the hammock, and I reach to stop him. My hand tightens around his wrist. "Please don't go. I want to know about the young Samuel McMahon. He's still part of you even though you have... transformed." I couldn't think of a better word.

"I've worked tirelessly not to be that person." His elbows rest on his knees, and I'm forced to release him. Samuel brings his hands to his face and rubs like he's expelling a memory.

"I'm sure they forgave you."

He groans into his hands.

"It's only sex, Samuel."

43

"I made a promise to one girl, and I never had sex with her." He pushes off the hammock and strides away. "It was a point in time I was lower than life. I had the blood of a demon in my veins."

"Wait." I scramble out and go to him.

Samuel hunches over the bench with his back to me.

"You're not a bad person, so what is it that has you putting space between us?"

His head hangs low between his arms, outstretched on the bench. "I'm disgusted with myself when I think back to what I did. And I don't want to talk about it. Can't without feeling nauseous." His voice is cut with a rasp.

I rub my hand in circles over his back. It's progress, and I know there's something stopping him from wanting to leave Ulara. For my sake and our baby's sake, I have to dig deeper. "Did you sort it out at all?"

"Not before she took her own life," he murmurs.

My hand stalls on his back before I consciously continue in a slower action. "You can't blame yourself."

"No. My friends and I were to blame. Now, can we please stop talking about this? As I said, I'm no longer the same person." He glances over his shoulder but won't turn to look at me.

"It's healthy to talk," I say gently.

"You mean repent. And I have done it over and over when drinking ayahuasca. I don't need to do it again." He straightens and pushes off the bench before striding past me toward the door.

"Where are you going?"

He freezes with his back to me. "In the garden to fucking cry. And no, I don't want you to come with me. It's something I need to do alone."

"No one has to cry alone." My heart breaks for him,

especially that he believes he can't cry about this in front of me. I wrap my arms around his back and rest my cheek on the spot where his heart beats inside his chest. "Please stay with me."

He doesn't move. His entire body is stiff, so I take his hand and tug gently to guide him back to the hammock. Keeping hold of his hand, I clamber in, and he follows my lead. He curls up beside me, his head on my shoulder. I take his hand and place it on my lower stomach. "No matter what, we will always love you."

"I buried that life a long time ago and refuse to be that person," he croaks. "I know what you're thinking, though I'm more disgusted with myself than anyone else could be. Telling you, the one person who loves me for me..." his voice cracks. "With everything else going on in my head, I'm not ready to tell you everything."

I keep stroking and holding him, but my mind is whirling. How can I do this—give birth to a child with a man I'm still getting to know?

Closing my eyes, I force the thought out. Of course, I can do this. I don't need years behind us to know he's the man for me. His past will not dictate our future. I also refuse to go back in time to being the weak woman I was before I met him. Together, we're stronger, and I can handle all he has to reveal. I need to if we're to move forward—together.

5

SAMUEL

Eden has bewitched Samuel.

He always knew the power of her love. Only tonight, she unearthed a crippling memory of his former self he'd kept locked away for years. Eden tried to pry it from him with loving tentacles, and the metal walls surrounding his heart melted like mercury. Raw and exposed, he wanted to run to his safe place in the shaman's garden and curl up in a ball until the sound of the shaman's voice released him from the hell playing over in his mind.

A time will come when he'll need to confess the horror of his past and why he was so screwed up living in his entitled world. He'd like to think he was brainwashed, but it wasn't so simple. He made choices and openly followed his friends and acted just like them without remorse for the consequences.

Until *Inesa*. She opened his mind and heart. Only it was too late to make it up to her. His apologetic words were meaningless. Her friends called her Nessie, and he had no right to call her by an affectionate title known to a select few. Yet, he hears Nessie's voice over and over in his head. He relives the tears and hears wails when her friends mourned her name. It took every ounce of his courage to attend her funeral alone. Samuel's friends declared their innocence to fuel any thoughts of her mental destruction. In the brief time he got to speak with Inesa, he could see how wrong they were.

Inesa instilled the power in him to change.

Eden has greater control over his soul, more so than anyone, including himself. Her power scares him more than any danger that lurks in the rainforest, not even the jungle herself.

🌴

"Stay with me tonight. I'm not up to eating any more yuca. Can I just have pizza?"

Samuel chuckles. "Capsicum and pineapple on flat yuca bread?"

"Funny." Her hand lingers at the curve of her pregnant body.

"Is everything okay?" He lifts her chin and directs her gaze to his.

"Yeah. I'm tired." Her hands wrap around his body. Her soft cheek presses against his chest, so he's forced to release her and rest his hands lightly on her shoulders.

"Would you like to lie down? I can fetch some fruit so you can snack on some food here."

"I'd love some fruit, please. And can you check if Kaikare has some of her special tea?" She walks to the hammock. Samuel assists her by lifting her feet for her to settle in the swing.

Samuel leaves to gather the fruit and bread and finds

Kaikare. "Eden is eating in our hut and asked for some of your special tea," he says in their native tongue.

Kaikare's eyes convey concern. Samuel places a hand on her shoulder understanding the two of them are close and explains she's tired, and it's natural for her to be so.

He returns with loaded palm leaves, including one carrying warmed fish, yet he can't shake the concern at the back of his mind that Eden isn't getting enough nutrition with her body being unacquainted with the rainforest. He's proud of her determination to be like the other Ularan ladies. The moment it conflicts with her well-being and their baby's safety, he'll intervene.

Eden pushes up in the hammock and uses her stomach as a table to rest some of the food on. "Do you remember the young couple? The lovers I told you about?" She bites pieces of fruit and waits to swallow before continuing, "I've noticed them together on several occasions and yesterday saw them holding hands near the fields. I think she was crying."

"Kapeá Tapire was crying?"

"Is that her name?"

Samuel slides in next to her, holding the palm leaf with the fish. "Yes, it is. And you should eat this."

"I don't think I can stomach it." She lifts a hand to her mouth.

"You don't have to eat it, although you haven't eaten protein in a while, which furthers my argument about us taking a trip to Ciudad Guayana for blood tests."

"There's a story about the young couple, isn't there?" she asks, changing the subject.

"There is." He takes the palm leaves from her and springs from the hammock.

"Wait." Eden pushes up onto her elbows, and the hammock wobbles. "I want to know."

Samuel chuckles and throws the palms outside. He seals the netting and takes his place beside her, curling in so he can take her in his arms.

Eden lifts her head to get comfortable and sighs. "I thought you were going to leave and not tell me."

He kisses her cheek and smiles. "There's nowhere else I'd rather be."

"Ha." She slaps his chest. "Tell me about the secret lovers."

"It's not so much a secret. Everyone simply turns a blind eye."

"I knew it."

"Okay, Detective Monteford, let me know when you're ready to hear the story."

Eden rolls her eyes. "Go ahead."

Samuel can't hide his smirk. "Her lover, Mari' Iwoi, was from the Watache tribe."

"Wait. Isn't that the bad tribe? The cannibals everyone fears?"

"Yes, and yet the real power is here. In the parameters of the village, you have nothing to fear, and you'll most likely never see a Watache warrior."

"Warrior? Are they the only ones who venture out?"

"Yes, usually to hunt."

"How did he come to be in Ulara?"

"By circumstance after a sacrifice. He was brought here by one of the women when he was left in the rainforest as a newborn. A sacrifice to their god, but our shaman and chief debated on what should happen to him."

"Really?"

He pulls her close to his side and kisses the crown of her head. "Mari' Iwoi translates to 'dancing snake,' a name the women gave him. At first, he wasn't to be trusted, and yet he was a content baby. Kaikare told me he moved his limbs a lot and giggled at the sound of their voices."

"Such weird names."

"Says the tortoise."

She punches him in the arm, and he chuckles. "What about the girl?"

"Kapeá Tapire was born on a red moon. It's what her name translates to."

"It doesn't explain the secrecy."

"Kapeá Tapire was promised to someone else. A jaguar attacked and killed the young man a few years back."

"A jaguar," she croaks.

"Again, it's something we rarely see, yet they do venture close. Everyone turns a blind eye, so to speak, as they believe their physical attraction is the spirits' doing. A Kanaima messing with the Ularans. Kapeá and Mari' are... cursed in their minds, and many believe what happens between them is the business of the gods."

"They hide their affair, and yet they probably don't need to?"

"They need to out of respect until the shaman gives his blessing, and then Mari' Iwoi moves his hammock into Kapeá Tapire's family hut."

"When will the shaman give his blessing?"

"Not until the jungle speaks to him. It's why he wants another ceremony as he says the jungle is talking about an unhappy balance."

Eden rests her cheek on Samuel's shoulder. "I'm glad the jungle approved of us."

Samuel closes his eyes and nods. He can no longer imagine his life without Eden.

🌴

The following morning, Samuel wakes early and creeps around the hut so as not to wake Eden. He understands her fatigue and the need for her to get adequate rest. He'd love nothing more than to lie with her, pretend it's a lazy Sunday, and spoon her until she stirs.

"Hey," she murmurs.

He stills and turns to check on her. "I was trying not to wake you."

"Our baby has been moving all night and kept me awake."

Samuel goes to her and places his hand on her abdomen. "Do you feel okay?"

"Ah-ha." She places her hand over his. "It wasn't just our baby. I had a dream last night and need to know about the Watache tribe, so I won't fabricate my own version of cannibalism."

Samuel takes Eden's hand in his, raises it to his lips, and kisses her knuckles. "I'll let nothing happen to you. Now come." He eases her up and out of the hammock and then guides Eden to the treatment table. "I'll tell you how it was explained to me." He takes the clay pot containing the balm and rubs it over her shoulders and neck. Her little moans remind him how much he loves her. He massages circles, his need building with each one, more and more.

"Were they always bad?"

Eden brings him back to the present, and he takes a moment to compose himself. "My interpretation is the stories originated in the early 1700s, but I could be wrong. The shaman described the Watache tribe as being descendants of an ancestral tribe known as the Kariña—famous for their violence because they were not good communicators. The Ularans are descendants of the Pemón, and the Pemón, Macuxi, and Kariña tribes are all descendants of the same tribe from hundreds of years ago. But the folk tales say the Kariña didn't develop the peaceful characteristics of the Pemón people. The Kariña believed they were the only 'true' people, and outsiders were considered unintelligent, animal-like, and inhuman if they didn't speak the same language. The phonics differed between tribes, and this language barrier gave reason for the Kariña to believe other tribes were not human and were therefore dangerous and should be hunted. They hunted foreigners like animals and ate the flesh of people outside their tribe."

"Oh my god." She shakes her head.

He rests a hand on her shoulder for reassurance. "They believed eating their victim was magic, and it gave them a sense of spiritual power. The Kariña believed the person's soul would remain in their body after consummation. Feeling indestructible, the Kariña would attack other tribes, accessing the villages by river. All tribes in the surrounding areas feared the Kariña, which, in return, gave them more power. In their mind, they were not eating other human beings as only actual people spoke the same language as them."

"I can't imagine ever having to eat another person," she murmurs.

He moves to her front and massages the balm along

her arms. "My point is they didn't intentionally eat humans."

She shrugs. "They decide someone isn't human because they talk differently and yet they have the same appearance. It's messed up."

"No more so than anywhere else. We have more monsters in what we think is a civilized world. This happened centuries ago, and stories are interpreted by the listener. Fear stems from what you want to believe."

Eden remains quiet for some time before she speaks again. "I'm thinking I should learn more Ularan words. Just the basics to help me get by when you're not around. I tried before, but I struggle to get my tongue around some phonics."

He chuckles lightly, and yet he's delighted she wants to learn their dialect. "I'll teach you a few more while I walk with you to the long house."

Beneath his delight, a dark thought lingers in her wanting to learn the language for safety reasons. Until now, his concern for Eden's well-being centered on her and their baby's health. He's aware their lives swing in a balance jeopardized by the things they can't see. It goes without saying dreams play a major role in this unique world, and maybe he should listen to Eden as her dreams could be a voice alerting her to the future.

Because he'd never forgive himself if anything happened to her.

6

EDEN

Two Days Later...

Sweat drips from my brow like a leaky tap.

I lean the axe on the ground while I flick beads of sweat from my forehead. The sun has shone all morning, and in the field's small clearing, I've relished the rays on my bare skin. I've removed the necklaces except for the one strand Kaikare made for me since all were too heavy for my shoulders and neck, especially with the added weight of Baby McMahon. Instead, I rely on my tangled locks to cover my breasts, but it fails, considering they have grown equally in size with my baby. How much I still care has surprised me. I'm fine here in the fields where many of the ladies, pregnant or not, don't cover-up. Yet when I'm around the men, I feel exposed, so I wear the beads at dinner but not out here.

Kaikare and I follow the line of women with woven baskets on their heads. We gather in the long house for lunch. There's a wild hunger in their eyes, and I hope the men will return with game to feed everyone in the village.

The teenage boys have caught a few monkeys over the past two weeks by hiding out in camouflaged cubby houses. Palm fronds built like a miniature tepee around their body conceals their presence. Inside the tiny space, they are armed with poison blowpipes and sit motionless for hours, hoping for a kill, providing a meal to prove they are worthy hunters.

When some teenage boys shout and kick a coconut along the ground, I recognize them as the young hunters. My shoulders fall in relief, happy they have returned empty-handed today. I'll never get used to the thought of eating monkey.

"Kuwata?" I ask Kaikare. I was quick to learn the word for monkey so I could decline the meat if offered.

"Awarö." She bows her head. *Bad.*

Wakü, I think to myself. *Good.*

"Oo?" She hands me the bread made from yuca.

"Waküpe-küruman." *Thank you.*

Her slim lips turn into a broad smile.

In the dirt, I draw a snake with a forked tongue and stripes. She studies it a moment. I tell her, "Snake."

"Iwoi," she replies. I repeat the word in my head.

Next, I draw a spider, remembering my encounter with a wandering spider in a bunch of bananas. "Spider."

"Spi-der," Kaikare repeats, and then adds, "Mojowai."

I say it over and over in my head. "Mojowai awarö." *Spider bad.*

"Are you asking for a list of everything you fear?" Samuel stands close by with a grin on his face. Damn him and his stealth skills that let him appear like a ghost.

"Did I tell you about the time a wandering spider almost bit me? It happened while you were away on your journey."

"Almost?" His eyes widen, and he crouches to listen to my story.

I tell him how Kaikare saved me and how freaked out I was to have my hand close to its fangs.

"I'm glad she was there, especially as we don't have an anti-venom here."

"Jesus, Samuel." I shake my head to rid the stressful thoughts coming to mind.

"The venom is toxic to the nervous system, and in men, a bite can cause a painful erection for days as the venom boosts nitric oxide, which increases blood flow. Then, sexual dysfunction can be for life if the poison doesn't kill you first."

"Seriously, what the hell am I doing here?" I raise my arms and act more dramatically than I intended.

Samuel raises a brow and waits a moment before I drop my arms to my side. "Do you have poisonous spiders in Australia?"

"Well, yeah, of course. It's Australia." Duh.

"No different from here, Eden."

My shoulders heave with a sigh. Every day I wait, and it's not with sugar-coated hope for Samuel to say he'll leave Ulara to be with me. It's glazed with fear that something bad will happen. Samuel's journey to the Ayuan Tepui hasn't gone unnoticed among the Ularans. I see it in their eyes. Only one warrior was brave enough to travel with him to the house of the devil—the home of Mawarí spirits. Will there be repercussions for upsetting the spirits?

"Hey." He waits for me to meet his caring gaze. "I think we'll take that trip to Ciudad next week, okay?"

"Okay," I say without argument. Kaikare is turning her head every time one of us speaks as though she's at a tennis match. She places a hand on my back, and I rest my head on her shoulder.

"Tamu'ne Akare wakü," I tell her. *White tortoise is good.*

"You're doing fine," Samuel says in a low, gentle voice. I don't miss the concern in his eyes. "You don't have to go back to the fields this afternoon."

"I enjoy spending time with her. Besides, I don't know how much longer I can work, and I want to prove my worth. The rate our baby is growing, I might be basket weaving with the men."

"That will be a first since it's not women's work." He grins. "Though, with you, anything is possible."

🌴

After a couple of hours of working in the fields, the girl who sneaks off with her lover, Kapeá Tapire, catches my eye when she wanders past the banana palms and into the rainforest. I grab Kaikare's attention, point to the trees, and then follow the girl since I also need to pee.

Vines slash my wrists as I forge a path in an attempt to be out of sight. My name suits me now as I move almost as slow as a tortoise, which is why I lost sight of Kapeá Tapire. Finding a large Kapok tree, I squat beside it and watch the ground for anything that crawls near my feet.

"Ahh." The wail doesn't sound far away. Is it Kapeá Tapire? Is she okay? I finish peeing and weave around a few trees, walking as fast as I can toward the sound. She crouches, one hand on the ground, the other holding her stomach. There's movement behind her, but I don't see who it is.

She continues to weep, so I make my way to her and

rest my palm on her back. "Kapeá Tapire wakü?" *Kapeá Tapire good?*

She raises her chin so her eyes meet mine. My heart sinks at the tears in her eyes. The Ularans don't feel emotions and not to this degree.

I asked if she was good, and knowing she's not, I'm lost as to how to communicate further.

"Are you hurt?" I ask, hoping my tone conveys meaning.

I'm barely capable of maneuvring to a full squat, so I lower myself with one hand on the tree for support. Her gaze lowers to my rounded stomach. She bursts into tears and runs the opposite way to the fields crying uncontrollably. Overhead, the sky turns dark, and a rumble sounds in the distance. This isn't good. I follow her, but I'm too slow to keep up.

"Kapeá Tapire," I call, pushing past several palm fronds. A loud crack and I scream, bobbing for cover. Within seconds, heavy sheets of water fall to blur everything beyond a few feet in front of me.

Bloody hell.

I raise my hands to my brow and try to work out which way to turn to find my way back to the field. I pivot a full 360 degrees and move to stand under the largest tree closest to me. Useless when the branches act like a waterfall, and I near drown when I look up. The already saturated ground has barely a chance to soak in the water, and it's pooling everywhere. I slush through the murky puddles with my head down and no idea if I'm walking toward the village.

"Samuel," I scream at the top of my lungs. Another *crack,* and my voice is smothered by thunder.

"Ahh." I turn in the direction of the scream. It has to

be Kapeá Tapire. I need to find my way back to the village for safety—to Samuel. But I can't leave her out here. Not alone. Not like this. I keep my head down, concentrating on every step so I don't slip and fall.

"I'm coming," I call back when the rain eases as quickly as it fell.

They appear out of nowhere like ghosts from behind the trees. Dark-skinned bodies with red-painted faces, so I can only see their eyes. The red paint continues down to their torso. A stick is pierced through each nose like a trademark to what tribe they belong. Long arrows point at my throat, a warning not to scream. Behind them, I make out Kapeá Tapire on the ground, her hands and feet being tied to bamboo, then three men lift the bamboo to their shoulders, and she's carried like a wild animal.

"Stop!" I scream and raise my hand.

Spears jut closer to my throat.

A taller man steps forward and eyes me. He speaks a different dialect and waves his hand to the men carrying Kapeá Tapire. She moans with the impact when they drop her to the ground. I turn toward the movement I see in my peripheral vision.

I hear the thump of stone on my skull before I feel it.

7

SAMUEL

After working in the shaman's medicinal garden, Samuel makes his way to the long house to search for Eden. He assumes she's resting in the hammock as the downpour ceased work in the fields. He intends to tell her not to overdo it to prove her merit when a high-pitched wail and more wails in a chant-like sequence have his feet moving quicker in the direction of the chief's hut.

Kaikare runs to him with panic in her voice, her words tripping over the other in near hysteria. His heart speeds up. She's not previously acted like this, not even when a jaguar stole one of their own. He raises his hands, trying to calm the alarm spreading in the village.

Kaikare pants as if she's hyperventilating. Samuel places a hand on her shoulders. "Awarö?" *Bad?*

She nods. "Watache Tamu'ne Akare."

"Jesus." He runs his hand through his hair and turns a full circle. He doesn't know which way to run. Why? How? None of it matters. He takes a few quick breaths to clear his thoughts. He points to the river.

She shakes her head vehemently before pointing to

the jungle and then to Kapeá Tapire, who's huddled in Mari' Iwoi's arms by the cooking fire.

Samuel sprints over to her and asks what happened.

She stops sobbing and nods. "Areku wokyry." *Angry men*. She shakes her hands and points to her feet, showing Samuel how they tied her to a pole. "Konopo Tamu'ne Akare." *Eden appeared out of the rain.*

"Watache topu upùpo." She acts out being hit in the head with a rock.

Samuel's eyes widen. "Tamu'ne Akare's upùpo?" *Eden's head?*

She nods and tells him it was under the two rubber trees.

Confirming the area, Samuel takes off into the jungle, swatting unruly vines and sharp branches aside. Is she unconscious? He turns when a chant comes from behind him, several warriors on his heels, jabbing spears to the heavens.

An old wound opens with the memory of failing someone when he is in a position to help. The scar will always be there.

Wayara meets Samuel's stride. With longer legs and his elite track training in college, Samuel is the fastest of the Ularans. He struggles for every breath, his throat tightening in fear—still, he wills his body to run faster, to find the strength.

He slows to a walk as they approach the two large trees that tower high amongst the canopy. Wayara holds out his hands to stop further movement and leans over to inspect the ground. Samuel spins and listens for the jungle to alert him of alien movement.

"Pona saküne," Wayara tells him and points to the puddles. *Seven men.*

There are signs of a struggle—several muddy footprints and scattered yellow beads that were around Eden's ankle.

Samuel does not know where the Watache village is located, and although the Ularans are peacemakers and keep to themselves, the warriors are spies for the chief. "Do you know where the village is?" he asks Wayara in Ularan.

Wayara tells him to follow the river path for two days and walk west for one. If they haven't moved camp.

"Fuck," Samuel screams to the trees. He falls to his knees and stifles a sob. "No, please, no."

The men circle him, chanting the same syllables he's never heard sung before. The spears shake toward the tepui, but the Mawarí spirit isn't to blame. Eden was in the wrong place at the wrong time, and Samuel wasn't there to protect her like he'd promised he would be. He closes his eyes and visualizes her face. In his mind, he searches for her soul in the depths of the jungle. His third eye sees his outstretched hand reaching into the darkness, his every nerve on alert seeking her energy. He needs a spark of hope. The black jaguar with the blue eyes growls only inches from his face. He topples back onto his rear.

He may have disappointed her grandmother, and yet it's the hope he seeks. Ivy's spirit is in the jungle.

Wayara gets up in his face, bringing him back, telling Samuel he thinks they can follow their tracks.

The one thing they have going for them is Eden will slow up the Watache men unless they don't care about her well-being. He pushes out the thought before his mind is trampled with images of them hurting her.

The men head back to the village to gather supplies and form a plan along with advice from the shaman.

"Wayara," Samuel calls out, and he won't apologize for his overbearing tone. He points to the ground inside the long house and draws a map of the tepuis, the rivers, Angel Falls, and Ulara. The men lean in, expressions of wonder on their faces at his knowledge of the land that stretches for hundreds of miles. He hands Wayara the stick and asks him to mark where the Watache village is located.

Samuel studies the location and rushes back to the paper map he hides in his briefcase. He spreads it out on the treatment table, and hope allows his chest to expand as he runs his finger east along the Carrao River. It's a slow journey using paddles with no motor but quicker than going on foot.

He stuffs the map into his pack, grabs a first-aid pack, including antibiotics and some bottled water before meeting the warriors by the long house. The women shove bowls of food in the warriors' hands, their backs laddered with arrows, spears, and blowpipes. The shaman sings a song, one so sweet as though it will calm any anger, promote clear minds as to what's the right behavior, and remind the warriors that killing for revenge isn't wise. It could start a war—one they have avoided. They've experienced centuries of peace by remaining hidden from the world, including other Pemón descendants.

What has Samuel caused?

He lifts his gaze to the chief. Deep lines are etched around his eyes. The young warriors chant before him, testosterone unrestrained compared to the calm, older, and wiser men.

A dozen children carry a long curiara, one Samuel has never seen or used in fishing. Its faded paint looks decades old. The warriors carry it to the river, where they are out in the open exposed to the rest of the world. His heart weighs heavily at the cost of this journey to the Ularans. When out of sight of the chief, Samuel joins in the chant, his voice louder than any other.

He knows what he needs to do—fight for the one who owns his soul.

8

EDEN

When my eyes shudder open, I reach for the side of my head to where it throbs. Then the nausea hits me. I cringe with every jolt coursing along my spine as though I'm on a poorly engineered rollercoaster.

Treetops pass and the clouds roll by.

I lean onto one elbow and, for a moment, think I'm in Asoo's curiara, only smaller and with no planked seats. But I'm not smoothly sailing on water as I'm swamped by trees.

Squinting in pain, I want to call out to put me down. The bumpy ride creates a sharp vibration in my skull. Before I do I make out three figures ahead, their red-painted bodies, and then recall following Kapeá Tapire before being surrounded by these men.

A whimper escapes my throat, and I quickly smother it before I scream. *Shit. Shit. Shit.* Are they Watache?

I'm so bloody scared right now.

What am I going to do? My thoughts cloud as fear builds inside of me.

How am I going to escape? My gut is tight with panic

and I'm breathing so fast it feels like I'm not getting any air.

My hand goes to my stomach and rubs reassuringly over the reason why I can't lose my shit.

I need to protect my baby.

Closing my eyes, I focus on slowing each breath. At this rate, I'll soon need a paper bag.

A single sob blurts out of me, and one of the men jogging ahead turns, and I duck before he sees I'm awake.

Thump.

Did someone just punch from underneath me?

God, my head is killing me.

I gently touch the side of my head and check my fingers for blood. It's sticky, and after dabbing my hair, I hope the bleeding has slowed. How long was I unconscious?

I should have stayed with Kaikare in the fields. No matter how scared I am I can't change the fact I'm in a situation and I need a plan.

To save my baby, I have to stay alive.

I can't escape. I couldn't take them on, and if I tried, well, then what? Even with a million-to-one chance of defeating these trained warriors, I'd be left to find my way home.

Think.

Assess.

As rough as the journey is, it's better than being slung like an animal to a pole or forced to walk endless miles. The only reassurance is Samuel *will* come looking for me. Until then, I need to stay alive and not do anything to provoke them.

Cannibals.

The explanation Samuel gave comes back to me.

Jesus.

Fear bubbles to the surface and disperses in waves over my body. A single quiver, then one after the other, and I can't control it. I'm curled on my side. My head bounces on one arm, the other under my stomach for support. My vision blurs with tears. Trees pass, one by one, nothing out of the ordinary, and nothing noteworthy to identify my location.

In a slow movement, I raise my leg to assess a sting on my calf. It's red from a graze, and my beaded anklet is gone.

Beads.

I touch the single strand of painted yellow and red beads on my chest.

Slowly, I rise onto an elbow and look around. Three men walk ahead of the men carrying me on their shoulders. No one walks behind.

Lifting the beads over my head, I pry the knotted ends apart with my teeth, slide several beads off the twine, and in a subtle movement, I throw one high in the air behind the canoe the men are carrying me in. I wait for the sound of it hitting a tree or the ground.

Nothing

And I couldn't be more grateful to the squawking creatures surrounding us. I wait for what seems like minutes before I toss another. It needs to be more strategic, so I count to five hundred before throwing the next and visualize Samuel finding the bead.

Clouds roll like a tumbleweed above me.

Shit.

If it rains, the beads will be washed away or be covered in muddy soot. I clamp my eyes shut and hug my baby. The negative voice in my head tells me this is in vain. I'll most likely die out here alone.

No. I make a silent vow to protect us.

My god, when was the last time my baby moved?

Rolling my palm over my stomach, I prod a couple of times and wait.

Please move. Please, please move.

Squeezing my eyes shut to stop the tears from coming, I try to clear my thoughts because I'd never forgive myself if anything happened to my unborn child. My only plan is to outwit these people because physical fighting or running is futile. I open my eyes to more sky from a clearing of trees. A potent stench of smoke makes me woozy for a moment. I cover my mouth.

Burned monkey fur. Ugh.

It doesn't smell like one or two monkeys. It's so strong it must be the whole damn howler monkey family.

Children scream with excitement.

I sigh in relief because I've always believed children are innocent until taught otherwise. And I hope they haven't watched someone die.

Yet.

The bounce in the capsule intensifies with the men running and screaming out a weird sound. With every reverberation of wood to my torso, I'm hit with another wave of nausea. My head continues to thump like a drum, so I wrap my arms around my head to protect my skull moments before I'm dropped to the ground.

The thud startles me, and I make an oomph sound combined with a groan, then reach for my stomach. Black hair framing red-painted faces block out the sky. Rounded white eyes peer down at me.

Several men shout in anger. "Stay calm. Stay calm," I

murmur to myself. I refuse to speak loud enough for them to hear my alien words. Because of Samuel's story, I know I have to act as an equal but not disrespect them to stay alive.

Their eyes hold fear and curiosity. I lift my head in the slightest movement, and they jump back. I freeze when spears are jabbed at my face, back and forth in warning. Fear, I assume, is what provokes their anger—or maybe it's a protective reaction.

The Ularans were curious by my white hair, skin, and blue eyes. They had some reservations about my spirit and whether I was evil even with Samuel in the village. These people have no outside influence and could believe I'm a threat.

Shit.

What do I do now?

The one thing the Ularans admired was Samuel's height. Willing my legs to move after endless hours of being curled in the same position, I unfurl my limbs until I'm crouching. The women and children stumble back. The men hurl unusual sounds in abuse, and tone is all I can go by. I continue to unroll, one vertebra at a time until I'm standing, looking down on the crowd. The women are tiny compared to the men, and if not for their breasts, quite difficult to distinguish from one another. The man closest to me yells, his venomous yellow eyes appear possessed, so I crouch to be less threatening. I'm at eye level with his naval and can't help a gasp at how his penis is stretched and flattened against his stomach. Red twine is wrapped around his hips, securing it almost in strangulation.

Appearance. First impressions.

My thoughts cluster into one mess. A bead of sweat

falls from my forehead. I will my heart to slow and concentrate on each breath to control the fight-or-flight response. I clench my fingers to hide the tremor, only it draws more shouting, and spears are raised toward my face. I imagine what Samuel would do, how he'd work through this. He taught me not to fear, to use my surroundings to my advantage.

"Upetoy," I say in a loud voice. *Friend*.

The women mumble something to me. Broken vowels spoken too quickly to comprehend. I focus on one lady with the least paint on her body.

"Waküperö." *Hello, how are you?*

She steps away from me as though I have singled her out, and the man standing beside her shouts, "Tamu'ne woryi awarö." *White woman bad.*

"Tamu'ne woryi wakü," I reply. *White woman good.*

A sudden movement at the back of my audience has them stepping apart like a zipper. Red, blue and yellow feathers strewn into a crown bob toward me. A leader. A shaman or chief. Either way, I know to stay on my knees and bow my head. I sneak a glance when the last man steps aside. A dozen long sticks protrude from the leader's cheeks like whiskers.

My throat tightens.

His face blurs as the tears well in my eyes.

Don't show fear.

I lower my gaze without bowing my head to keep him in my peripheral vision. My heart thumps in my chest. It beats so hard the pain in my head worsens. I'm doing what I can not to let the fear bubble to the surface, knowing he's staring at me, determining my fate.

Focus on one thing.

Feathers are sewn together in a cape, draped over his

shoulders and falls to his knees. One red and one yellow feather threaded through each ear lobe protrude at odd angles.

Is he a bird spirit?

The shaman.

My baby moves inside me.

My shoulders slump in relief.

"Thank you," I murmur to my god, the universe, the jungle, or whoever is watching over me.

I yearn to touch my stomach in comfort but know better than to bring attention to something vulnerable inside me when I could be perceived as a demon. The majority of the tribe have protruding stomachs like me only not all are pregnant.

My grandmother's face fills my thoughts. I pray for her to give me the strength she found in the jungle.

"Tamùne woryi wypy," he says to his audience along with other incomprehensible words. *White woman mountain.*

Shit, he thinks I'm a bad spirit from the tepui. Or is it because I'm taller than his people? Please let it be the latter. I've never been so happy to be called a mountain because of my size.

I close my eyes and keep praying to God or anyone who can hear me.

Samuel.

I focus on his spirit—his love. Picture his love protecting me like a colored aura. I open my eyes to black eyes close to my nose. I stifle a scream and fall back onto my rear.

The raw belly laughter rises in the air and incites the monkeys to squeal from the treetops. Confirming I'm not a threat, I bow my head not only in respect, but the throb near my temple is getting worse. I raise a finger and touch the goo of old blood. When I meet the shaman's gaze, there's a hint of a snicker behind his painted expression. He waves his hand and shouts to the crowd, then grabs a handful of my hair and leans down to sniff it. He yanks hard, so I'm forced onto all fours, and he turns to walk away, my hair acting like a dog chain.

I scramble out of the capsule and stumble behind him, hunched over with my face to the ground. When I lift my chin, the feathers of his cape block my view to where he's taking me. I have an awareness of no one following.

From the force of him pulling and a sudden release of hair, I stagger into a hut and fall onto my knees. Dirt puffs up around me, and I close my eyes and cough, one hand protecting my stomach. His voice comes from behind. I adjust my hair to fall over my chest and sit on my legs, my head bowed. Words are shouted. He's lost the cape and no longer appears threatening. Mid-thirties maybe, he's young to be a shaman. Skinny, with paint covering every inch of his skin. Like the other men, his penis is tied around his waist, only he has a bamboo-like tube to protect his package.

With dust coating my throat, I need water. I cough and make an action like drinking. Regardless of what's offered if I don't hydrate soon, I'm putting both my baby and me at risk. He stands and grabs a stainless-steel cup and scoops the water from a bowl. In the corner is a collection of foreign items, including a machete and gold jewelry hanging from a pot.

"Sweet Jesus," I murmur. Did the people who offered these gifts survive? Are they trophies? At least the Watache have seen civilized people. He hands me the cup, and despite the cloudy appearance of the contents, I guzzle the water down, then hand it back. He refills it. I take it without hesitation and cough again when it hits my empty stomach. I have no idea how long I was out or how long we traveled, depriving my body of food and fluid. The chance of Samuel finding me is slim, and the reality hits me like another blow to the head.

I slide onto my side, resting my head on my arm in case I pass out. The Watache shaman squats and fixes his gaze on me as though he doesn't trust me to look away. I close my eyes, ignoring the female voices at the doorway.

I did what Samuel advised. I stayed out of the jungle at night when predators hunted. Daytime is supposed to be relatively safe. Only these people aren't nocturnal hunters. They do what it takes to survive, and I'm a means to an end. I'm unsure as to how I'll benefit them, be it food or bargaining or pleasure. The thought eats away at my soul, and I do my best to shut off my mind to the world and seep into the earth.

A shaking of my shoulder rouses me. He shoves bananas and passionfruit in my face. I sit and nod, taking the food from him. Backing away, he squats to watch me eat. Twilight has filled the hut. Through the door space and in the distance, a fire flickers. Again, I'm hit with the smell of meat. The jungle shrieks with life, a warning on high volume as though the trees are talking to me.

A woman enters the hut, full-rounded belly, black body paint, same hairstyle as everyone else. She moves in a way that suggests she's almost at the term of her pregnancy. She shoves a handful of meat in my face as if I'm a nuisance. Even in the failing light, the red flesh stands out.

Don't eat it!

I cover my mouth with my hand.

She shouts a few incomprehensible words before jerking the meat closer to my face. Samuel had warned me refusing food is a sign of disrespect, so I take it from her and eat it so fast, imagining it to be chicken because, hell, everything is supposed to taste like bloody chicken. I refuse to think of the possibilities of the source and signal again for more water.

My stomach growls, and not long after, I'm hit with sharp jabs of pain.

Sliding my arm through the dirt, I lay my head on my arm, and close my eyes, praying when I next wake, it will be sunlight.

At least I would have survived another day.

9

EDEN

It's not the sun that wakes me.

I throw myself onto all fours with an excruciating spasm in my gut.

"Please, no. Not my baby," I whimper.

The Watache shaman's quiet snores alert me to where I am.

Oh God, I need a toilet. If I don't find a bush and fast, I'll make a mess of myself.

Enough moonlight shines into the hut to see him curled on his side. He seems younger or perhaps vulnerable in his sleep.

The stench of poop hits me, and it's not mine. I heave then cover my mouth. The pong comes from his corner of the hut like something is dead, and I have to get out before I lose control. On my first step, I stumble, then stop to steady my balance and take a deep breath when the room spins. I must have moaned because the Watache shaman springs to his feet and yells out to me. I jab a finger at my bum because I have no idea how to say toilet. I doubt he even knows what a restroom is. He grabs my arm, and I yank it out of his grip and groan, clutching my gut. He stares down at my abdomen as if for the first time understanding the roundness. He follows me out, shouting. Deep murmurs come from near the fire as people stir from sleep.

The full moon casts enough light where the central fire lags. There are two large, open-walled huts on either side of the fire. I keep walking past the women and children in one hut. In the other hut, the men lie huddled, side by side. Legs and arms are wrapped around each other, and abdomens are used as pillows. All lay close and not a woman among them.

Movement catches my eye. Thrusts in sync. Gentle moans of pleasure. I look away and turn to the opposite side, where women sleep peacefully with their children. Many of them are pregnant, yet the men find pleasure and comfort with each other. There's no sign of a family huddled together.

The shaman shouts again, and this time, some men spring to their feet. I make my way to the closest edge of the jungle, one hand clutching my stomach, the other flexed straight in warning not to follow me. I rush forward with faint awareness they didn't stop me.

When I reach the closest tree, I lower in a wide squat, one hand on the trunk for support. The flatulence alone is enough warning for no one to come close until the pain has tears falling from my eyes. I blink the tears away, hearing sniggers from the men on the other side of the tree.

When I immerse from the dark jungle, the men chuckle and point to the shaman, making a circle shape with their hands. "Sano, sano," they repeat.

Mother.

The shaman's expression sours, and he yells before gripping my hair, and again, I'm stumbling behind him. Did he think I was going into labor? Hopefully, he believes I'm a well-fed white woman with a gastric bug.

Inside his hut, he releases his grip, yells more words, and points to the corner.

Does he expect me to poop in the corner?

It explains the stench coming from his side of the hut.

When I lower myself to the ground, I'm coated with dirt as it adheres to my limbs. There's no regard to hygiene, and it's only a matter of time before microbes will feast on me.

The odds of survival are stacking against me.

🌴

Faint light fills the hut.

Soft sounds drift in from the village coming to life—hushed voices, not threats of fierce cannibals I imagine them to be in my mind. I survived one night, although not from the mosquitoes. The itch from the bites covering my arms and back drove me half mad through the night.

I ache all over. Lethargy weighs down every part of my body, and I'm losing the will to fight for what seems like an inevitable ending. I close my eyes and wait for *him* to summon me.

The Ularan shaman would be in the medicinal garden at the break of dawn. He cared for every Ularan as if they were his responsibility. While this man sleeps the morning away, it seems he only cares for himself.

Ugh, my dry, scratchy throat is on fire. I'm not

convinced water is the cure. I recall coughing through the night—hard coughing capable of cracking a rib.

This isn't how I want to die.

I feel so helpless, lost in my mind about how to save myself. An urge to sob, really sob, overwhelms me. Holding it back has my throat burning. I squeeze my eyes shut to stop the tears and push out every scary thought of death because the hysteria is clawing at my chest. A shiver washes over me and then another. I open my eyes and interlace my fingers to stop my hands from shaking, and the terror taking over my thoughts.

Block it out. Think of our baby.

I can't let the Watache shaman see my fear.

Closing my eyes, I focus on the forest, the trees, and many months ago when I connected with a jungle spirit in an ayahuasca ceremony.

Breathe.

Slowly, in for a count to seven and release for a count of seven.

Clear my mind.

Close down the chatter and negative thoughts.

The voice telling me this is all for nothing.

I. Am. Not. Going. To. Die.

Clear my mind.

Breathe.

I envisage my third eye seeking guidance from the unseen spirits surrounding us. At night, the decaying leaves are moist under my feet as I pad through the pulsing dark forest. Walking blind toward a presence, something draws me closer. Not a bright light as one would describe death but another soul—one that can provide protection.

A pair of eyes shine through the trees. They're not

yellow or white like other animals. These are blue and mesmerizing, bewitching me to come closer. As I move closer, the dark silhouette morphs into a cat—a black jaguar. My heart lurches out of my chest only to be lulled into quietness, and a serene calmness surrounds me. The animal pads toward me and then circles not as though I'm prey, more in warning for anything lurking beyond the trees to stay away. The jaguar is protecting me.

Breathe.

Hold the image.

I allow the vision to wrap around me like a protective cloak.

Slowly, I open my eyes.

The Watache shaman is squatting, staring at me. God knows how long he's been doing it. His eyes hold suspicion, as though I could magically disappear at any moment.

The whole magic thing has me weighing up what to do. Should I take the I-am-powerful path or prove I'm not a threat?

I push up, change my position, and signal for some water to soothe the burn even though the cloudy water could be the source of my abdominal pain. He stills, eyes fixed on me. Suspicion evaporates, and there's no fear in his eyes. Instead, lust glimmers in his eyes, a universal longing recognized in all humans. His bamboo pipe bobs around his waist. I glance down to my exposed breasts, full and round unlike those of the women in the village.

Sex is carefree and permissible whenever and with whoever. I witnessed that last night.

I point to the water and mime drinking from a cup. He brings it to me, and as I drink, he flicks my hair over my shoulders and takes his fill. I keep drinking despite the cup being empty rather than meet his dark eyes. He squeezes both breasts. Sandpaper hands roll over my skin. I gulp air in revolt and fear.

I bow my head and hand him the glass, afraid to look him in the eye. I point to my mouth and hope he gets the message. He stands, his erection obvious even hidden in the bamboo.

He scoops water and brings it to me, turns to yell at the two women standing in the doorway holding fruit. He takes it from them and pushes on their backs to shoo them away. Then he squats directly in front of me. A long pointy nail pierces the skin of the passionfruit. He sucks out half of the fruit and then hands it to me. My head screams *no* with his filthy nail and his black teeth sucking on it first.

I suck the remaining pulp greedily. One taste and I'm craving more. I point to the other fruits, and he hands me a banana, and we eat, him watching my every move. He peels the entire banana and holds the fruit in dirt-covered fingers. I stick to what I know and handle less with my hands, though, at this point, it all seems pointless.

My thoughts wander, and I can't help imagining my heart being offered as a sacrifice to the others to eat and ingest my spirit power.

A spine-tingling scream comes from outside. I freeze. What now? The shaman's face glares at me as though he doesn't trust me enough to leave. The screaming continues, and he dashes through the doorway. I move to get a better view. A woman bounces with a small child limp in her arms. My thoughts tick over to the cause of the child's illness, but damn, it could be anything, including last night's meal.

"Iwoi. Iwoi," she wallows. *Snake.*

Behind her, a young boy holds a limp green snake, killed too late. Her cries of loss fill my heart. She refuses to hand over her limp child, his head now dangling from her arms. Beyond the cries of the other women, the men shout, "Tamu'ne woryi mawarí," jutting their spears to the sky. *White woman spirit.*

Painted red faces turn in my direction, their eyes as venomous as the snake. There's more yelling, and I don't need to comprehend the meaning. It turns into a chant and continues long enough for panic to build until a woman explodes from the jungle, screaming and pointing. The attention falls from me as the men dash into the tangle of green vines. The shaman spins, comes at me, and shoves my shoulder.

I stumble back and retreat to my side of the hut. He stands over me, machete in hand. "Not now," I rasp, my throat still on fire. God, I no longer have the energy to resist.

I fall to my knees and bow my head. "Tamu'ne woryi wakü." *White woman good.*

My last words.

I close my eyes and picture the ones I love. Samuel's voice cries out to me. I sigh even though the shouting sounds real.

"Eden."

The shaman and I turn to the doorway, and I see a flash of white hair.

Please let it be him.

"Tamu'ne woryi wakü," I repeat louder, hoping to be heard. *White woman good.*

The shaman spins toward me. His gaze is fixed, watching me carefully. A low hum rolls over the village, a song of low monotonous notes. The machete hangs low in the shaman's grip.

Samuel rushes to the door panting with every breath.

"Eden," he shouts in a combination of relief and panic.

Samuel's presence doesn't concern him. His gaze doesn't falter.

I don't look at Samuel in fear of taking my eyes off the shaman.

When the shaman sneaks a sideways glance, so do I.

Stupid because I witnessed the fear on his face, glimpsed the spears pointed at him and the Ularan warriors.

I fall apart piece by piece. Quiet sobs choke every breath. I don't have to hold on any longer because Samuel *is* here.

In a low, calm voice, Samuel speaks to him. I recognize some words. "Waküpe-küruman, upetoy." *Thanks, friend.* He lurches with an outstretched arm, something shiny dangling from his fingertips.

"Are you hurt?" His gentle words help to calm me even though he hasn't risked taking his eyes from the shaman as he takes slow, deliberate steps closer to him.

"No," I manage. I hurt everywhere, but *no* was the easiest word to say.

Samuel demonstrates how to wear the watch, vying for the shaman's attention. Pulling rolled paper from the twine around his waist tie, he reveals a map. He unfolds it and lays it on the ground. "Here," Samuel commands and points to an area on the map. The shaman speaks to Samuel, and they both hover over the map, pointing and shaking their heads.

"Samuel," I wail, my breath becoming weaker.

"Breathe," he rasps out the instruction without looking at me.

He holds out a hand and sidesteps slowly until he can touch me. With his legs bent like he's balancing on a surfboard, he passes me a bottle of water, keeping both the shaman and me in his line of sight.

I don't have the energy to twist the lid or hold the bottle to my lips. So I just hold it and focus on trying not to pass out.

"I'm sorry." The strain in his voice comes from his chest. "Wayara," he calls to the Ularan warrior.

He takes the bottle from me and holds it to my mouth. I swallow each mouthful slowly, allowing my stomach to adjust.

"Oh, Eden," Samuel croaks, as though he too is hanging on by thread. He strokes my hair. "Are you in pain?" He lifts a finger to catch my tears with his fingertips.

"My throat is closing up." I fall into his arms, my face on his shoulder to stifle further sobs so as not to alarm the Watache shaman.

"I'm so sorry," he says into my hair. My shoulders slump, the tenderness wrapping around me with each gentle stroke of my tangled mane. "You're alive. You're safe now, and I'm getting you out of here."

10

SAMUEL

Shit. Shit. Shit. Samuel has mere seconds to think.

Thank God, he found her, but her strength is fading, and time isn't on his side. His heart is racing as quick as his thoughts because he has no clue if their plan will work. He can't panic, not now when Eden needs him to get her out of here. Before they do anything, he has to first assess her and determine what she needs to stay alive.

"You're going to be okay," he tells her and kisses the top of her head. Eden is limp in his arms, and he needs to get her somewhere safe.

Wayara is puffing when he enters the doorway. Samuel asks Wayara to speak to the shaman, as he is a better communicator—calm and powerful. He listens for the right moment to make his exit. Samuel stands with Eden in his arms, and Wayara explains to the shaman that Samuel is tending to her wounds.

He carries Eden to a stream close to the village, and he assumes it's why they chose this location. Several Watache warriors maintain a safe distance behind them, all with spears pointed and primed to kill. The small stream is the Watache's water source since the main river is a half-mile from their makeshift village. Hidden under palms and with no crops, he assumes they plan to move on since these huts won't last the next rainy season.

"We're at a stream, and I'm going to carry you in," he tells Eden.

She hasn't opened her eyes since he lifted her into his arms. The water takes her weight so he releases one hand and strokes her cheek to calm her. "You're going to be okay, my love. Just hold on a little longer." He can't lose her. He just can't.

She clutches the water bottle as though it's a lifeline. It is for now. One reason he didn't want her to stay in Ulara was the high risk of dehydration when he had no adequate place to store intravenous fluids. He's thankful Asoo delivered extra water bottles last week, the ones he ordered in case of an emergency. Before rushing into the jungle, he packed antibiotics and other drugs in his small backpack. He was prepared for the worst. Now he's counting on Wayara's negotiating skills, so when he returns, they can get the hell out of here.

"Tilt your head back," he whispers to wash the funky smell from her hair. She has slept in the dirt and God knows what else. He needs to clean her skin to treat her bites and inspect her for possible skin infections. It's what he can't see that stirs concern. Gastroenteritis, he expects —a possible cause of her dehydration. There's the risk of mosquito-transmitted diseases other than the ones for which she is vaccinated. The list grows. His thoughts wander to their baby and her mindset. Eden's life has to come first, and much of it relies on Wayara getting them out safe and fast. He's aware they are being watched and prays nothing spooks the warriors to react and come charging while he attends to Eden.

Samuel assists her up onto the rocky bank and sits her on a boulder, so he can retrieve the leaves from a nearby plant. The foliage soothes the skin and acts as a natural repellent. In gentle swirls, he massages her back, arms, and shoulders in the sap. "Thank you," she murmurs. "I didn't think I'd see you again."

"Of course, I'd find you." His voice finds strength within his fear. "I had Wayara to guide me."

Her lips curl. It's slight, yet he sees it. She opens her eyes, and a single tear falls to her cheek. "I don't think I'll make it home," she croaks. "I can't walk. I'm too weak... and my throat." Her hands go to her neck.

"Open your mouth." He angles her chin and notices the yellow dots at the back of her mouth.

He ruffles through his waist pouch, grabs a high-energy bar, and rips open the wrapper. "Little bites, Eden. You'll feel better soon. And you won't have to do anything because we'll help you." He has one antibiotic blister pack in his pouch. Punching out two tablets, he holds them in front of her face. "Can you swallow these?"

"What is it?" she croaks.

"Penicillin. Take them, and then we can get out of here."

Her brow furrows. "I don't want to go back there," she says in a stronger voice.

Only now he hears the chants and turns to the trees where bodies camouflaged in paint hold their spears like javelins. "No one is going to hurt you." Regardless of the underlying threat, she's in his arms, and he's not letting her go.

"We have to go back. You're with me and are safe."

She pushes up, and he helps her to stand. Together, they inch their way back to the village. By the time they reach the shaman's hut, Eden has slumped forward.

"I can't..." she moans, "... take another step."

"Wayara," Samuel shouts.

Wayara steps out of the hut, the shaman keeping watch.

Samuel tells him they need to get Eden out of the village.

Wayara has negotiated a trade and calls to Timenneng. "Bring the wild pig and Samuel's hammock," he says in Ularan.

"What's happening?" Eden groans. "I'm scared," she whispers.

Samuel tightens his arms around her shoulders. "There's no need to be afraid. Focus your energy on you. Just rest, my love."

"I can't relax here. I'm tired. So tired, but I'm scared to fall asleep. What if—"

"No what-ifs, okay?" He kisses the top of her head and understands her fear as his heart is still racing in his chest. "We killed a wild pig near the river." Despite the Ularans craving meat themselves, the pig's purpose is to use it as a bargain for Eden's safety. "It is a..." he refrains from mentioning the word trade, "... a gift."

Timenneng went into the jungle with another warrior and three Watache men in tow.

"Please hurry," he whispers, aware every minute is crucial. "Hey." Samuel strokes Eden's face. "Are you still with me?"

She nods once. It's slight, yet it's enough.

Wayara exits the hut. He announces the shaman has commanded Samuel to explain the map. He wants to know the magic of the pictures. Wayara enlightens him on the Watache plan and how fire destroyed their home. Wayara explains the Watache are searching for a new place to live. Years ago, they found one by the river, but illegal mining nearby had poisoned the water and their food source. The elderly remained too tired to walk any further, including the shaman's father. Divided, hungry, and tired, they need to keep searching.

But there's more. The shaman remains bitter about his cousin being raised by the Ularans. Eye for an eye, they were taking the woman with his cousin's child. Then Eden stumbled into the scene, and they thought she was the ultimate sacrifice to the Mawarí spirits.

Wayara stops speaking when Samuel's shoulders slump. He stares down at Eden and hopes she doesn't feel his heart racing in his chest.

The shaman likes Eden, which is why Wayara sent for the pig. Another gift along with Samuel's wristwatch and the map. She's alive because she was going to become another wife to the shaman.

Samuel tells Wayara he's not taking Eden inside the hut. Wayara tells him to use his *Paranakyry pyjai*.

White-European medicine.

Everything in his pack is for Eden.

"Wayara will stay with you, okay. I won't be long." Panic rises in his gut as she falls into Wayara's arms without caring. She needs medical assistance now. "Hold the water bottle for her to drink," he tells Wayara in Ularan before striding into the hut.

Samuel clears his mind to negotiate with the man that has nearly killed the love of his life. The bitterness is bubbling inside of him like a volcano ready to explode. He has to keep calm and save his energy because Eden needs him. Now isn't the time to do something rash or revengeful. Samuel inhales a deep breath and points to their location. He tells the shaman they took the picture from the heavens. He points out the tepuis and the rivers and circles the place where the Watache elders remain— the place Wayara was leading them and why they almost didn't find Eden. They had no choice but to move on when the elders held no clue to their descendants' whereabouts. They were at peace and prepared to die, unable to continue to wander the forest. On the return journey in the curiara, Timenneng spied smoke rising above the trees.

He leans close to point out the places where illegal gold mines dotted the rivers. He jerks back when the sharp sticks protruding from the shaman's cheek prick his nose. The shaman grins, believing he still has the upper hand. Ignoring the glare from red-painted eyes, Samuel continues to reveal all his knowledge of the river and jungle and the caves that could lead the Watache through the tepui to the other side.

The shaman's eyes narrow in suspicion. He suggests certain parts of the jungle where they would be safe and says they should remain close to the Peruvian border. He tells them to stay out of the sight of the miners and metal birds that fly in the sky.

Cheering comes from beyond the hut. Samuel's head dips, and he takes a moment to offer thanks to the gods. Both men stand to see the pig—legs tied to bamboo— carried into the village and placed over the fire.

Samuel shows the shaman how to fold the map. He drops it in the corner along with his other prized collections, including Samuel's wristwatch.

The shaman leaves him to inspect the pig. The

Watache are hungry and distracted, allowing the Ularans to creep to the edge of the jungle. From here, they secure Eden in the hammock and carry her through the jungle without saying goodbye. In minutes, they reach the curiara parked under a tree on the narrow sandy bank.

Samuel barks instructions to Timenneng. He pushes the curiara off the bank and then hurls himself into the canoe. Wayara paddles with the strength of an Olympian with three other warriors paddling up front. Wooden paddles hit the water with loud *thwaps*, each nudging the canoe further from the bank. Shouting comes from the shore.

"Faster," Samuel says, only in panic he yells in English instead of Ularan. He points to the trees where painted bodies sprint out with spears over the shoulders. Several spears fly, whizzing on the descent. "Noo," Samuel calls out, then springs up to blanket Eden with his body, hovering on his knees. He leans his forehead on hers and squeezes his eyes closed for a moment. "Please, no," he moans in a raspy cry. The curiara tilts sideways with everyone scrambling to dodge a spear when it lands inches from the boat. He lifts his head to maintain his balance and not fall sideways and expose Eden to the danger. Spears spiral into the mud-colored river in a series of *tink, tink, tink sounds*. They steer the nose toward the middle of the stream until the current surges the curiara away.

Samuel glances down at Eden. "Are you okay?" He wipes matted hair away from Eden's eyes. She's already asleep. He places a finger on the pulse in her neck. Fast yet thready.

She's leaving him.

The walls of the green jungle close in around them

like a green jail cell offering reassurance they are on their way home.

The torment eats at him. Every breath is a step closer to her going home. The river current takes control of his thoughts when he imagines her caught in the rapids and being swept away—far away to another world, one where she belongs.

Home, safe with her family.

11

EDEN

"I'm okay," I whisper as I blink away the haze. My throat is dry, and it burns when I speak. I tilt the bottle again, taking small sips as Samuel instructed.

"Shh." The tips of his fingers stroke my cheek.

"Thank you," I croak, again. Every time I've opened my eyes, they're the only words I've whispered before slipping back into sleep.

"I want you to remain here," he tells me. "I'll grab our bags, and we're heading straight to Canaima. I'll stabilize you there before we fly out to Ciudad."

I didn't argue. My body aches and my head hurts as though someone has hit me with a hammer. The last thing I want to do is be upright.

I keep my eyes open and stare at the blue sky with ribbons of white clouds. Yet experience has taught me not to be tricked, for in minutes, Mother Nature will sucker-punch you with violent wind and rain. The walls of the dense jungle canopy pass by. A small amount of me bursts with pride how I can now identify the coral trees, wild cashew, and my favorite white and orange flowers of the beauty leaf. Even from here, her brilliant leaves stand out against other foliage.

The Ularan warriors stand with perfected balance, the canoe steady beneath their feet. One push of the paddle and it hits the bottom, so we coast into a turn. The other men row and steer us toward the familiar sandy banks of Ulara.

Shouts sound from the bank. I lift my head to a dozen men and Kaikare.

"I won't be long." Samuel hurdles the edge of the canoe and speaks to Kaikare. She points to our quarantine camp. Asoo stands away from everyone else. They speak, and then Samuel takes off in a sprint, and in seconds, I lose him to the trees.

Kaikare boards the curiara. It rocks gently as she kneels before me. She strokes my face, and I manage a weak smile. She speaks to me, although I'm too exhausted to comprehend any words. Two hands cup my belly, and she closes her eyes as though she's listening for a sign or concentrating on touching. She opens her eyes, her face serious. "Wakü." *Good.*

"My baby is okay?"

She nods, yet I sense she means, *for now*.

Asoo stands at the nose of the curiara. "I sorry, Eden. When I visit yesterday, Kaikare tell me. So I stay in your camp and wait." He points to the makeshift campsite. "I take you to Canaima."

"Thank you." It's all I can manage for now, yet in my daze, I comprehend the enormity of him staying here the night.

My eyelids flutter with the weight of lead forcing

them to close while Kaikare squeezes my hand. I fight to stay awake, afraid of seeing the Watache shaman's face when trapped in a feverish dream. A battle I'm losing for the red faces with sticks protruding like animal whiskers take over my thoughts.

Lost to the dreams and reliving the nightmare, I know I'm lucky as it could've been worse. Much worse.

The canoe rocks with Samuel loading our bags onto the other curiara. "You're back," I say and smile.

He leans over me and brushes my cheek. Sweat beads dot his forehead. Hot air caresses my face with every pant passing his lips.

Asoo speaks to Samuel, and they switch back to talking in Spanish. Kaikare squeezes my hand one last time before she jumps ashore. Samuel tilts the bottle for me to take another sip, then helps reposition me at the front of Asoo's curiara with our bags placed around me for support. I close my eyes and allow the sound of the motor to lull me into sleep.

The next time I open my eyes, the jungle is no longer a dense wall. It takes a moment to come around. I'm lying between Samuel's legs, my head in his lap.

I stare up at his beautiful face—dirt-smeared cheeks, hair tangled into knots, the lines near his eyes etched deeper on his thinning face, and still beautiful in a masculine way.

"Where are we?" I murmur.

Bloodshot eyes hold my gaze. "Hey. We're not far out of Canaima." He hands me another two tablets. "Can you swallow these?"

"Sure." I attempt to push up. Samuel takes my weight and supports me while I drink several mouthfuls of water.

I clutch my stomach as I drink. Everything is an effort. Everything hurts.

I close my eyes—then open them when I hear a helicopter overhead.

"They're flying closer to the river and closer to Ulara," Samuel says without checking if I'm listening. He watches its path as it heads for the opposite side of the tepui to Angel Falls.

"Why?" I rasp.

"More explorers are coming here seeking adventure. Looking for the caves or attempting to climb the tepui or even search for gold." He shakes his head. "Flying low enough for the Ularans to see them. The shaman asked me about the metal birds and if they were our Mawarí."

"Did you explain it couldn't hurt them?" I murmur.

His eyes meet mine. He strokes my jawline several times. "Yes, but the reality is if they see the village, the repercussions could hurt the Ularans. Years ago, no one flew close to the mountain range near that part of the jungle, but only now people are seeking their own adventure, dare devils taking bigger risks."

"You hear the aircraft before you see it, so you teach the Ularans to hide," I whisper, clutching my throat.

"They're going to have to find somewhere new," he says. "In the opposite direction to where we're sending the Watache."

"Where would they go?"

"Southwest and deeper into the rainforest. I'm sorry, I'm talking out loud, and it's not important right now." His fingers rest on my pulse. "I'll head straight to Victor and arrange a flight for you. I can check how long a medical flight will take to get here. If you can cope sitting up, then we can take one of the Cessnas, and I'll pay the pilot double."

"My throat is a little better."

"The antibiotics are working, but you're going to need a series of tests for the sake of you and our baby."

"Meaning?"

"Expect to be in the hospital for some time," he says it as though it's a difficult thing to endure.

"It has to be better than my last accommodation."

Samuel offers a weak smile, then pushes the hair out of my eyes. "Some hospitals have fewer supplies than I do in Ulara. They can't afford soap to clean, some don't have drugs like antibiotics or clean running water."

"What?" I croak.

"I'm taking you to a private one where I have briefly worked. It's well funded, and I've met many of the specialists."

Shades of pink streak across the eastern sky. A golden crown glows behind the resort creating a shimmer as if glitter has been sprinkled over the buildings. It's a fairy castle compared to where I spent the previous night.

Samuel carries me to his room while Asoo dashes to reception to alert Victor of our plans. Samuel runs a bath, and while I soak, he showers, then steps into the bedroom to use his cell.

The bubble foam cleanses the surface of my body. Beneath the skin, my joints ache. It's deep, as though the goodness in my bones is being drenched of nutrients for my deprived body to stay alive. My legs are heavy like steel. I barely have enough energy to lift my arms to wash my hair. In the other room, the bed calls for me to climb onto its softness and sleep for a thousand hours.

Samuel's voice turns deeper, engaged in a battle of

words in Spanish. Before I move a single muscle, the bathroom door swings open.

"We have a problem." Samuel lowers to his knees and takes my hand. He circles his fingers over my skin to calm me. "There's no pilot to fly the plane until morning. I tried to arrange an emergency—"

"It's fine, and I'm feeling much better. I'll survive another night." I smile at him, trying humor to lighten his mood.

He rests a hand on my stomach as though he's holding our baby. His eyes meet mine, and I'm not prepared for the anguish building inside of him. "The health system has changed. Many hospitals are closed or, if open, there are no doctors. There are stories of women giving birth out in the parking lot and waiting rooms. Now there are limited supplies of the treatment you need—"

"What do you want me to do?" I rasp.

"I'm failing you. I—"

I reach for his hand and squeeze it. "None of this was your fault."

"I'm sorry." His expression falters, then he scrubs his hands over his face, although the pained mask remains. "I know a guy in Guyana... Georgetown, and you'll have good private care. We need to get to Ciudad Guayana first, then fly to Guyana, so you'll need your passport."

"Everything is in the small bag that I left with Victor."

"We'll fly out first thing in the morning and then catch a connecting flight to Georgetown. For now, I'll get us some food, and then you need to rest."

Samuel helps me out of the bath, dabs the towel over me, tenderly drying my skin, and then helps me onto the bed. He kisses my cheek before he leaves. "You're going to be fine," he whispers.

I need to believe him, for the way my muscles hurt, it feels like I'm slowly letting go. Every bruise is ingrained deep. Beyond the surface, my soul is scarred. Each scar has torn at my faith in surviving out here and keeping my baby safe.

I'm hanging on to my own life by a thread.

12

SAMUEL

A steady *beep* comes from the monitor beside Eden's bed. Her blood pressure and blood oxygen levels remain stable. He stands to check out the intravenous infusion pump even though the nurse left the room mere minutes ago. Medication and intravenous fluids have treated her dehydration and bacterial infections, and yet it hasn't stopped him from worrying and analysing the slightest change in her blood pressure.

The chair by her bed is where he's slept in short bursts, too afraid to close his eyes for long periods in case she needs him. How she has gotten through the ordeal is beyond him.

Dr. Jagdeo closes the door with a slight click. Samuel gives him an appreciative nod for not disturbing Eden.

"I'll let you know when her blood results are back. The obstetrician will be here soon to take an ultrasound of the baby. From there, we'll decide if further tests are necessary. As for Eden—"

"Can you write up some forms for fecal samples? I want to cover all bases," Samuel says impatiently.

Dr. Jagdeo places a hand on Samuel's shoulder. "Patience, Samuel, you know some blood results take longer than others. We'll cover everything on your list." Dr. Jagdeo pauses and meets Samuel's gaze. "Do you want her to speak to a psychologist when she wakes?"

Samuel had told his friend every detail, as he's one of the few medical specialists aware of Samuel living with the Ularans. He was working with Samuel when he voiced his desire to do voluntary work with the remote Indigenous communities.

"I'll assess her first. She's stronger than anyone I know." Samuel turns to the woman who has captured his heart and soul. Lord knows what he'd do if he lost her. Watching her battle through the fever was difficult, but he knows something more sinister could be swirling in the depths of her mind. He's barely held onto his own sanity through the ordeal, not knowing what they did to her and if he was ever going to find her. Waiting for the tests is torture. His mind grows silent with panic as though he's trapped in a car as it plunges into a river, the water immersing the space. Every minute drags him closer to drowning.

Opening her bag, he retrieves her photocopied travel papers and finds copies of the yellow fever certificate and vaccinations she had before her venture with her girlfriends. If only he could rewind time and stay the hell away from her. He was the worst thing to happen to her, and yet she was the very best thing that's happened to him. She thinks he's strong, and yet time and time again, she has proven her resilience and love with an open heart without fear.

"I think this is everything." He hands the documents to Dr. Jagdeo.

"Thank you. I'll come back and check on Eden soon."

Samuel releases a long breath when the door thuds closed.

His eyes sweep over the bones of her face. She's a beautiful woman, only he notices the gaunt cheeks, her chapped lips, and slight scratches above her brow. He clamps his eyes shut, knowing what has to be done. He has to protect the two most precious loves in his life.

"I'm going to miss you every day," he whispers.

A squeaky wheel disturbs him. He opens his eyes and greets the doctor in a white coat pushing the machine on a trolley.

"Eden," Samuel says gently to wake her.

Her eyes flutter open. "Hi," she says wearily.

The obstetrician checks her identification wristband. "I'm Dr. Vásquez. I won't disturb you for long. We need to check on your baby."

"Thank you." She pushes up onto her elbows and groans, gripping her abdomen. "Argh. This pain... I keep getting these contractions." She stares up at Samuel and grimaces.

"I assume she's having Braxton Hicks contractions," he tells Dr. Vásquez.

"Have you learned breathing techniques at antenatal classes?" Dr. Vásquez asks.

"No," she murmurs.

"I can teach her," Samuel adds. He squeezes her hand reassuringly and then counts with her as she takes some deep breaths.

"Thank you," she says and rolls closer for Dr. Vásquez to examine her.

The doctor squeezes gel over Eden's abdomen and prepares the wand.

She giggles. "It's cold."

Samuel grips Eden's hand when a soft whoosh echoes from the monitor. He bows his head and sighs in relief at the beautiful sound of their baby's heartbeat.

"There," Dr. Vásquez turns the screen so both parents can view the image of their baby.

"Oh, wow," Eden says and gasps. She swipes tears from her eyes and then meets Samuel's gaze.

He shakes his head in wonder. For years he believed he was destined to live out his life alone. Seeing their baby for the first time is similar to an out-of-body experience with a sensation of floating from the pure joy pumping through his body. He leans down and kisses Eden's lips, the woman who has saved him. "I love you," he whispers.

Her happiness bubbles through muffled sobs. "I love you too."

Dr. Vásquez focuses on hitting buttons. "I'll print a sonogram for you to keep."

"You're the bravest mother in the world," he tells Eden.

Her gaze returns to the screen. "It's our baby." The light burns bright in her eyes, reminding him of dawn, a time of day when the best is yet to come.

"You estimate the baby to be twenty-eight weeks?"

Eden's brow pinches as she tries to gather her thoughts.

"Yes," Samuel answers for Eden.

"By the scan, your baby has grown remarkably, and I'd work with a possible mid-January date."

"Oh." Eden's eyes widen. "So, can you see the sex of our baby?" she asks. She glances at Samuel. "Do you want to know?"

"I... well, yes, if that's what you want?"

Dr. Vásquez's lips pull tight into a smile. "It's a girl."

"A girl," Eden says in a high-pitched voice. "Oh, Samuel."

Samuel chuckles. "I imagine she's going to be as beautiful as her mother." He shakes his head. "And yeah, I can't believe it." The thought of him almost losing both of his girls triggers the demons inside of him.

A voice he has fought hard to ignore.

You're a failure.

Dr. Vásquez's phone dings. "Excuse me a moment." He exits the room to take a call, leaving Eden and Samuel alone.

Samuel stands and walks to the window, only he can't open it for the fresh air he urgently needs. The last two days have played over in his mind again and again. He was dangerously close to losing Eden and their child. He doesn't have the stamina to fight the guilt. His eyes well as the emotion takes hold of his body. Eden can't see him like this when she needs his support more than ever.

"Are you okay?"

Samuel dips his chin, takes a deep breath, and looks over his shoulder. "Do you know how amazing you are?"

She tilts her head. "What's wrong?"

Samuel shakes his head. "I could've lost you."

"But you didn't."

"No." His voice cuts out as his demeanor cracks. One sob escapes him. He strides to her, collapses to his knees, and rests his head on the bed.

She runs her fingers through his hair to soothe him. "I'm fine. We're going to be okay."

His past and present collide, every thought undoing him until his entire body shakes. Every painful memory of his life is sucked into a vortex as the tornado rips out his heart.

"I'm so sorry," he weeps. "I almost failed you too."

"You saved me," she says gently.

Samuel shakes his head. "I saw everything I care about slipping away." He shakes his head. "You were out there alone, and I wanted to trade places with you. I kept thinking back to our time in Brazil. I wanted to go back to that day on the beach and not leave my room. I wish you never found me. Because of me, you almost died."

"Stop. Finding you was the best thing that's happened to me," she croaks and squeezes his fingers. "You can't blame yourself for what happened. I shouldn't have ventured out alone."

Wiping tears from his face, he then dots her fingers with kisses. "And you can't blame yourself when you had to pee. Something we all do."

A single laugh burst from her. She pats the bed beside her. "Lay with me."

Samuel slides on his side and lays beside her, taking up the smallest amount of room on the single bed. Everything has changed, and there's no going back to how things were before. They have days to contemplate what to do.

She runs her feeble fingers over his chin, catching on his stubble. "What are you thinking?"

"Sorry for interrupting," Dr. Vásquez chirps. "I'll let you rest, and we'll do another check in the morning."

Samuel walks the doctor out of the room to discuss further treatment and finds Dr. Jagdeo at the nurses' station. "I'm grateful to have Eden in a private room," he tells him. "It's a smaller hospital than in Venezuela. My concern here is if Eden went into premature labor, do you have enough incubators?"

"My friend, much has changed over the years. The medical system was failing in Venezuela, so I packed up my family and came to Guyana. This hospital is small, but we're better off here."

"How bad did it get?"

Dr. Jagdeo scratches his jawline. "I was told about a young girl who went into labor in her village. A friend took her on the motorbike across three rivers, then she caught two buses to get to a hospital. No one would see her as they had no incubators, and her baby was coming early. She tried several others. She slept on the street, cried for her baby as her labor pains worsened. Eventually, she banged on one hospital door and then passed out. They admitted her, and she gave birth to a little girl. The baby died hours later as she didn't have insurance, and they did not have an incubator in this particular hospital, but the young lady lived. She left the baby in the morgue as they didn't issue a death certificate, and she had no money for a burial. Maternal deaths rose, and infant mortality increased in that year. So, my friend, I'm glad you brought your special lady to me."

For a moment, Samuel has no words. His thoughts had jumped into overdrive thinking ahead to what they'll need. "When we leave, I'll require more sterilized products. Can I buy them through you?"

Dr. Jagdeo smiles. "I know of someone who can help."

Samuel gives a knowing nod. "I knew I could count on you."

13

EDEN

"Nooo," I wail with nothing left to give.

My heartbeat fills the dark space around me. It's all I hear, and every pulse is becoming weaker and slower.

Icy fingers claw at my chest. Cold tentacles spread the chill through my body. My arms are heavy as if a slab of steel restricts my movement, and I can't escape.

"Samuel," I rasp. He's not here. I'd feel him if he were here. I'm going to die alone. I'm so fucking scared.

I suck air in like it's my last breath.

"Where are you?" I shout to Samuel, only my throat constricts, and no sound comes out. "Please, Samuel."

He's the one person I need by my side to hold my hand even if I'm not okay, and the thought of him not with me scares me more than death itself. I imagine I'm home, safe with my family, yet my heart still yearns for a man who shares my heart. Through time and space, I'm searching for his soul, knowing we are one. Despite the short time we spent together, it was our destiny to find one another.

The air thins. My gut wrenches knowing I'm slipping away, and Samuel is completely unaware.

"Samuel," I rasp to the dark, empty space.

The life inside of me dies, and in those seconds, every face of those I love flashes before me. Faith, on her wedding day. Mum and Dad at Christmas lunch with my father making his traditional toast to our family. My girlfriends when we were on the beach in Rio. The darkness envelops me, and I'm among the stars, aware of another presence.

Gran.

Her gentle blue eyes hold an enormous amount of love for me. Her soft hand takes mine as she walks along the beachfront talking about what home means to your heart. How I'm about to give life to a new soul. She smiles, and a light shines around her.

The intense brightness forces my eyes to open.

A light reflects from the monitor.

My heart pounds with enough force to break a rib. Not a weak pulse.

A dream.

I'm cold and alone. Every part of me is trembling. It's the closest I've come to death despite it being a dream. It felt real, like a part of my subconscious the ayahuasca had accessed.

A warning.

Or a vision telling me not to leave him.

🌴

The following day, I'm discharged from the hospital, and we book into a hotel overlooking the Demerara River and the Atlantic Ocean while I recuperate, and we wait for the remaining blood results.

Sweeping the curtain aside, I take a moment to enjoy

the view and inhale a deep, cleansing breath of fresh ocean air.

The seaside city reminds me of home.

I close my eyes with the ache in my chest of missing my family and friends.

I glance over my shoulder to where Samuel had placed my phone on the table to call them, only I don't have the strength to speak to anyone without my voice cracking. Especially if they ask how I am because I'm too weak to fake a strong voice, and they'll see straight through me.

I lift the hem of my long blue dress that Samuel bought for me at the nearby Stabroek Market. He purchased new T-shirts for himself and some loose dresses that flare for me, bright-colored Boho dresses with beautiful patterns to lift my spirit.

It worked.

I'm still weak but don't want to be cooped up in a room after four long days in a hospital bed, especially after my dream. I cup my stomach and whisper, "We both need sunshine."

Taking a seat on the balcony, I inhale the fresh ocean air and gaze down to the sparkling blue hotel pool where Samuel swims lap after lap.

My gaze moves back to the beach. "You're going to love the beach," I tell my daughter. The beach is one of my most favorite places in the world. The ocean is the place I've missed the most, knowing the warm months in Adelaide are when my friends are having fun.

God, I can almost feel the sand between my toes.

The door behind me creaks. I turn to Samuel entering our room with a towel draped around his waist.

Good God.

I see his bare chest every day, but today, droplets glisten on his golden shoulders where light streams through the window highlighting his sculpted physique.

We meet in the center of the room.

"You look..."

"I've washed and dried my hair." I grin at him, knowing he doesn't understand how one small thing can do wonders for my morale.

"That's not it. Your cheeks are flushed."

"It's the effect you have on me." I take his face in my hands and taste the pool water on his lips. I taste more until our tongues collide with love and silent apology. "I need you," I say against his lips with an overwhelming desire to be adored by the one person who can destroy me and put me back together all by his love.

"Eden..." He pulls away and shakes his head.

"I need to feel again," I plead. Love will heal me quicker than any drug. "We haven't been intimate for a long time. Let's not waste another day where we don't put a comfortable bed to good use."

He lifts and carries me to the mattress. "Give me a moment."

It's the quickest shower for I've barely stripped my clothes before he's back, hair dripping and body glistening with moisture. His lips meet mine in gentle kisses, bathing my skin from my neck to my shoulders and then to my lips. He hovers over me with far too much space between our bodies. Every minute, he slowly eases closer as though not trusting himself not to break me.

My vagina works just fine, I want to tell him even though slow and gentle is all I can cope with right now. He's not only worried about the parts of my anatomy, it's the bruises to my heart, my soul, and the hurt deep in my mind where the demons hide.

If only he was aware how his lips are like heaven, and every touch has me floating on the clouds above as he breathes new life into my bones. His love awakens me and makes me truly feel alive.

🌴

The afternoon sun beats down on my bare shoulders as I take tender steps toward the ocean. Samuel has a tight hold on my hand as though he's ready if I stumble.

Small steps.

Deep breaths.

"Let's just sit," I say. He assists me to lower until my rear lands in the sand. "It's beautiful in Adelaide at this time of year. I can't wait for you to visit then." I'm aware it won't be this year. "A hot, dry Christmas by the beach." I smile, hoping he can imagine our future like I do. "Dad has a spread of seafood, although Mum still likes to have some roast meats and vegetables. There are too many choices considering Faith and Jake don't stay for dinner. They share themselves between families and go to his parents for the evening."

"It's how I imagined you spending your Christmas with your family." His tone is off, and I know what he's about to say.

"By coming here, I chose not to have Christmas with my family," I say firmly. "I wanted to be with you and then leave before the airlines refuse my travel."

Samuel stares at the ocean. "Everything is different now. Christmas is a month away, and you're thirty weeks pregnant. We need to talk about what's best for you and the baby, not what is best for us."

"What about us?" I wait for him to look at me. "I need to know we have a future together and where that will be. Our baby will have grandparents in two different countries." His gaze drifts back to the ocean the moment I mention his parents. "We need to talk about many things," I whisper. "It's time you level up and be honest not only with me but to yourself."

He stands, brushes the sand from his rear, and offers me a hand. "Let's start by you making some phone calls home. I'm sure everyone is worried about you."

"I'll make the phone calls if you promise to talk later." I don't give him my hand until he nods. When I'm upright, I kiss him on the cheek. "We promised each other *no secrets*," I remind him. "Some of your painful memories might be before my time, but we can't move forward unless you share them with me."

While drinking a glass of ice water, I make my way through the long list of text messages from my family and friends. Most are updating me with their lives with 'stay safe' at the end of the message.

I start with the easiest call to build the strength to speak to the others. I sigh in relief when Bree's phone switches to voice mail. I expected it, considering the long hours she works.

"Hey, Bree. Hope you're shaking it up in Sydney's most prestigious hospital. I know you're doing great and just wanted to leave a message to let you know that I'm okay. Love you and can't wait to kiss ya face."

The screen goes blank, and I wait a moment before calling Yasmine. Again, it goes to voicemail.

"Yas, it's Eden. Just wanted to check in and let you know I'm okay." My throat turns dry, thinking back to only a few days ago. A ghost of the woman she knows. "I'm so jealous thinking about you all partying at night at The Bay and hanging out at the beach on weekends. And I can't wait to hear about your new job. Love you, babe."

I sink onto the bed and hug the pillow before I call Amy. *Hey, remember when...* is how she starts each message. I do, Amy. I remember all the fun times we had together.

"Finally," she says on the other end.

I smile as though we're in Adelaide, and she's been nagging me to come out on a Saturday night with her. "It's good to hear your voice."

"Is everything okay? With you, the baby, and how's Samuel?"

"We're g-good." I swallow a few mouthfuls of water. "I had an ultrasound. Do you want to know what I'm having?"

"Fuck, yeah," she yells, and my shoulders relax.

My cracked lips stretch into a big smile, only it hurts, so I try not to smile so hard. "A girl."

"I knew it!"

We both laugh. "You'd say that if I said it's a boy."

Amy chuckles. "It's good to hear your voice."

"Same." I close my eyes and imagine us in the same room together. If we were, Amy would see right through me. "I hear Yasmine has a new job."

"She does, and she's been working weekends, so we haven't caught up in weeks. Trust me, you haven't missed out on much here. It's been bloody cold."

"Serious?"

"It's shit and not at all spring weather. I want to come back to South America. I don't suppose you're allowed another visitor?"

The reality of where I am hits me. "Amy, I told you it's complicated—" A sob escapes, and I cough to cover the sound.

"What's going on, Edes?"

"Nothing, I'm fine," I blurt.

Silence.

"You're keeping something from me."

"Oh, Amy, I was so fucking scared. I almost died." I let out another sob until the tears keep coming.

"Fuck, what?"

"I'm okay now," I rasp out. Even though I still have a long way to go because my thoughts are messed up. I wish Amy was here to hug me and tell me I'm doing the right thing because after what happened, I'm feeling shitty with myself.

"Hey. I'm here, babe. Tell me what happened."

I nod even though she can't see me. "I wish you were really here."

I tell her what happened and how I'm now in Georgetown, Guyana.

Amy cries with me.

"Come home," she croaks.

In my heart, I know it's what I need to do, but I also don't have the strength to leave Samuel.

"Have you booked your flight?"

"There's no way I could sit on a plane and be at airports for the next thirty-odd hours. I haven't got the strength."

"Samuel would accompany you, right?"

"He can't right now."

"Bull... shiiit," she draws out. "That's it. I'm coming to you."

"You can't." My shoulders slump. "When the time is right, I'll come home. Samuel will make sure I'm safe, only it can't be now. When I know, then I'll let you know."

"You'd better, Edes. And he better be doing the right thing by you."

"He is," I whisper. I knew of Samuel's commitment before I returned, and I don't expect anyone else to understand him as I do. "I have to go, Ames. I still need to call Mum, Dad and Faith."

"Text me soon," she demands.

"I will."

"Love you."

"I love you too."

"Eden—"

"Yeah?" I say, placing the phone back to my ear.

"Please be careful."

"I will."

I end the call. My fingers tremble as though I've run ten miles and sprinted to the finish. I close my eyes with my phone in my hand. I need to rest before talking to my family.

14

SAMUEL

"You should call your parents," Samuel says after returning from the market with fresh food for lunch.

Eden shakes her head. "It's too late with the time difference. I'm lucky Amy was awake. I sent a text and intend to call them tomorrow."

Samuel gives her a look as though he'll keep her to that promise.

"What do you think my parents will say?"

The question throws him. "I expect your father to say—"

"Come home?" she finishes. "Why is it you're concerned about my parents, and yet you skip over any details for yours?"

"I'm not the one who was hospitalized, so my parents have no need for concern." He places the paper bag on the table and unpacks apples, bananas, strawberries, and oranges.

"They should be concerned." Eden slides onto the chair at the other end of the table. "You've been living in the jungle for years on your own."

"On my own?" Samuel arches his brow. "Last time I checked, I was living in a community."

"It's not a normal community." Eden folds her arms over her chest. "And I bet they are concerned because when was the last time you spoke to them?"

"Normal. What's normal, Eden?" He shakes his head. "Talking about *normal,* most of your tests have come back, and all are within acceptable limits except your iron levels are low. Although I may need to challenge the pathology on your iron levels. You don't sound tired at all."

"You're not funny."

A laugh escapes him. "I could debate with you all day. On a serious note, I'll find a pharmacy to fill your prescription."

"Explains why I'm craving a steak."

He takes a plate of fresh fruit and places it in front of her.

"I eat *this* every day," she moans.

"*This* is what's good for your body, and it's just a starter. If you're up to it, I'll take you out for dinner tomorrow night."

"On a date?"

"Yes, Eden, a date. It's what *normal* couples do."

"We're not a normal couple." She takes a handful of strawberries and nibbles on one. "It's not a bad thing, but I know we can't do what other couples do."

His hand stills with a knife, ready to cut the orange in half. "We can." He drops the knife and sits beside Eden, taking both her hands in his. "You want to go out?"

"My God, yes. It's like prison has released me on probation, and there's so much to see—"

"Prison?" he chokes. "No one has forced you to stay in

Ulara." Her words hurt, for it's the place where he feels free, and he thought she understood him.

"When we're there, we aren't free to do what we choose."

"Every society has rules."

Her eyes flick over his face. "Right."

"You know Dr. Jagdeo asked me if you wanted to speak to someone confidentially."

"Like a psychologist?" She pulls her hands from his and wraps them over her pregnant belly.

"I said I'd run it by you. The option is there."

"What do I tell them? Cannibals kidnapped me? They'll think I'm delusional."

"It's for you to decide what to tell them."

"You know I'd feel a lot better if my, my... what are you to me? A boyfriend?"

"What? No. We're more than..." He stops himself and runs his fingers up and down her arms before looking up to meet her gaze. "You mean everything to me. *Everything*. You know that, right?"

She holds his gaze but doesn't answer him.

"Before you, I barely lived. I had no idea how I survived in the dark until that sunny day on the beach in Salvador when the light radiating from you almost blinded me. You're the sun and the moon together, and I need your light, your warmth, and your magnetic energy to survive every day."

Eden caresses his face, pushes long strands of hair out of his eyes. "And yet you're about to send me home, aren't you?"

He understands why she was defensive in their conversation. "It's the safest option."

"No. What I need is to be with the father of my baby. I

have another month to decide what to do. I want to be with you."

He pulls her onto his lap. "Let's get something straight. I never considered our commitment to each other to be decided by a piece of paper or a ring on your finger, but I can arrange for it to happen tomorrow."

Her eyes pop. "Just like that, you would marry me?"

Taking her chin between his fingers, he raises her face until she's looking him in the eye. "Yes." He kisses her cheek and wraps his arms around her.

"You're right. Paper and rings aren't a symbol of our love, and if I'm honest, if we were to be married, I'd want it to be in front of our family and friends."

"If we do this now, it would be for you and me. We could have another celebration later."

She takes his hand and places it over her heart. "It's reckless for you to have my heart racing after all it's been through."

Samuel slides down onto one knee. "Eden. You steal my breath, and I'm often lost for words just by the sight of you. I know what I feel in my heart, and it beats only for you." He takes her hand and places it over his heart in the same gesture. "I want to spend the rest of my life with you. Will you marry me?"

She kisses him again and again. "A thousand times, yes."

🌴

Samuel assists Eden from the taxi and takes her hand as they enter the hotel foyer. Dinner at a romantic restaurant is what Eden had needed. They chatted about her family and friends while dodging the topic of her return home. Tonight, he'll gently coax her into doing what's right, and it's not returning to Ulara with him.

He expects she'll be tired and want to fall asleep. The remaining pathology results should be back tomorrow, so he'll arrange for her to go home in the next week.

While Eden sleeps, he can research flights. He had overlooked the effort for her to come to him. Her flight to Sydney was a couple of hours. Then she took an international flight to Santiago, Chile, which was almost eighteen hours in duration. It took several flights from Santiago to reach him in Venezuela, all before boarding the curiara for the boat ride.

Their baby is growing. Flying for many hours can be problematic and not only for comfort. He's concerned about deep vein thrombosis.

Eden showers before bed, and he smiles at how she's showering at least three times a day while she can.

He opens his phone and scrolls through the news. Eden has forced his hand to face what's happening in the world. He has only answered to the shaman for several years and thought every country's leader insignificant to his chosen lifestyle. There's political unrest *everywhere.* He had researched what his friend told him about Venezuela and was shocked to read how thousands of physicians had fled the country. Even in Chile, people sleep in airports where flights have been delayed because of an imposed curfew. He'll fly as far as he can with her to Santiago before returning to Ulara to his quarantine camp. He doesn't want to think about Eden leaving, the lonely nights and the days blending as one.

Every day she has chipped away at his armor, leaving his life and love exposed and his heart vulnerable. He wants nothing more than to be with her, spend the rest of his days with her, and until then, it's his responsibility to keep her safe.

Samuel closes his phone when Eden exits the bathroom with a towel on her head and one draped over her breasts. The swell of her stomach gives the most beautiful shape to her curves, one he never expected to see on a woman who had captured his heart.

He falls to his knees where she stands, opens the towels and kisses her thighs, the dark line of her linea nigra, and turns his head as though listening to their baby.

Eden runs her fingers over his scalp. "You'll only hear my belly complaining I ate far too much."

He gazes up at her. "Do you mind if I have a word?"

Eden tilts her head and smiles.

"I'm yet to meet you, and already you have fulfilled my life in a way you'll never know. As your father, I vow to do what's best for you and your mother, even if it means sacrificing what's best for me. So forgive me for sending you away when all I want is to be there when you come into the world. Your mother will take care of you until we can be a family."

Eden clutches his hair and tilts his head until their eyes meet. A single tear rolls down her cheek. "No," she murmurs. "Please don't do this."

"I need you to be safe."

Eden backs away, so his hands fall to his sides. "No."

"I'm doing this for us."

"Then come with us. Come with us now, and be with me in Australia when I have our baby."

15

EDEN

"In Australia…"

Samuel remains on his knees, head bowed.

I wait for an apology, a confession.

"I can't," he whispers. "Not yet."

Gah.

I storm to the minibar and shake the bottle of whiskey. "You know this is when I miss drinking."

He's beside me, and I didn't hear him move. "I have to finish up my work, complete my contract, and then I'll be on the first flight to you."

"It concerns me how you don't want to be there when I have our baby. I mean, what if things go wrong, and I can't contact you—"

"Don't. Don't do that." He places both hands on her shoulders and leans, so his forehead touches hers.

"And it's not just me." God, he has unleashed the bitch inside of me. I can't control my voice to discuss anything calmly with the urge to yell at him until he gives in. Only he won't. I know it's the part he struggles with— a side of him hung up on failure. And I'm destroying him by allowing him to think he's failing me when he's doing his best to keep us safe. "Your parents. Why haven't you told them they are going to be grandparents?"

"I can email them now."

"Christ, Samuel, listen to yourself. *Email*. When was the last time you spoke to them?"

He backs away from me until his legs hit the bed, and he sits on the edge. He slouches so his elbows rest on his knees. "We don't have that sort of relationship, but if it's what you want, I'll do it."

"I have to call my parents," I tell him. "We'll do it together. I'll call from the bathroom, and you do it from here." I check the world clock. It's nine at night, so it's around five in the afternoon in LA and nine in the morning in Adelaide. His face turns ghostly white, yet I stand my ground waiting for him to pick up the phone.

"Are you going to police the call?" he asks. I ignore it because these are all steps to melting the armor to why he believes his life is in Ulara.

"Only until they answer, and then I'll make my calls."

I wait until he presses buttons, then he turns the screen.

Mom.

A woman's voice answers.

"Samuel?" Her voice sounds excited yet confused.

His free hand supports his forehead. "Hey. I'm sorry it's taken this long to call..."

I leave him and head into the bathroom to call my parents. I decide to buzz Mum in case Dad's in a work meeting.

"Eden."

The warmth of her voice wraps around me like a blanket comforting and protecting in equal measures.

"Hi, Mum."

"It's good to hear your voice. I'm at Faith's now helping her with the baby. Seb, stop. Mummy can't do that while she's holding the baby. Come here, and Nanna will do it for you. Wait, love, I'll put you on speaker. Say hello to Aunty Eden."

She doesn't question my safety, so it makes it easy to account for my well-being. I love hearing her interact with her grandchildren and look forward to the day she'll have a special relationship with my baby.

"Seb." I focus on my nephew. "Aunty Eden misses you. Do you want me to bring home a surprise?"

"Tell Eden you miss her. He's showing you his dinosaur figurine. Darling, Eden can't see it. Growl, growl, roarrr. Yes, that's right, darling. Oh, now we have a lion toy."

"Hi, Eden," Faith calls out from the background. "Welcome to my madhouse."

"How are you, Faith? And baby James?"

"I'm good. Busy coping with a two-year-old and a two-month-old. Wait, no he's ten weeks now."

I never knew why mothers counted in weeks.

"Great. Well, I just wanted to check in. Everything is wonderful here. I thought I'd call while I have internet. Sometimes it's hard, and the weather has changed, so it just rains nonstop." I hold my tongue, not wanting them to panic about any little thing. "It's annoying, that's all. Makes for a boring day sitting in the hut. I'll check in soon, okay? Oh, and I had a scan..."

"Is everything okay?" Mum asks quickly.

"Of course. But I wanted to let you all know I'm having a little girl, and everything is fine." I'm amazed by my acting skills and how together I sound.

"Oh, Eden, that's wonderful. I'm so happy for you. When are you coming home?" Mum asks.

"I'm not sure, Mum. In a month or less. I'm working out Christmas festivities with Samuel now. I love you. I'll talk soon, okay."

"Stay safe, Edes," Faith says quickly.

"Bye." I end the call and take a deep, healing breath. The hardest call is to Dad, and I'm waiting for tomorrow to speak to him. Beyond the door, I hear the murmur of Samuel's voice. He's still on the phone. So I stay in the bathroom to give him the privacy he needs and scroll through the few photos on my phone. There are some of the jungle and others on the curiara with Asoo and Samuel. I send them to Amy, then to Faith with a text asking her to show them to Mum and Dad.

I open up Instagram. Scroll. Close it. Facebook. Scroll. I feel out of touch with everything I'm reading. An unsettling sensation creeps over my skin as though I'm lost in another dimension, and the world keeps spinning without me. I open up the Netflix app. Damn, there are so many shows I haven't seen. If I were home, I wouldn't have missed them. Did I watch half the shows so I felt like part of the mob and excited?

Everything I did then seems insignificant when compared to my life here.

The room next door is silent. I open the door enough to see out a gap. Samuel is lying on his back with his arm over his eyes.

"Are you okay?" I ask in a gentle voice.

"Y-Yeah." His voice cracks, and his arm remains over his face.

I slide onto the bed next to him. "Were they glad to hear your voice?"

"They want to meet you."

I smile even though he can't see it and remain quiet, hoping he'll say more.

"They want to know when I'm coming home. The conversation started well until they berated me for not having a career and a home for you and the baby. They questioned my sanity as to why I'm here and putting you in danger. It made sense, and yet it opened up a gaping hole of emptiness at the thought of going home to live the same life as them. Always living to their standards and never being enough."

"You're enough. You're an amazing man, and I'm proud of what you're doing. Your work makes a difference to many lives." Holding my stomach, I roll onto my side so I can look at him, touch him. I rest my hand over his heart. "I know how big your heart is for all of us."

We haven't resolved some issues, and yet he took some steps in reassessing what he needs in his life. I know it's my baby and me. And it might not be his home in LA, which is fine by me. I'd like to think he was on good terms with his parents so they would want to come and visit us. I'm yet to find out what really pushed him to come to the jungle, and I know it had something to do with his parents and a girl while he was at college.

But this is enough for one day. I'm exhausted, and we both need to call it a night.

🌴

"Eden."

I open my eyes and try to focus. Is it morning already?

Samuel hands me his phone. "It's Dr. Jagdeo." He's dressed, showered, and shaved. I'm still in bed.

"What time is it?"

"Eight thirty."

And I have an overwhelming urgency. I wave my hand at him to take the phone. "I have to pee."

Samuel chuckles before he speaks. "She needs to pee."

Argh. Did he have to tell him?

"Sure, I'll pass on her results."

My bladder hasn't been the same this past week. I'm sure our daughter takes pleasure dancing on my organs.

When I exit the bathroom, Samuel has ended the call. "Did you want to talk to him because you can call him back?"

"Do I need to?"

"Your bloods are fine, and your fecal samples have come back negative for blood or any worms."

"Worms?" I cough.

"There are worse things than worms. He wants you to stay on the iron tablets until you have the baby."

"Those tablets make my..."

"No need to explain." Samuel grins at me. "It's best for now. You should have a repeat blood test in another month to compare."

Another month. For now, I'm not sure where that will be. All I know is I want to be wherever Samuel is and not *alone*. "Hey, can we go out for coffee?" It's a luxury to do these things with him, and I'm trying to show him what our future could look like."

"I'll do whatever you want since it's our last day here."

"Are all my results back?"

He nods once.

I'm not discussing anything right now. "Book a taxi for an hour. Maybe we can eat lunch in a quirky café."

"Quirky..." He shakes his head.

"And maybe you can get a haircut," I tell him.

The look on his face has me giggling as I head to the shower.

"I need a date, Eden." He taps away on his phone. "We're booking your flight home today."

The smile has evaporated from my lips. "No." I shake my head several times. "You promised me one month."

"Okay. One month. Give me a day." His steely eyes fix on me.

"Fine. Two days after Christmas so we get to celebrate together."

"Eden." He lowers the phone from his face. "You are required to fly before you're thirty-six weeks pregnant. Now that your date is mid-January—"

"But the authorities don't know that. They still have my January 30 date from my gynecologist. Please, give me Christmas."

It gives me the extra time to convince him to make the journey home with me.

16

SAMUEL

Two Days Later...

Eden had convinced Samuel to stay in Canaima for a week to quarantine in his room, yet not so far from a Cessna if she needs to fly out. He was also comforted knowing his order of supplies will arrive, and he'd have enough medication and sterile instruments on hand.

"Samuel."

He turns to his friend who's calling his name outside the room. Eden is asleep on the bed, so he sneaks out to speak with Asoo, remaining a few yards apart.

"The miners you speak of along the Carrao River. They talk of burning forests and building mines, look for hidden gold in river. In tepui. Garimpeiros will come work. Everyone needs money."

"Mine near the tepui?"

"Yes, my friend."

"Christ. Where did you hear this?"

Asoo points to the restaurant. "They stay here. They eat here."

"When?"

"Three days ago." He holds up four fingers.

"Where are they now?"

"Getting chain saws and guns."

"You need to warn your friends, all the Pemón communities, not to work for these men. Ask the elders to explain the damage and how they'd be slaves."

He assumes it will be months before the mine opens, yet he knows the shaman has to be notified. The mine will be on the opposite side of the tepui, but the mine leaders will risk Pemón lives with no regard to Indian values and destroy everything that's sacred.

"Asoo, please bring me a map of the area from reception."

Asoo nods before heading to the office building.

It's time the chief and shaman saw his paper map.

He returns to his room and sits on the bed where Eden sleeps, opening the news app on his phone. Many countries remain hostile, and civilization is still competing to be the most beautiful, the most famous, or the biggest jerk. There's a part of him that vowed never to return to society, and it creates an internal battle with his love for Eden.

She makes a sound from her throat. A sharp sob. Is she dreaming?

Samuel takes hold of her hand and gives a gentle squeeze to indicate she's safe. It's enough to rouse her, and she opens her eyes, closes them as though relieved to be with him.

"What are you dreaming about?" he asks gently.

"Their faces," she murmurs. "I keep seeing the sticks in their cheeks, mouth, and nose and the way his dark eyes stared at me as though I was an animal."

Sliding down the covers to be closer, he pulls her to his side. "Appearances are measured differently in every society. What you find beautiful, they may find offensive. The Indians are in tune with the jungle. She's a source of life and not feared or considered a hostile place."

"I don't think the jungle is hostile. I just... don't know it well, so it's dangerous in that respect."

"I know, and you're looking more relaxed with every week you stay. I'm explaining how the Watache respect all creatures of the jungle, including the most venomous. Those sticks in the shaman's face? It's his way of dressing like a cat. He believes it helps him to hunt more effectively and move quietly through the jungle."

"Like the jaguar."

He strokes her long white tresses, now tamed after days of brushing and repeated washes. "Your hair would've freaked them out. A white-haired woman would be sent from the spirits. You would be equally disturbing to them as they were to you."

"I've never been more flattered to be called ugly," she murmurs.

He offers a weak smile, knowing her nightmares may go on and cause her other grief.

"The jaguar... I see it too. It's in my dreams only I'm not afraid, which is weird," she murmurs.

"Why is it weird?"

"It's the one animal the Indians fear even though they respect everything about the jungle. My brain must work backward because I'm afraid of the things you mention can help, and what everyone else fears, I'm like... meh."

"Dreams and reality are two different things. There must be something about it that's talking to you," he prompts.

"It has the most hypnotizing blue eyes. It watches me. It's not like I'm its next meal or anything, it's more like..." she shrugs, "... it sounds crazy but as though it's protecting me."

"Not crazy," he says. Samuel thought her grandmother's spirit might look out for her granddaughter. "The jungle speaks to us in many forms."

"It's another reason I want to stay. There's a voice calling me, and I feel like the jungle isn't done with me yet. I hope it's not the Mawarí enticing me back to seek revenge." She holds his gaze. "I've made mistakes before, but this feels different."

"It's not the Mawarí." He kisses the top of her head. "I have something to tell you. While you were sleeping, I emailed the pharmaceutical company's HR explaining I won't be renewing my contract for another year. One more journey to the tepui to retrieve the flower along with the roots, and once I've sent the samples to Caracas, my contract can be terminated."

"What about your duty to the Ularans?"

"You and our baby will be my responsibility."

For a long moment, Eden stares at him. "You'll struggle to say goodbye."

"I will," he says, his throat suddenly tight. Fear runs along his spine at the thought of returning to society to the place that caused him years of unhappiness. Back then, he had no soul. He's no longer that man, thanks to the beautiful woman beside him. Yet that dark voice whispers to him, reminding him of his past.

A failure.

And Eden is better off without him.

He has built a life in Ulara. A life he loves.

Now it comes down to a choice.

And he'll always choose her.

Regardless of the consequences on him.

17

EDEN

The following morning, Samuel left to meet with Asoo. He says they need to discuss business and to call him if I need him. I have a couple of hours to spare, so I wander out to the gardens and stroll a short distance along the path.

It's truly paradise, and the postcard view lifts my spirits. Closing my eyes, I visualize the animals and their sounds echoing from the rainforest. Howler monkeys high in the treetops. The macaws deathly screech. The constant clicking of insects, and now the buzzing above my head. I head back to Samuel's room intending to nap. If only I had a book to read.

It's been a couple of weeks since I opened Gran's diary. I retrieve it from my backpack and slide onto the bed with a piece of chikoo fruit. Samuel insists this fruit should be part of my daily diet because it's a super food that has everything our daughter and I need. He also emphasized that it will help my body heal quicker than most drugs people have been shoving at me. Since it tastes similar to a pear, I'm not objecting, and it's easier to eat than some foods I've been offered in Ulara.

Relaxing with a book feels much like home.

The thought comforts me.

Until I clasp my chest and burp out air. Ugh, this heartburn is annoying.

Another thing, when did I stop being a lady? Because at night, I giggle, thinking how air just sneaks out of me.

"What are you doing to me?" I say affectionately to our baby. A smile stretches my lips, knowing we're going to be okay. Staring at Gran's diary, I wonder about her pregnancy and what support she had from the shaman because she didn't have someone like Samuel to guide and support her through it. I imagine my Gran being strong like the other Ularan women. I have her blood pumping through my veins. Her strength is with my spirit, and she'll help and guide me while I'm in the jungle, doing what she did decades ago.

Mum said she had blessed me when I was born. Maybe she had some power to see my future and visualize this moment where we'd connect even though times separate our journey. A different level of consciousness unites us.

15th May 1961

What's wrong with me?
I'm a nurse, for God's sake, and I can't even cope with a baby. I know my skills. I have the knowledge only the black hole keeps threatening to swallow me up every night. Every night I'm scared to close my eyes. It is not the fear of dying. It's the demons waiting for me, whispering that it is all a lie. It

shouldn't bother me, but no sooner do I close my eyes and Winston starts crying, I'm up pacing the floor with him in my arms.

Last night I was so tired I walked around in zombie form, and I almost dropped him. There was a moment I wished I did because then all the crying would stop. And I've hated myself since because it's not how I feel. I love my baby. I've just stopped loving myself because I'm trying to find that mother-baby connection.

It's not there.

My heart is empty.

I tried to talk to Albert this morning.

He brushed me off and said all mothers are tired, and I'm going through a stage. He didn't even offer to help.

19th May 1961

I haven't showered in two days, and I'm wearing the same pajamas.

Winston isn't crying as much, so I can't even blame the colic. What sort of life can I offer him when I can't even manage to change my clothes? I see the sideways glances from Albert. He notices, yet he doesn't say anything. I know he thinks I'm a terrible mother.

3rd June 1961

Brenda is getting married. I'm thrilled for her as it's her dream, and she wants babies more than anyone.

I showered before she came to visit me and pinned my hair to the top of my head in a classic roll. The guilt stops me from telling her the truth.

I wanted to share in her happiness. When she asked me to be her Maid of Honor, I cried. She thought it was tears of joy.

How am I going to pull myself together in three months?

I need a miracle to get me out of this cave.

"Gran." I wipe a single tear before it cascades over my cheek. I don't want to keep reading, only I need to know she got through this and found her way out of the darkness because it's the darkness that scares me too.

I remember the day Gran died. It was the same time we heard of the Haiti earthquake in January 2010. I remember the devastation of Dad telling Faith and me that Gran had passed in her sleep from a heart attack. Then the world grieved with the devastation of Mother Nature's wrath. I was around fifteen at the time, and I couldn't fathom life without Gran.

She had never mentioned being in the jungle, although her stories of life lessons made sense, especially her love of nature and every creature on earth. I got my spider phobia from my mum's side of the family because Gran loved to keep the huntsman spiders in her house.

"*Henry is eating the flies and mosquitoes for me,*" she'd say.

I lean up on my elbow and look around the stunning vista surrounding me. *God, she must have loved this place.*

My stomach tightens, and I groan before breathing through the Braxton Hicks contraction. "You can practice all you like," I tell my daughter. "I'm not ready for you to make any surprise appearances just yet."

23rd September 1961

It's Brenda's wedding day. I'm so excited for her. Albert bought me the dress for the wedding, and I feel excited to finally wear it.

I have had time to think and consider the guilt that cripples my thoughts. It is not being a mother that I struggle with most, and it's not working and being financially independent. I miss caring for my patients, knowing I'm doing some good in the world. Winston doesn't need someone like me. Anyone can feed him and change a nappy. He'll appreciate his mother when he's older.

I'm going to ask Albert if I can at least take on the bookkeeping for the hotel. He'll need to teach me. Then he could care for Winston while I do a day's work.

I'm going to ask him tonight after the wedding when he's in a good mood.

28th September 1961

Albert told me he didn't need my help to run the hotel. I should just do what I'm good at and be a mother for Winston and cook his dinner every night.

I've cried myself to sleep the past five nights.

I don't have a purpose. There has to be more to life than this. After completing my nursing, I have so much to offer. Why do

I have to act like it no longer matters? Albert said my role is to be a good wife and obey my husband.
We have one shot at life, and this isn't the life I choose.
I'm an awful person.
I should be happy. I have a home, a husband who loves and cares for me, and a beautiful son.
When did I become ungrateful?

Date: 10th October 1961

Today I received a letter from Dr. Anderson.
I hid it from Albert and waited until he was in the office until I read it.
I can't stop shaking.
It's the best news to feel valued. Only it is pointless. I can't go. There's no way I can leave Winston and Albert to do something like volunteer in an indigenous community in Venezuela. He'd call me selfish. And it's true. Only I can't stop dreaming about it.
I'll keep the letter as a reminder someone values my work and me.

I'm holding my breath. Despite my heart breaking for the pain she's suffering through, I'm struck with the realization this is the letter that invites her to come here fifty-eight years ago.

My whole body tingles. I hold the diary to my chest.

I want to feel the excitement and sense of adventure my Gran would've experienced. Mum mentioned her time in the jungle is documented in a journal, which her friend Brenda knows about. I vaguely remember Brenda at Gran's funeral, dressed in black with red shoes and handbag. I remember thinking why red?

Our advances in medicine have come a long way since the 1960s. Yet, she endured the hardship. She survived for a couple of years as I'm not sure of her time volunteering before she discovered Ulara. In that time, she gave birth to a baby in the jungle with more than likely no help from anyone. Remembering Gran as a strong-minded lady and slightly stubborn, her determination to be included in the community and be as one with Ularans with no special benefits isn't surprising. The energy explodes within me with the lightbulb moment. This is my destiny. Gran lives in me, her spirit has remained here, and if Gran could give birth in the jungle like many other women, it's not outrageous for me to have my baby here with my daughter's father by my side. Apart from the improvement in medicine and having extra supplies on hand, Samuel *is* a doctor, and he'll be with me during the birth—an advantage over Gran who would've wandered from the village, squatted over a hole, and delivered Kaikare herself, going by their tradition. Maybe some women were there to help.

Nonetheless, I'm in a far better position than her.

I'll have the baby here—in Ulara.

18

SAMUEL

Samuel took commitment as serious as a vow.

Years ago, he took an oath to keep the location of Ulara a secret. The people's safety was of utmost importance, and he promised the shaman he'd work alongside him to provide medicine and advise him on the science Samuel had learned in his medical studies. Although science isn't a word he could use, and it came down to his people, where he was born. Now *his people* are about to illegally mine an area close to the tepuis—a dangerous undertaking for those workers with the unpredictability of the tepui formation and how those in command treat the workers. He hopes his fear of the mine affecting Ulara is only that—a fear. Other mines have poisoned the local river systems with mercury leaching into the water and soil. It not only destroys the environment and water surrounding the mine but thanks to the poisoned fish, all the communities further down the river have been known to fall ill. He prays the government hears about the illegal mine and stops it before it destroys the surrounding ecosystem.

Overbearing all other fears is someone stumbling across Ulara. Their primitive minds and ways of life will be mocked, and he understands the mindset of outsiders. Other tribes have been bullied into change and tried to be saved with the way of God.

Their beliefs, lifestyle, and superior connection to the jungle would be perceived as being crazy, and they'd be thought of as inferior beings. The thought of bullying and enforcing change, then the suffering of the people he loves, has his chest tightening in fear. Especially knowing the Ularans have no immunity to many diseases outsiders will bring.

Even though the sun has barely encroached the horizon, he makes out Asoo throwing a bag into the curiara.

"Buenos días," Samuel greets Asoo. He leaps into the curiara and distributes the waterproofed bags evenly under the seats. "What happened here?" He points to a section where several planked seats have been removed.

"Eden to rest," he says, as though Samuel should understand. "Eden in pain last time."

Samuel hesitates, wanting to tell him Eden will not be traveling in the curiara. She's resting in Canaima before traveling home. The gut feeling she'll fight him on this halts his words. For now, she is healthy and safe. Victor will check on her during the day while Samuel investigates the location of the proposed mine with Asoo. He doesn't expect any complications. However, he left instructions with Victor on who to call if there's an emergency.

The risk holds more danger than he cares to contemplate. Both men are aware their presence needs to be hidden at all costs. They have fishing lines and bait to use as an alibi in case they are questioned.

To further strengthen their camouflage as hunters searching for food, the men have no phones or cameras. An action to prove they aren't spying so as not to cause a reaction if they are caught out or anything untoward happens, Victor is the sole person aware of their venture, and they have no means of contacting any other authority.

Samuel opens the map and spreads it out on the wooden seat. He marks the location of the small Pemón communities dotted along the river. With the latest rainfall, another tributary formed with the overflow of surplus water from the tepui, and it snaked a path to join the Carrao River. The tributary is their destination. Some of these smaller offshoots disappear in the dry season. It is a risk yet perfect for the mine to be invisible since barely anyone would know the location unless they are planning to dam the water supply from another source.

"You have sent word?" Samuel says as they sail along Canaima lagoon.

"Everyone want money," Asoo says, his expression serious.

Samuel understands the difficulty in convincing the communities the small pay for slave labor isn't worth risking their lives. Money is survival to these communities as many have forgotten the way of their ancestors by relying on the land for survival. Western lifestyle has influenced their lives, and money controls their life. It's no longer simply hard work and toil in the fields to sustain their well-being.

They sail along the Carrao River, navigating the

Mayupa rapids and onto Orchid Island. They pass the fork to the Churun River, which leads them to Angel Falls and Ulara. Instead, they continue east, then north on the Carrao River, and when the sun is high in the sky, they pass the first curiara anchored to the bank with a makeshift tent onboard, supported by poles. A long rope secures the temporary barge to nearby trees. Three hammocks hang beneath the canopy as well as a line with towels drying. Between the trees is a small opening leading into the jungle.

Asoo shakes his head, and they continue their journey. Several of these unsafe barges dot the shores of the river. The water is a dull caramel color, and there's evidence of sedimentation from the mines.

The curiara hits something hard in the river, and Samuel's body slams forward. Asoo kills the engine and leans over the edge to investigate the cause. Closer to the shore, there are artificial sand mounds caused by the mine drenching the riverbed searching for gold. Not far ahead along the river edge is a barge constructed of ropes and plastic bottles acting as a flotation device supporting the machines that do the damage.

Asoo hands Samuel a paddle, and the men steer the curiara toward the shore. They drag their curiara onto the sand and creep toward the sound of a clicking motor.

They barely make it one hundred yards before a bare-chested man wearing long shorts calls out to Asoo.

"Stay here," Asoo tells Samuel.

Samuel watches as the two men talk for a few minutes until the other raises his voice and uses his arms to dramatize his response. Although Samuel is fluent in Spanish and Pemón, the men are speaking fast and over each other. The dark-haired man turns and glares at Samuel, halting Samuel from taking a further step. Instead, he leaves the men to speak in private and takes shade under a tree. He reaches to lean a weary arm on the trunk and, in a reflex action, snaps his arm away. From the ground to the canopy, organized lines of bullet ants carry leaves in their pinchers. Samuel springs back, checking the ground for the nest. He dusts himself and stamps his feet, then glances up to both men smiling in his direction. Ten days away from the rainforest, and he has forgotten the ways.

Asoo weaves around the wild cashew trees and waves Samuel toward the curiara.

"We go now," he says with underlying urgency.

"What did you see?" Samuel pushes the curiara into the water while Asoo mans the motor.

"Nothing." When they are in the middle of the river, Asoo speaks over the sound of the engine. "Other bad men. Diego do nothing wrong. He say he Pemón and this our land. We mine our own land so he not..." he pauses a moment, "... breaking law."

"I'm aware many people break the law, but this isn't about the law. It's about the damage to the environment and poisoning the water. You've seen first-hand what the mercury does, and we don't want radioactive green lagoons that will kill the fish, your primary source of protein." Samuel curses under his breath. Asoo isn't the person to lecture.

"He's earning six American dollars a month. He has to feed his family."

"He is risking his life and destroying his water system for a mere six bucks a month?"

"It good money, my friend. Most earn two dollars."

Samuel shakes his head. "The younger generation needs to be educated about the benefits of living off the land. We don't want them to think this is what they have to do to survive."

Asoo's shoulders slump. "His wife coming to cook for men. His children will help sift. He get more money in gold."

"Where will they live? On those makeshift barges on the river? If the government finds out—"

"He tells me I no understand. I have job. The government made him broke. This our land. He needs to feed his family."

"So the children's education will cease?"

"We fight another way, my friend. If we stay and his boss return, we all die."

"I'm guessing his boss isn't Pemón?"

"No."

Asoo remains quiet for a while. Both men are aware the dry season is when more mines will pop up, and operation will be at night under the lights of gasoline burners.

This fight is bigger than one or two men. Samuel hopes Asoo can warn the communities not to fall prey to these mines. He needs him to directly influence other employment using their farming skills or even their craft work including basket weaving for the tourists—if tourists return. Only with no tourists...

Samuel focuses on the impact to the Ularan people. In time, their migration to find another home is inevitable.

West.

That's the way he'd have to send them. It's the only safe direction. It's the same direction he sent the Watache, only deeper into the jungle.

A journey the shaman would expect him to do with them.

But would he find his way out alone?

19

EDEN

I'm almost asleep when there's a bang on the door.

I jump up, expecting Samuel.

"Oh, Victor." I lean a hand into my lower back and stretch out.

"Sorry, Miss Eden. I hope I didn't disturb you?"

I shake my head, not wanting to admit he got me out of bed. I saw him before dinner, and he wasn't this pale. "No, I'm just resting."

"Is Samuel here?" He moves his weight side to side while waiting for an answer.

"Sorry, no. Wait, you haven't seen them either? I expected them to be here by now."

Victor scratches his ear without looking at me. "Please ask Samuel to speak to me when they get back."

"Should I be concerned about something?"

"No, Miss Eden." He waves both hands at me as though to erase any stress. "Everything fine. Samuel will be back soon."

He takes off along the garden path and disappears

into the night. Beyond the lodge, Canaima Lake is still peaceful. There's no sound of a motor, only the constant croak of frogs and chirping insects. A buzzing at my ear has me swatting the air, then pushing the door closed. I adjust the mosquito net and climb into bed even though I'm no longer tired.

This is what it will be like when we're apart—Samuel out trying to save everyone, me worrying about the danger and whether he'll even return. It's why I begged him not to go until he explained the reason, and I understood his concern. Only I know this isn't something he and Asoo can fix in one day.

Pressing fingertips to my temples, I massage tiny circles. I can't allow my mind to jump into a negative cycle and think the worst. There's strength in optimism. Samuel is an intelligent man, and Asoo knows the river like the back of his hand.

Positive thoughts. I rub my hand over my baby bump. *Everything will be fine.*

Eventually, I fall asleep, but I'm woken with the discomfort of gas. I am learning the many discomforts associated with being pregnant. When I rise to head to the bathroom, I notice the space beside me is still empty. I check the time on my phone—two o'clock in the morning.

Damn you, Samuel.

How am I to sleep knowing he's out there somewhere and possibly in the hands of criminals.

I switch on the light and pad to the bathroom. Then I climb back into bed, and before I switch off the bedside lamp, a sound chimes from my phone, and it's not the usual ringtone.

I dive on it, thinking it could be Samuel when, in reality, where he's traveling doesn't have connection service.

Snapchat?

I swipe the screen to accept the group Snapchat video call. One by one, my friends' faces appear on the screen.

"You answered," Amy screams. I can't help the smirk in reaction to her big, bright smile.

"Hi, girls," I sing. "Checking in on me?"

"Damn right," Yasmine says and blows me a kiss. "When Amy said you could still be in Canaima, we thought let's do a group chat."

"Where are you?"

"Having a late lunch at Yasmine's," Amy responds. "What time is it there?"

"After two."

"Shit, tell Samuel we're sorry," Yasmine says. "Hi, Samuel." She waves.

"He's not here." Before I explain, Yasmine's brows tighten.

"He's left you alone, again?"

"He's supposed to be back by now. He is with Asoo looking into..." I decide not to explain the situation to my friends. I shake my head. "It's not important. He'll be home soon. Hey, do you want to see my baby bump?"

"Hell, yes," Amy says.

I stand and tug up my tank top and angle the camera for my friends to see the swell of my abdomen.

"You're huge." Amy laughs.

"You look beautiful," Yasmine says in a gentle voice. "I wish you were here so we could experience it with you."

"Yeah... I miss you both." I take a breath and force the

emotion from building in my chest. "One good thing, I haven't had to spend a shitload of money on an entire new maternity wardrobe while in the jungle."

Amy chuckles. "No fun in that."

"How are you really?" Yasmine asks.

I fake a sincere smile. "I'm good. We're both healthy. The time has passed so quickly, and it won't be long until I'm home again."

"I miss us," Amy says. "I miss going to the Shores, just the three of us for cocktail Fridays."

"Even if I were there—"

"I know, I know," Amy says quickly. "Stay safe and hurry home." She wipes an eye, and my stomach drops to my feet.

"Soon, the three of us will be taking long walks along the beach behind a carriage," Yasmine chimes in.

I can picture it clearly and smile at the thought. "We have plenty of good times ahead of us with a plus one."

"You mean plus two," Amy corrects.

"I'm still working on him," I reply honestly.

Yasmine's eyes widen.

"He has some work to do first but hopes to make it back to Australia in time for the birth," I lie.

Yasmine's lips press thin. As though she senses my apprehension, she smiles at Amy. "Have you told her about your new guy?"

"No, he's not my new guy. He's my guy for now."

Yasmine and I both chuckle.

"Yet you have a date in an hour," Yasmine adds.

"Get ready, Ames." I smile at my friends. "When I'm next in Canaima, we'll do this again."

"Do you know when that will be?" Yasmine frowns at me.

This time, I opt for the truth. "No."

🌴

At first light, I push out of bed, ignoring the lethargy weighing down my legs. I refuse to lay here while Samuel could be in danger. My first instinct is to pull back the blind and peer out to the vast green jungle bordered by prehistoric mountains to where Samuel could be. I move the blind aside, and my God, there's a body curled up in the hammock on my porch.

I creep out despite only wearing a tank top and panties and lift the mosquito net to touch his shoulder.

Dirt smears his face, bare arms, and legs, and it reminds me of our life in Ulara. Sliding my fingers through his already unruly hair, my nails catch in knotted ends. "Samuel," I whisper. "Come inside."

"I need to shower," he mumbles. "I didn't want to disturb you."

"Well, I didn't sleep well without you, so please come inside." I take his hand and tug lightly.

He lets out a groan, swings his legs over the side, and rubs his dirty hands over his face. "Is it dawn already?"

"How long have you been here?"

"A couple of hours."

I take his hand to pull him up, and there's smeared blood over his shins. "What happened to you?"

"I'll shower first. Then sleep. Then we'll talk."

With his hand on my shoulder, I walk with him to the shower realizing how much the trip took everything out of him. He rips off his T-shirt and cargo shorts. "These can go in the trash," he grunts.

I pull my tank top over my head and toss it aside. I

slide off my panties and step into the shower with him. "Here." I place both his hands on the wall and then lather soap to wash over his back, arms, and shoulders. I miss these sensual moments. Even if he's exhausted, I'm not passing up an opportunity to run my hands over the smooth muscles of his body. After filling the palm of my hand with shampoo, I lather it into his hair. "Can you bend down so I can massage your scalp?"

"God, that feels good."

A soft laugh comes from me. "It's nice to reverse the roles. You can rinse it now."

Eyes closed, he tilts his head and pushes the last of the shampoo out of his hair. I focus on his face. His expression is a combination of pleasure and relief. The bones of his cheek are more prominent than they were when we first met. Lines are etched deeper near his eyes. The slight stubble of fair hair dots his chin. I prefer him without a beard, but I'll take Samuel any way I can.

He rubs both hands over his face and opens his eyes. I gasp. So many emotions roll off him—so much pain. Even though his love for me is there, I sense more.

A man seeking understanding.

A man crumbling with the walls of his demeanor cracking.

A heart that wants to give and give until...

"What happened yesterday?"

His eyes flick over my face.

"Don't give me an edited version. I can handle it."

"I know you can." He places a hand on my cheek. "But you've been through enough."

"Apart from going crazy last night knowing you could be in danger, I'm fine," I emphasize. "You don't have to carry the burden alone." I take his hands and place them on the swell of my body. "Talk to me because we're here for you."

His gaze fixes on my ever-growing stomach. He lowers to his knees and kisses my stomach before placing his ear to the mound. "Yes," he whispers. "I know your mother can be stubborn. I agree." His gaze lifts and meets mine, and he's smirking. "We're both tired, and we need to sleep."

I smile at his effort to distract me. I turn off the tap and hand him a towel. While I dry off, I keep a close eye on him. He groans when he bends to run the towel along his long limbs. I push up to my toes and ruffle his hair with a towel. "I'm going to cut your hair before we leave."

"When you say we leave, where do you think we're going to go?"

I take his hand and lead him back to the bed. "Ulara."

He says nothing, yet I feel the tension in him.

"Another thing to discuss after you sleep," I add.

I climb under the sheet with him and roll, so my head is close to his, although my stomach keeps us apart.

He edges closer to kiss me on the lips. "Let me sleep so at least I can put up some argument about keeping you safe."

It doesn't take long for Samuel to fall asleep. While he rests, I think more and more about the future. Our future. How far we have come as a couple.

Thinking back to the times I was with Ethan, there was an element of flirtation, a lot of sexting, and every weekend we went out, drank a lot, which led to drunk sex. Yet during the night, he remained with the guys and I with my friends until it was time to go home.

In a short time, I've learned what love is while being with Samuel. We don't need the flirting. Take everything away, his touch, his kisses, the sex, and still that deep feeling of what he means to me remains.

How far I will go for him.

It will be tough when we're apart. I'll give it my all to convince him to come home with me after the baby is born, although already I know there are certain tasks he needs to fulfill, including another trip to the tepui. The thought of him making the journey and leaving me alone in the village again freaks me out. So I accept he'll do the trip when I'm gone. After everything we have been through, I believe we can overcome any obstacle thrown at us. It will take time, and thankfully, I'm learning to be a patient person.

Except while we're here in Canaima with my erratic hormones controlling my thoughts. My fingers skim over his muscled abs, stalling at the dent of the 'V' pointing down to where the sheet sits on his naked hips. I slip one finger under the edge of the sheet.

I want all the sex while we're here because admittedly, there's a lot to be said for a comfortable bed and having access to a shower. As much as I want to wake him and throw my leg over his hips so I'm strategically placed to arouse him, I have to focus on relaxing him so he'll talk to me.

Perhaps there's a point to having sex first.

Allowing him time to sleep, I roll onto my side, close my eyes, and relax alongside him.

"Eden," Samuel whispers.

My eyes flutter open.

Warm breath blows in my ear. "You were talking in your sleep," he says in a low, sexy voice.

"What did I say?" I murmur, rolling with one hand to cover my eyes.

"It's not what you were saying but more the noises you were making."

Noises. I wipe my mouth. "Was I snoring?"

"Were you dreaming?"

I know what I was dreaming about. I open my eyes, and the way his gaze heats, he knows.

"You..."

"Was I doing this?" He flips onto all fours and trails kisses from my shoulder to my breast. My breath hitches the moment he takes my breast in his mouth, and his tongue toys with my already hard nipple.

"Maybe..." I rasp.

"Or this?" His fingers slide to my hips and then to my legs. He gently prises my thighs apart and finds me ready for him.

My breath comes hard. "More," I manage to say between breaths.

He leans close to my ear while his fingers keep building me to climax. "Let's get one thing straight. For you, I'll give everything and more. At the very least, you have the whole of me." His kisses dot over the swell of my stomach and lower.

"Oh," I murmur when his kisses my clit, then slides his tongue over my labia. I buck my hips. Large hands rest gently on my thighs. I look up to catch a glimpse of Samuel's beautiful face between my legs before I flop back on the pillow, my abs too weak. His fingers find the delicious spot while his mouth teases my clit. He sucks, flicks and licks, and I moan through the rapture.

I cry out when the colors of ecstasy fill my mind. It's more beautiful than ayahuasca's kaleidoscope.

Samuel gives me a moment to catch my breath. I place a hand on his cheek. "I want you," I tell him. "Now and always."

He turns his head and kisses the palm of my hand. "You owned me from the moment I laid eyes on you."

20

SAMUEL

Samuel's heart doesn't want to slow.

His body calls to hers, the boom vibrating in his ear as loud as the 125 decibels of the white bellbird's mating call. No matter how many times they make love, how close her body lies to his, he'll never get enough of Eden.

For years, he embraced his safety in loneliness. He appreciates those years of being alone to truly experience the pleasure of Eden in his life.

The old Samuel still lives within him, and the same instincts of understanding a woman's needs haven't been lost.

When he used to go out to bars and nightclubs, he could spot the woman needing extra attention from across the room—a woman dragged out by her friends. Tell-tale signs included the way she had to hold something in her hands. Her gaze would flit around the room as though she was assessing her surroundings, and she'd nervously chug down her drink.

Those women craved to be like their friends, and he

gave them the confidence to be more in tune with their bodies. Rarely did a woman say no to him. As a young man, Samuel's good looks bewitched women. His friends also possessed unique talents. Michael spoke in French or Spanish, and the ladies became putty in his hands. Given the opportunity, Harrison would remove his shirt to bare his football-muscled body, and women flocked to him.

"What is it?" he asks when Eden winces, a hand reaching beneath her abdomen.

"Braxton Hicks contractions, I assume. Ugh. They burn." Rolling onto her side, she brings her legs to her stomach.

His gut tightens, and his thoughts roll over to all the possibilities that could cause her discomfort. He'll do what he can to reduce her suffering since her pain can bring him to his knees. Sliding her hands away, he gently massages the tight muscles of her abdomen. "Breathe through it."

"I know it's going to get a damn sight worst," she mumbles. "But, ugh."

"It is, and the days are passing fast. We need to discuss—"

Pushing his hands away, she uncurls. The movement is slow. "I've already thought it through." Eden repositions herself to meet his gaze. "I'm going to stay and extend my visa."

He closes his eyes momentarily while images flash through his mind of the worst possible outcome.

"Samuel." Her hand brushes his cheek. "I need to be with you. If you can't return to Australia with me, then I'm staying here with you."

Are the antimalarial drugs clouding her thoughts? "It's no longer safe."

"Really? Is it more dangerous than the time you left me in the jungle to fend on my own when I first found you? Or when I was captured by the cannibals?" Her brow pinches, and she lets out an exasperated sound.

"Yes," he murmurs. "These people are by far more dangerous than the Watache. There's no reasoning with them. They'd rather shoot first and think after."

"Well, I won't be anywhere near those mines, which brings me back to my second part of the argument. If you're in danger, then I don't want you here. You should accompany me back to Australia so you can be with our daughter and me."

Samuel's gut tightens. Eden is even more stubborn than when they first met. Does he have to place her on the damn plane himself to keep her safe?

"I'm going to book your flight, and I don't want to hear another word." He gives her a stern look, but she meets him with a glare reflecting equal determination.

"And if you're not stepping onto that plane with me, you don't have a flying fuck of a chance of sending me away."

He flinches at her words and her tone.

"Take my blood pressure now, I bloody dare you." She awkwardly pushes up from the bed with both hands on her lower back to stretch out her spine. Throwing another glare over her shoulder, she opens her mouth. Closes it. Changes her mind. "It seems I'm the only one committed in this relationship. I gave up everything for you. However, you're still trying to save the bloody world and be the hero to everyone else but me. It's so easy for you to send me home. Keep me safe so you can go about doing whatever it is you're trying to prove to yourself to some... some bloody ghost." She throws her hand in the air to make a point.

His heartbeat thuds behind his ears, and like her, his temper is rising despite years of training to withhold emotion.

She walks to the door and yanks it open, then slams it so hard behind her that the window rattles with the bang. The small print hanging above his dresser slides down the wall and hits the wood with a thud.

Maybe this is what's best for Eden. He can handle her anger if it's what it takes to convince her the safest place for her and their daughter is far away from him.

For how long?

Without her in his life, he'll barely survive. Yet, living in a society where he no longer fits scares him.

Does she expect him to don a shirt, tie, and pants and continue to work as a doctor in the very way he needed to escape?

Samuel closes his eyes and tries to imagine his future with Eden in a world where he doesn't belong. But he has to try for her and their baby.

An hour has passed, and Eden hasn't returned.

There's no perfect solution for either of them. He leaves his room and takes the path toward the restaurant. The vista of the tepuis and Canaima Lake is one of his favorite places, and he smiles, appreciating the place he calls home. Her voice echoes ahead. She's on a bench seat under a tree, looking out to the lake. She is talking on her cell. He approaches cautiously, not wanting to overhear a conversation not intended for him.

Eden turns as if sensing him and holds his gaze. "Yes, I'm fine." She pauses. "Of course. I love you too. I'll speak to you soon." She lowers the cell from her ear. "I have informed my family I'm safe and staying longer."

"What do they think of me?"

Eden tilts her head. "What do you mean?"

"Only a selfish man would keep his pregnant wife in a place that's not safe. So, I can only imagine what their opinion is."

"I told them the decision is mine and that you want me to leave." She pushes up from the seat. "I want more time here. I don't know when I'll see Kaikare again, so please give me this. Yes, I want to stay with you, but there are also other reasons why I'm not leaving yet."

He takes her hand and guides her back down to the seat.

"How long? I'll be comforted if we can book your flight home and work with a date. If we have to change it, then fine, but I don't want to risk not getting on all the connecting flights in time."

Eden nods, and he's relieved she has not fought him on this. She looks out to the lake before responding. "I want to spend Christmas with you."

"Christmas will be more enjoyable with your family." Her head snaps back to meet his gaze. "Only because it will be just another day in the village. The Ularans know nothing of Christmas, and I have never tried to explain our celebrations to them."

"Of course." She takes his hand and rests it on her lap.

"But we'd know. We would be together, and that means something, right? I mean, when was the last time you spent Christmas with someone you cared about?"

"I care about the Ularan people even though I don't celebrate what our society has taught us. The gesture is appreciated, but please understand, I want you to be surrounded by family celebrating something *you* believe in."

"When was the last time?" she asks again.

He ponders the question. "Five years. Longer away from family."

She exhales loud enough for him to hear. "I refuse to allow you to spend another Christmas alone."

"Eden."

"No. It's unnecessary, and you no longer *have to* be alone."

Samuel remains quiet so as not to fuel her contention. "What if we have our own Christmas celebration before you leave, so you're home to celebrate with your family?"

Eden remains quiet. At least she doesn't object.

"I'll agree to book a flight if you promise to tell me everything."

He gives her a sideways glance.

"Everything about what happened yesterday at the mines and why it's so dangerous and about the girl you promised to give up your life for."

Samuel's stomach hits the grass beneath his feet. "The mines yesterday," he begins on the subject that doesn't rip his soul apart. "Asoo's friend was shot for talking to us. He's okay," he adds when she stiffens beside him. "His blood was on me. We applied pressure on his wound in the boat until we arrived back in his community. The doctor on site treated him. Luckily, it was a surface wound, yet the warning was clear... keep your mouth shut. He's being blackmailed and has to return to the mines to work. Otherwise, they'll go after his family."

She nods. "That's horrible. Why can't you call the police?"

"Victor informed us gold is being smuggled out on the planes. We're in way over our heads to try to stop this, and we don't know who's involved, including corrupt police and government officials. If we stop this mine, then another will appear elsewhere along the river system. Everyone wants to make money fast. It's getting to a point..." he swallows down the lump of truth at the back of his throat, "... the Ularans will have to migrate west, toward Colombia, only it's where I sent the Watache."

Eden makes an exasperated sound, and he can see the concern in her eyes.

"They should travel toward northern Brazil until they are closer to the Peruvian jungle."

"You have given this considerable thought."

"I have." Samuel hesitates on disclosing more—especially the part where when the time comes, he feels obligated to accompany the Ularans on a safe voyage since he has maps and a satellite cell.

"They are lucky to have you looking out for them. I know they're like your family now..." Something stops Eden from continuing.

He lifts her hand to his lips.

"But now you have us."

"I do. And I'm thankful for it every day."

"But it's not enough for you to return to Australia with me yet, is it?"

He takes her face in his hands and kisses her. "That day is close, only it isn't for Christmas as you hoped."

She nods slowly as though she understands. "Okay. Book my flight for three and a half weeks so that I'm under the thirty-six-week deadline. And I want you to book a flight as well. A date where you promise to return to me."

21

EDEN

Last night I slept the best I have in weeks.

Whether it was knowing it was my last night in a comfortable bed for a while or whether Samuel and I came to some agreement about our future, it was the most relaxed I have felt in a long time. All I know is I'm sitting on the curiara heading back to Ulara with Samuel and Asoo, and I'm as excited as if I'm on a luxury cruiser sailing the Mediterranean.

Samuel and Asoo fall into easy conversation. I have no clue what about since they are conversing in Spanish, but the tone is calm.

The forest curtain surrounding me reminds me of green lava pouring out of the tepuis and covering everything it touches. It's familiar and comforting. I close my eyes and snuggle into the cushions Asoo has provided for me.

The journey must be uneventful as I don't wake again until we're gliding into the sandy embankment of Ulara.

Samuel hoists me up from behind, and it's awkward

with a bulging stomach. We wave goodbye to Asoo, and Samuel makes arrangements for his next visit.

"We'll quarantine in my hut," he tells me as we stroll toward Ulara. "Or at least try to keep some distance from everyone. I'll get Kaikare to make you some purifying tea after I speak to the chief and Shaman."

"Please tell Kaikare I'll see her soon."

"Of course, she'll be looking forward to seeing you."

We remain quiet as we pass the village, and as soon as we reach his hut, he plops our bags down and grabs our skirts and beads before taking my hand and leading me to the stream.

"You know we haven't discussed names. Do you have a preference?"

"Whatever you like." He smiles at me.

"No, that isn't how this works. We decide on a name together."

"Please don't think I haven't considered names. I want to run something by you." Samuel places our skirts on a rounded boulder. He pulls his T-shirt over his head. I gather up my long dress and pull it up and over my head. It will be weeks before I wear it again, which is a pity because I love the bright colors and the printed mandala swirls. He pushes his shorts down his thighs and steps out, giving me a moment to appreciate all of him. I kick my panties aside, and before I have time to respond, he has swept me up in his arms, and we meander into the water as though he's dancing with me in his arms.

I giggle and loop my arms around his neck before we both plunge into the cold water up to our necks. I can't help but yelp in shock at the change of temperature on my skin. It only takes seconds for me to relax in his arms. He's smiling as he wades through the gentle current, and instinctively, I kiss him. Samuel glances down at me, the desire he has for me swirls behind those beautiful blue hues. Today the color has specks of hyacinth blue, and it reminds me of the macaw's feathers, and if it's his jungle spirit, now he's *home*.

"What did you want to run past me?" I murmur and then kiss him again.

The moment he breaks the kiss, his eyes hold mine captive. "Do you remember how I told you in Ulara you're given two names? The first is a traditional Ularan name the parents and the shaman and child acknowledge, not to be shared with anyone else. I've been thinking about this name and the personal meaning, rather than a name everyone else will know our daughter by. And you Aussies..." he smiles at me, "... will more than likely change it, abbreviate it, right? So regardless of what name we give our daughter, family and friends will change it."

"Are you referring to my friends calling me Edes instead of Eden or Monts instead of Monteford?"

"Exactly, and I heard an Aussie call me Macca after a few hours of meeting me."

I giggle loudly as Macca does not suit him. "Okay, Doctor McMahon, what names are you considering for our daughter?"

Samuel takes hold of my hand. "Float on your back," he says. "It's therapeutic with the water supporting your weight." He guides my head to rest on his shoulder, and my body rises to the surface. "Stretch out your arms and close your eyes."

I do what he asks, and it feels almost sensual. With my eyes closed, the surrounding sounds are amplified—the trickle of water over boulders and the birdlife in the trees.

"Arukuma Turùpo," he whispers close to my ear. "Star of our heart."

With my eyes remaining closed, I picture the stars, a tiny bundle of warmth in my arms, and my heart lost forever to our unborn child.

"Her name is only for us and our daughter's ears. Our secret, her private treasure."

"I think it's perfect," I whisper. Reaching behind me, I feel for his head and guide his lips to mine.

🌴

"It tastes rank," I tell Samuel after one mouthful of the tonic or the tea, as he describes it, used to purify our immune system. I understand the need for it, but it doesn't make it any easier to swallow.

Samuel chuckles.

"No, seriously. How long did it take for you to drink it without shuddering?"

Samuel shrugs. "It never bothered me. I visualize the good it does for my body, and it's enough to block out the unusual taste."

"*Unusual.*" I roll my eyes. "Well, I guess my visualization skills suck balls."

Samuel coughs and chokes on his last mouthful of tea.

I laugh at his reaction. "Did I shock you, Macca?"

His brows pinch. "Eden, I'm warning you—"

"Eden, I'm warning you," I parrot in a deep voice.

In a flash, he's beside me, mouth close to my ear, hands around my waist. "In another world, I'd silence you in another way, one where my mouth is on yours until you slowly give in to lust."

"Another world? That's my world every damn day. I live for your kisses, your touch." Suddenly, my tea is placed on the ground, and I'm whisked up into the hammock. Thankfully, with us in quarantine, the Ularans will keep their distance from us tonight.

🌴

Four days later, Samuel walks with me to the stream. I'm swimming twice daily, especially to ease the pressure in my back and to move a little in the water. I compare it to hydrotherapy as one would indulge in back home.

When we return to the village, the women have gathered around the fire, along with the men.

"What's happening?" I ask Samuel and tighten my hand in his.

"I don't know." He lets go of me and steps into the circle with the men. Kaikare turns and comes to me. She wraps her arms around my neck and lays her cheek on my shoulder. I pat her back affectionately. It's the best way for us to communicate the family love between us.

"Wakü," I tell her. *Good.*

She lifts her head and stares into my eyes as though she needs to assess my well-being herself. Her hands press to my bulging stomach as though she's holding a glass ball and can foresee the future. She glances up at me and smiles.

I'm relieved to see her smile. Kaikare and her father both have a divine presence about them, and I trust her unique wisdom.

Samuel asks me to mentally take notes when the baby moves. It's something I have to monitor every day, and Samuel has to take my blood pressure.

We talk about keeping the fluid down in my ankles by resting in the hammock frequently. And, of course, he has banned me from wandering into the forest alone. Even to pee—last night he stood a good distance away to give me some privacy but also to keep guard. I'm not going to object because I've vowed never to wander off on my own again.

The memory hits me at the same time I lock eyes with Kapeá Tapire. *Red Moon.* Her stomach is more pronounced since I was last in the village. I can still picture her strung to the bamboo like a wild animal ready to be carted away. It's like an understanding passes between us, one where I saved her life.

She smiles at me, and I give her a subtle nod in return.

Kaikare turns to where my focus is and smiles. She takes my hand and leads me to Kapeá Tapire. Kaikare speaks to her, and then the young girl, like Kaikare, wraps her arms around my neck and lays her cheek on my shoulder. This is now our universal way of showing gratitude.

When she releases me, I reach out and touch her stomach with one hand. She mirrors my action on my stomach. "Wakü?"

She nods once and smiles at Kaikare, then at me.

"During our absence, the shaman granted Mari' Iwoi permission to move his hammock to her family hut," Samuel announces.

"So Dancing Snake is free to... well, literally do that," I say and giggle.

Samuel shakes his head at me. "Do you reference everything to sex?"

"Says Väi Uarati Kún-imá," I say and laugh again.

"Seriously, how can I not with some of these names. At least you kept our daughter's name clean."

"Eden," he says in a reprimanding tone. "The discussions with the men are serious. Someone passed along the river while we were gone. They hope the intruders didn't see the smoke rising above the trees from the cooking fires. There's tension in the village, and you're giggling with Kaikare and Kapeá Tapire."

"To be fair, nobody informed me about the discussions. And both ladies are happy to see me so, of course, we're going to be smiling."

"I understand." He takes my hand and leads me to the fire where the women are frying bread. Kaikare steps ahead and picks up some flat bread and hands it to me.

"Oo?"

"Waküpe-küruman," I tell her. *Thank you.*

Samuel takes me aside and sits me away from everyone else. "My fear is the people cruising the river in boats are those working for the mines and that they're finding secret places along the river too. It also means they'll carry guns and disease, and even if they set up camp further along the river, the mine will poison the water in these parts. I need to get word to Asoo. Some of the nearby communities have inside information. We need to know if Ulara is on their map to mine.

22

EDEN

The following morning, I search my bag for my antimalarial tablets as I only take them once a week. That way, it's less harmful to the fetus—that's how my doctor described the medication. Cupping my hand under my belly, I consider my baby as already real and not a medical term. I'm yet to decide on a name that suits her, although I want it to reflect my grandmother, so maybe her middle name should be Ivy as in hindsight, that also signifies the jungle. My name is also connected to the jungle in the sense of a biblical garden or paradise. I smile with memories of my gran, and with that, I pull out the diary and open it to the page where I last read.

24ʰ October 1961

Albert and I have fought every day for the last two weeks. Tonight, in anger, I told him about my letter and how I wish I hadn't met him and wish I was going to volunteer and help

people who needed me, people who were genuinely poor and
sick and in desperate need of medical help.
He got upset and told me that he and Winston needed my help
in other ways and why I couldn't see it. Why must I keep
fighting him on this? Why do I find it hard to just be his wife
and a mother?
It opened up a can of worms, and now I'm doubting my ability
to be both. I'm a terrible mother and wife.
In the end, we went to bed crying and made love. It's the first
time in months that he has touched me.
I promised him I'd try harder.

I turn the page.

24th November 1961

I'm trying.
Every day I try to be who they want me to be.
I love them. Deep in my heart, I know I do, yet I'm fighting a
dark, empty space inside of me that keeps clawing at my
confidence, telling me I am worthless.
Maybe Albert should've married someone who could be a
better wife to him than I could ever be. Not a woman who's
more interested in caring for visitors if they are stung by
jellyfish or have a fishing hook in their finger.
I'm not going to drown in the black ocean threatening to
swallow me whole. All I can do is keep swimming and hold my
face above the water.

There it is. Her postnatal depression just like Faith had told me.

20th December 1961

Tonight, Albert took Winston and me on a picnic by the water. Thankfully, we didn't have far to walk.
I stayed with Winston while he walked up the stairs to our apartment and carried down the picnic basket and wine glasses. We snuck in some wine while the sun set over the ocean. Albert asked me to make a wish, and then he asked what I'd like for Christmas.
I couldn't honestly tell him what my heart craved. Instead, I told him I didn't want anything because I was thankful to have a loving husband, a healthy baby boy, and a beautiful home that also was our livelihood as a business.
It's how I should think and be grateful for my blessings.
Not cry myself to sleep like I do every other night.

25th December 1961

My hand is shaking while I'm writing this entry.
I can't believe it.
Albert gave me my gift after I put Winston in his crib.
It was a note.
One that told me he knew I needed to go away and finish the part of my nursing that still lived inside of me. Until I 'got it out of my system,' I'd never be entirely happy.
He wants me to reply to the letter from Dr. Anderson and tell him I can volunteer for twelve months, then return to him

hopefully more settled and ready to be a good wife and mother.

I said no.

I couldn't possibly leave him and Winston for twelve months. Albert insisted as he couldn't handle hearing me cry at night anymore.

My heart sunk. When I let go at night, I thought he was asleep.

He reassured me he and Winston would be fine, and his parents would help while I'm away.

No wonder his Mum has barely spoken to me. Albert must have told her his plan, and she must think of me as an awful mother. Can't blame her.

I am.

But he's right.

This is a yearning my heart won't let go of, and it's as though a strange force is pulling me away from my family.

I promised I'd do anything he asked.

Is this a dream? I still can't believe it.

But I'm writing the letter to Dr. Anderson tonight before Albert changes his mind.

So that's how my grandfather agreed to let Gran go.

The rest is all history.

I flip the pages, and there are only a couple of more entries, and then there's a wad of blank pages now a creamier color, tarnished over time.

Resting her diary on my chest, I close my eyes and imagine what it was like here fifty-eight years ago.

I need to find Brenda when I return home and ask for Gran's journal of when she was in the jungle.

The burden of the secret no longer has to be Brenda's alone. I wonder how much she knows and whether she too was sworn to secrecy.

A dark blanket has fallen over the village, and the deafening chatter of insects and creatures is enough to keep me awake. My heartbeat refuses to slow, despite my efforts to remain calm. I'm no longer naïve. I'm aware of the predators lurking beyond the village boundary. Even though I've convinced myself the Watache have moved on in the direction on the map where Samuel has sent them, my thoughts snowball with the possibilities of potential threats. Beyond the doorway of our hut, the darkness pulsates with life, death to preserve life, and a hunger by every species to survive.

I'm just a number.

A statistic.

No more important than any other individual or animal in surviving what life throws at us.

Why am I still alive?

What purpose do I hold?

What good can I do besides feed my selfish need to be with Samuel?

It's the first time I've been alone in the village at night since my ordeal, and my subconscious is playing havoc with my mind.

I wouldn't even know if something or someone were sneaking up on me or even outside the hut because the bloody monkeys and insects are deafening right now.

The clicking and mindless chatter stops. My hearing

pricks and thoughts sharpen. I listen intently as it usually means there's a predator close by.

When the raucous returns, my shoulders slump, and I let out a long breath, hoping the danger has passed.

I need to pee, and I'm struggling to wait any longer for Samuel to return from the waipa.

Stepping carefully down the few steps of his hut, I pad toward the green web enticing me closer. Spinning in a full circle, I assess no one is around, so I squat the best I can, and as far as my stomach will allow, and simply pee.

Nothing is simple, and I pass the loudest fart ever.

"That wasn't me. That was you," I whisper to my daughter.

"It makes finding you easy with flatulence like an elephant." Samuel's voice comes from behind me.

"Oh God, did you hear that?"

"I think every animal in a mile radius heard. You stunned the jungle into silence for a brief second."

I stand and cover my face with my hands even though Samuel can't see me. "I tried to hang on as long as I could waiting for you to come home."

"I'm sorry." His silhouette is before me. "The ceremony took longer than the shaman expected."

"Did he find the answers he's searching for?"

"Yes and no. He's not sharing much at the moment, so I fear it's not all good news." He places an arm around my waist and leads me back to his hut. "The shaman mentioned more rain is on the horizon."

"More?" I moan.

"He said the Mawarí's cooking pots on the tepui are full and will overflow."

"Are you concerned about the village flooding?" We

reach his hut, and I kick off my sneakers and slide into the hammock. Samuel secures the netting around us.

"Yes. Tomorrow we continue to build more huts in the trees. The crops will be harvested, so we have plenty of food for now. The canoes are for getting around in the upcoming wet season. He believes it will be the most rainfall in decades. What concerns me is if it begins early and while you're still here, there's a risk of disease to you and the baby, and returning to Canaima will not be as easy."

It never was.

🌴

The following morning, Samuel lifts my arm and inspects the skin. His fingers trail lightly over it, and I moan, savoring his touch even though I want to scratch. He lifts my hair and touches my neck, and I shiver. He plants a kiss on my shoulder.

"I hope you don't do this to all your patients?" I ask.

He chuckles lightly.

"We have three weeks to decide how we're going to celebrate Christmas," I say to lighten his mood. "My creative skills will be tested, but I can decorate the room with acai berries and use flowers like monkey brush, orchids, passionflower, and heliconias," I say dreamily. "The ferns are no mistletoe, but... well, there's an abundance of ivy." I smile at him, hoping he's the least bit excited, but he's distracted by something on the side of my abdomen.

With a gentle touch, he runs his fingertips over the skin to the side of my ribs. "How long have you had these?"

"Ouch." I scratch where he touches. "I'm not sure what it is, but it's itchy and a little tender."

"It's some sort of bite. There's no inflammation, but I'll monitor it." He grabs the stethoscope and listens to my heart. "Take some deep breaths."

I do so and scratch an itch near my eye. His gaze follows where I scratch. He stops listening and pushes strands of hair out of my eyes.

His brow pinches together. "And how long has this been itchy?"

For a few seconds, I scrutinize his tight expression. "I'm not sure. I have a rash almost all over me and thought it was just a heat rash, but now you're touching it, I want to squint because it's tender."

"I only hope it's not triatomine bugs, known as kissing bugs."

"So, you did hear me when I mentioned mistletoe." I chuckle. "Or maybe you bit me?"

"Eden, it's serious." He stretches my skin, studying the bite. "Kissing bugs cause Chagas disease."

"And that can do what?"

He leans back and meets my gaze. He hesitates, and I assume he screens his response. "Do you have any fatigue, headaches, a fever, or body aches?"

"Really? Of course, I do. I'm carrying a baby, and I'm living in the damn jungle." I ignore his frown. "My back hurts because of obvious reasons, my hips ache because things are expanding around there, and I'm permanently bloody hot, so I wouldn't know if it's a mild fever. And tick the headaches as well, as I think I kinked my neck sleeping in the hammock. What were the other symptoms? Oh yes, fatigue... what do you think?"

His expression is unreadable.

"What?" I snap.

"I understand how you're feeling, but there are hundreds of symptoms I'm looking out for. I hope none lead to serious disease."

"I've had vaccinations for—"

"I'm aware. Don't assume because you've had vaccinations against yellow fever and others, and you're taking antimalarial meds that you're safe. Many other diseases are caused by fungal pathogens and parasites as well as the bacterial and viral ones you're vaccinated against. There's a risk of Chagas disease, adiaspiromycosis, and now leishmaniasis, especially with the surrounding mines clogging the waterways." Taking my chin in his hand, he tilts my head slightly and peers closely into my eyes. "Onchocerciasis, an eye disease," he whispers while concentrating before releasing me and scooping up my foot. He brushes away dried mud before angling my foot to inspect it.

"I swear you're trying to scare me."

He releases my foot and then cages me in, leaning both arms on either side of the treatment table so we're nose to nose. "Eden."

I swallow hard, acknowledging the seriousness in his eyes.

"You scare me by merely being here, especially with the wet weather coming. Everything is exacerbated in my mind, and you and our baby are my responsibility."

23

SAMUEL

"Asoo is bringing your cell," Samuel informs Eden. "I asked him to pack it every trip to check your messages and send word back to your family. You need to account for your safety."

"Of course," Eden says.

Eden has been quiet for the last couple of days. He hopes he has educated her on the dangers other than the visible ones she may face.

"He's also bringing more medical supplies."

"For me or you?"

"Both. I'm heading there now to meet him. Do you feel well enough to join me?"

"As long as you can handle my slower pace." She takes his hand, and they meander through the village.

"Did I mention there's a ceremony tonight?"

"No. What type of ceremony?"

He holds her hand while she balances to step over an exposed root. "I know how you worry when I take ayahuasca, only tonight is special. I'm drinking the tea *with* the shaman. Together we hope to find answers."

Eden stops walking. "Have you done this before? I mean with the shaman. He usually guides you, right? Will your minds be locked together in, I don't know, some weird dimension?"

"I haven't, still it's not necessary to worry." Samuel rests his hand on her cheek. "I won't be far away. Kaikare is overseeing the ceremony."

"Don't for one minute assume I'll be sleeping while you're puking your guts up and stuck in some universe. I'll be there with you, at least physically and emotionally."

"Eden, I—"

"No. Don't tell me not to come. I. Will. Be. There."

"It could go well into the early hours of the morning."

"I expect it will."

For now, there's no changing her mind. He takes her hand and continues toward the river. "Is there anything you want to request from Asoo? Cushions? Even pillows to sleep with in the hammock? Do you need support under your stomach or between your legs for comfort?"

"Is it hygienic to have those things here? I didn't think the Ularans used anything like that from the Western world."

"No, they don't."

"Then neither will I. You know I want to do this like the other ladies in the village and my Gran."

"Is that what this is about? To prove you're as strong as your grandmother? I understand you're trying to connect with her on some level, but you need to remember everyone's journey is different. Every pregnancy is different. What do you need to support you through the next few weeks?"

"You."

It's all Eden says before turning on her heel and striding to the river bank without Samuel.

He jogs to catch up, and the *putt-putt* of a motor echoes from the trees on the riverbend. The sharp point of the curiara appears first, then Asoo's smiling face comes into view.

"Samuel. Miss Eden." Asoo waves his hand in a large rainbow arc.

Samuel stands aside when the point of the curiara rams onto the embankment. Wading into the water, Samuel takes the packages Asoo hands him and lays them on the sand.

Eden wanders out and stands near the edge. "Is there anything I can help you with?"

"I have mail." Asoo scurries through his backpack and retrieves a wad of envelopes and hands it to Eden.

"One is for me," she says with an elevated voice. She tucks the papers under her arm while she tears open the envelope. "Oh, Amy wrote to me."

Out of the corner of his eye, Samuel observes her body language. When she giggles loudly, his stomach relaxes.

"Wait here while I deliver some of the boxes to the village. Chat with Asoo and read your messages. Prepare more texts to send for when Asoo reaches Canaima." Samuel packs up several boxes to carry back to the village and leaves Eden with Asoo.

When he reaches his hut, he piles the boxes in the corner then breaks into a jog toward the river. Closer, the motor of the curiara purrs in the distance. Asoo must be eager to leave. He picks up speed, and before he steps beyond the trees, another curiara is cruising by, the driver looking at Asoo's boat.

He darts backward and searches for Eden and Asoo. Fifty feet away, they both crouch behind trees and bromeliads, well hidden from the driver. The man steers toward the sandy beach—Samuel assumes it's to inspect Asoo's curiara. The hiss of a spear whirls out into the water and lands several feet from the boat.

A warning.

The driver curses and jumps to the side, ready to turn the boat in an arc. Another spear whizzes closer this time. Samuel turns to his right. Timenneng prepares another. Samuel waves his hand, slamming it to his side in a chopping action.

Timenneng places the spear at his side, then turns his focus to the imposter.

In a scurry, the Caucasian man turns the curiara, revs the motor, and then disappears around the bend.

Asoo uncurls and straightens. He yanks Eden to stand. Bent at the waist, they creep out from the ferns and myrtles and peek when they get to the opening on the sandy embankment.

This could've been another situation where Eden's safety was compromised. A sense of urgency grows inside of him to keep Eden safe and to get her out of here as soon as possible. Samuel jogs over to them and wraps his arms around Eden. "Are you okay?"

"Of course."

"Did you recognize him?" he asks Asoo.

"No." He shakes his head vehemently. "My friends will know. I ask them."

Samuel holds Eden to his chest. "We need to get you back to my hut."

"Wait. I threw the mail in the boat when Asoo told me to run. I'm sorry it's probably important, but I panicked."

"It's fine, Eden. Nothing is more important than your safety."

Conversing in Pémon, Samuel instructs Asoo to be careful in his travels back to Canaima and to find out as much as possible without being obvious he's prying. He collects the remainder of his parcels from Caracas while Eden carries the mail, and they head back to Ulara.

She doesn't say anything.

Yet, he assumes the silence stems from fear.

🌴

The chief is unhappy with the intruders being close to Ulara. He's aware no one is at fault except those who survive on greed with no knowledge of the land. The gods will punish everyone surrounding the tepui, and Samuel assumes the upcoming rain season, predicted as torrential, will be the act of unhappy gods.

He sprints back to his hut, to Eden. If the situation worsens, he'll send her home immediately regardless of her stubborn desire to stay.

Back in his hut, he tears open his mail.

A letter from Caracas catches his eye.

The pharmaceutical company has commenced testing his plant—the purple flower, and they're now requesting more. His hope was for the shaman to speak to the trees and be guided on how to prepare the flower for health benefits for the Ularan people. The Western world is jumping at the opportunity to study the benefits, especially in healing diseases like diabetes and blood cancer. The request stands out like blood drops on white paper.

More samples required.

They are successfully growing the flower here, although it has not grown enough to cut the flower for samples without possibly killing it.

The only way is for another trek to the tepui, which he refuses to commit to while Eden is in the village.

His contract with the pharmaceutical company is ending.

He promised Eden he'd not sign on for another year.

The Ularans need to migrate west, especially after today's threat. If the thugs come back with semi-automatic weapons, then it will end badly for both parties. The Ularans are camouflaged, and their blowpipes with poison-tipped darts kill in seconds. Never has he seen darts hit their target as they do with the precision of the Ularans.

The major threat is guns. To his knowledge, the Ularans have not witnessed the firing of bullets or the intimidating roar of a gun, and it could have devastating results.

He gazes up to the universe, closes his eyes, and prays for nothing to happen while Eden is here.

At twilight, Samuel sits beside Eden while she eats fish, oo bread, and a berry paste dip.

"Is the fish satisfactory?"

She nods.

"I see you've acquired a taste for the ants."

Eden shrugs. "I couldn't be bothered picking them off."

Samuel slides closer to her to wrap his arm around her waist. "You're afraid. I understand," he whispers.

"I'm only tired," she murmurs.

He assumed she'd deny it. "If you want to vent to me, then go ahead."

"No need. I'm good." She pushes the palm leaf aside with her meal only half-finished. "Can we go? I want to drink some water before I accompany you to the waipa."

"There's no rush. Finish your meal first. The shaman is still to tell his story."

Samuel sips his tea while waiting for Eden. It must spur her to eat more as she finishes the meal quickly.

"Let's leave," she says and stands before the shaman has started his story.

Samuel gets to his feet and brushes the dirt from the back of his thighs. He bows at the shaman and chief before leading Eden to his hut.

He pulls Eden into his arms and mashes his lips with hers. "You don't have to be brave all the time," he says against her lips.

"Neither do you." She pulls away from him and steps to the table holding their water bowl. Eden scoops out a cup and chugs it down. She drinks another three cups before placing the clay mug aside. "Do you want any?"

"No, thank you. I'll have Wayara go to the stream and refill it for you."

"Thanks. I'll need it when we return in the early hours of the morning."

"Lay with me," he says and tugs her gently until he's sitting on the edge of the hammock. "We have time to close our eyes and just be present with each other."

Samuel senses her resistance and assumes she's tired enough to fall asleep if she stops moving. It's what he wants—for her to rest.

"Five minutes." She clambers in with him with even less grace than she did when she first arrived in the village.

"Here. Allow me." He springs up, grabs her feet, and

swings her legs around while taking her weight. "Your feet will thank you in a few hours."

Clambering into the hammock beside her, Samuel stretches his arm behind her head and listens to her breaths as they slow. He places a gentle kiss on her forehead so as not to disturb her, then his fingers trail lightly up and down her arms until her head is heavy on his chest.

The jungle choir has lifted a notch with darkness around the village. His eyes adjust to the darkness and the faint moonlight streaming into the doorway of the hut. He cups Eden's stomach with his free hand and sends a silent message to his unborn child.

I want you to know I love you with every fiber of my being.

It may be months before I get to see you, and I'll struggle with the thought every day.

You'll be surrounded by love and safe in a beautiful country.

I'll count the days until we meet, but I'm blessed to watch you grow inside your mother and feel your presence within her.

I'll be forever your father and will love you always.

Samuel pictures the day when Eden is holding their baby in her arms, smiling and full of joy. She'll make a wonderful mother, and he can't wait for the day he will join them.

A steady drumbeat brings him out of his thoughts.

It's time.

24

EDEN

Kneeling beside Samuel in the waipa, I'm reminded of many months ago when I was here.

The round hut holds an ethereal essence—a calming sensation with the small fires dotted around it, flickering like candles providing an ambience similar to what I'd indulge in when I was home taking a relaxing bath.

It feels spiritual. I don't doubt there's a *presence* here since the shaman began his prayers calling to the forest before we even arrived. The shaman is taking the tea with Samuel, and to be honest, the notion of two great minds connecting simultaneously with the spirits freaks me out. Yet, in the gentle breeze, there's an aroma of herbs and an earthy scent wafting in from the rainforest.

I turn and look to the green cavern, unusually quiet and still at present.

Samuel touches my knee, and I turn back to the shaman blessing the tea. He hums a tune, the same syllables over and over.

From a bamboo pipe, he sucks in smoke, blows it over the tea, and continues chanting.

Much of the preparation was completed before our arrival since the shaman himself isn't overseeing the ceremony.

Kaikare is.

It strikes me that Kaikare is in charge and the enormity of the responsibility for her to lead two of the most powerful and influential men in the community. Kaikare is preparing to be a shaman and has studied all her life to follow in her father's footsteps. My stomach drops, knowing what could've been.

Kaikare is my aunty.

Her life might have been very different if my gran had brought her back to Australia. She'd have grown up alongside my father in a world different from this.

I imagine all the places we could've traveled together —attended football games, visited shopping centers, and—

Kaikare snaps her head in my direction as though she senses my thoughts. I give her a tight smile, trying to empty my mind and focus on what's happening, but maybe it's in here where our world collides with the spiritual one that *what if* is challenged.

Is it my ego talking? Is my selfishness surfacing with wanting Kaikare to be part of my world and not part of her father's where she was born?

Would she be any happier in my world?

The point is, she's happy here. She knows of nothing else.

Her world lured Samuel to leave society—the selfish, material world where money rules. A world where happiness is more about wealth, what you own, and power in the form of stardom.

I bow my head and concentrate on letting go of my ego, superiority, privileged upbringing, and just be in the moment.

Who am I to say one way of living is more prestigious than the other, especially for happiness and our purpose?

I glance at Samuel and see him for who he really is. Not my lover or the father of my baby, but the doctor. The man who heals and cares for other humans. The man who has given up everything I know to be important in our world to live here in what I initially thought was a substandard way. Only now, I know the Ularan way is far more superior.

The Ularans understand life, live with nature, and protect the earth only taking what they need without destroying their surroundings. They have a social set of rules like we do, only it's obeyed, knowing it brings happiness and harmony within the community. They are peaceful, spiritual beings in tune with the universe and who wouldn't hurt a soul. Well, unless the Watache kidnapped someone, but even then, they didn't want to harm anyone. A peaceful resolution was their first approach.

The Watache.

I'm scarred by those memories. Yet when I think back on those moments, they acted out by what they knew, and now I question if their shaman would've hurt me. After hearing about their village being burned to the ground by Caucasian men, no wonder they were afraid and reacted the way they did.

If I weren't pregnant or a privileged white girl, my body may have coped better with their food. The Watache shaman gave me food and water and treated me similarly to everyone else. I just wasn't used to sleeping on dirt, eating raw meat, or pooping right in front of everyone. Their ways are different from mine, but does that make them wrong or of less importance?

We all do what we need to survive in this world.

We're given one chance at life, and we have to make the most of it.

I came to South America hoping to find myself, and although I did, I also found Samuel. Could the shaman, or even Gran, have influenced destiny?

It's something we'll never know.

Only now, I'm questioning whether I have the right to pressure Samuel into making a choice—whether the baby and I should have priority over his life here. My ego says it's the right thing for him to do—be a responsible father and be with us.

Here in the waipa, my ego is silenced even without taking ayahuasca. We're two people compared to a village. He was happy and content before he met me. He has tried to explain—without falling apart—why he preferred to be here. I understand we all have secrets locked away in the back of our mind to stop the memories from crushing our souls.

Maybe it's this life. The sense of purpose. The happiness of life and nature and living in harmony with the earth. Maybe my world truly scares Samuel. He has tried to explain how unhappy he is in our society, and I assumed by being with me, all would be okay.

Shit.

Who the hell do I think I am?

"Eden, you don't have to be here," Samuel says softly and places a hand on my knee.

What?

Are they mind readers?

Realizing he's referring to the ceremony, I straighten my shoulders and bow my head. "Sorry. I'll focus now. It's just baby brain." Or is it a spiritual power here, surrounding us in the waipa, questioning my motivation?

He offers a slight smile before bowing his head once more, and we're both charmed by the shaman's prayers.

Samuel takes the tea from Kaikare and swallows the entire cup in one go. He wipes his mouth and bows his head.

He didn't flinch.

Ugh, I remember the vile taste. Earthy and bitter.

Kaikare hands another bowl to her father, then to Samuel. The shaman bows his head, raises the bowl high, and continues with the chant before swallowing the tea. Neither Samuel nor the shaman shudder or react.

Wow.

Many bowls later, the shaman holds up his hand to Kaikare.

Joining our circle, she lowers to her knees and bows her head. Her eyes now closed, the shaman continues to sing. He sways gently side to side, chanting the same syllables over and over.

What I'd give to know what he's visualizing.

Samuel also has his eyes closed and his brow is pinched. I place a hand on his knee yet say nothing, not wanting to distract his thoughts. We remain like this for some time for the tea to infuse their blood and brain. Kaikare pushes up to her feet, retrieves a cane mat, and rolls it out for her father. I follow her lead and lay out a mat beside Samuel. We gather empty bowls, much larger than those served with the tea, and place them beside the men.

Now we wait.

Samuel remains on all fours, panting, waiting for his fifth purge.

I'm aware it's to expel negative energy and the pathways of our past lives to lead the way into the next stage of the ceremony. Only it seems brutal to me. I mean, who likes puking?

Kaikare breaks out into song—a harmonic tune that speaks to my heart.

To my surprise, the shaman has puked only once. Then again, this is something he practices regularly, and it's part of their culture. And I assume the rituals provide him with cleansed, purified energy pathways.

I leave Samuel to empty the bowl outside the round hut and return to sit beside him. He curls up onto the mat, and I move away so my presence doesn't interfere with his aura and energy.

Homing in on Kaikare's beautiful voice, I allow the repeated syllables to infiltrate my mind, absorb the song of healing into my cells just as Samuel and the shaman do. Even without the presence of ayahuasca, my entire self feels present, and I close my eyes and allow the serenity to envelop my aura.

There's no light show, no kaleidoscope of color in my mind, and yet I detect a powerful presence around us.

There is a pull from beyond the waipa, a pulsing life, energy, and growth. Life seeks more life to be as one. The rainforest calls to all of us to understand what we need to survive, and now the shaman is calling to the trees in the most powerful way known to man.

Samuel's heavy breaths jolt me out of the trance.

Light flickers from the fire and casts an eery shadow around the room. Yet I make out his pain. His eyes are tightly closed, and deep lines highlight his brow. He pants quick breaths like one would in labor.

Samuel groans. At first, I believe it's from nausea or his stomach twisting in pain from the tea. I know that feeling—he doesn't know which part of his body will try to eject the poison next. Only the way Samuel's fingers grip his long locks makes me freeze. Could there be more to his pain?

His breaths amplify into grunts with sounds of fear and panic equally mixed. I shoot Kaikare a questioning look, asking whether I should do something, at the very least touch him and whisper consoling words?

Only her eyes are closed, her song continues without alarm. Are her visions within our space as strong as the shaman's?

Breathe.

Be patient.

The minutes pass, and Samuel is moaning, yelling incomprehensible words. To me, it's clear something is wrong, but neither the shaman nor Kaikare flinch at Samuel's reaction.

I have to do something.

What if he's in trouble, and they're both—I don't know—maybe in another dimension, another realm and are beyond helping him?

His breaths come faster. His chest is racing. I place my fingers over his pulse point on his wrist just like he does to me. His pulse is pounding. It's so fast I can barely keep up.

Shit, now he's hyperventilating!

Think.

Shit. Shit. Shit.

What the hell is happening?

25

EDEN

Kaikare stops singing.

She creeps over to where Samuel lies in the fetal position and places a hand on his shoulder. Her father remains in a trance. With his legs crossed, his seated position reminds me of a buddha, only his eyes are open, staring out to the forest.

Kaikare shoots me a look and then gently shakes Samuel's shoulder.

A single second, and yet in the flickering light, her eyes communicate concern. When she uncurls and stands, I lean over and whisper in his ear, "I'm here, Samuel. You're not alone."

Kaikare raises her arms and sings to the jungle. She doesn't stop me, so I take it as a green light.

"You're safe, my love. I'm here. And your daughter, Arukuma Turùpo, is with you."

He twitches—the reaction I hoped for. Whispering our daughter's name over and over is my way of penetrating any walls the spirits have constructed to keep me out. I glance up to Kaikare.

She gives me a nod. She leans over and places a hand on his shoulder. "Piriki'ki," she says firmly. "Piriki'ki," she repeats. She looks to the jungle. A rumbling growl overpowers the sound of every other creature—every hunter. Did it come from the dark, pulsating wilderness or the space around us?

Eyes. I see a pair of eyes, blue and unblinking on the ground. I turn to Kaikare, unmoving. Is she frozen in fear that it's a jaguar and our men's minds are temporarily paralyzed from the tea? The creature's eyes convey emotion, and I feel it with every fiber of my being. Anger? No, frustration.

What's Kaikare waiting for?

Moving onto all fours, I remain in front of Samuel, protecting him from whatever it is out there.

Kaikare breaks into another song, and it tricks my mind into relaxing. She nods to the trees. There's another set of eyes staring back at us. It hoots a soft sound.

"An owl?" I ask.

She nods. "Piriki'ki."

Right.

A flapping of winds comes from behind me, and I duck my head as I catch a flash of red, blue, and yellow before it disappears in the dark. Yet, it was enough time for me to realize the macaw is heading toward the owl.

"Kawak," Kaikare states. *Macaw*.

I nod. *Kawak*.

Kaikare bends down, touches Samuel's shoulder, and points toward the trees. "Kawak, Piriki'ki, Väi Uarati Kún-imá."

Wait. Väi Uarati Kún-imá is Samuel's name. I shake my head for my thoughts to unravel. Is she telling me Samuel is the macaw and the owl? I stroke his beautiful face. His eyes remain closed only now there's a peacefulness surrounding him.

Yet we have overlooked there is a jaguar crouched beyond the dense foliage.

I point. "Timenneng." *Jaguar.* Recently, I learned the warrior and friend Timenneng's name is the word for jaguar, and he's the most fearless of all the Ularan young men.

"Tykaraije Timenneng." *Black jaguar.*

My chest tightens with every breath.

Another set of fierce eyes, this time yellow in color, join the black jaguar, and a growl echoes through the trees. A clear warning these powerful cats are a threat to every creature. The noise of the jungle fades into the distance as the throb of my racing heart echoes behind my ears.

What's happening?

A smaller feline springs out from the ferns. Wild, with the same frustration reflected in its blue eyes. The larger jaguar roars, and it tumbles and retreats to crouch at their sides.

What the hell have we done?

I can't breathe. My chest heaves with each breath as though the forest is angered and has sucked all the oxygen out of the waipa.

"Kaikare," I murmur with my hand on my chest until I can't take anymore.

I lay alongside Samuel, my lover, close my eyes, and will my heart to slow.

26

SAMUEL

A low hum sounds from the jungle. The first light of dawn breaks through the trees and into the waipa.

Samuel opens his eyes.

Eden.

She lies beside him. She has a hand under her cheek with a peaceful expression on her face. There's not a hint of distress evident from the previous night.

Flashes come back to him. He pushes up onto his elbow. The dotted fires around the waipa have been reduced to nothing but glowing embers. The shaman sleeps. Kaikare rises from her mat as though sensing his presence.

She creeps over to him and places a hand on his shoulder. Kaikare stares at Eden, her eyes reflecting compassion and love. When her gaze meets Samuel's, his memory jolts again.

"Mawari? Kanaima?" he whispers.

Kaikare tells him a negative entity had entered the waipa while the shaman's spirit was deep in the forest. Kaikare's spirit was there in the waipa preventing it from taking hold of him, although she wasn't strong enough yet.

She smiles and bows her head. Kaikare explains her mother returned to protect Samuel, the shaman, and Eden.

"Eden?" he whispers.

Kaikare nods, confirming her danger. She explains the shaman's spirit returned from the forest and stood beside Eden, but he couldn't enter the waipa. Eden unconsciously released her spirit, a young jaguar. Eden passed out, and it was the moment her spirit entered the waipa and stood alongside Kaikare. Together they were powerful enough to force the entity back into the jungle to where her father and mother awaited.

My god.

He had no idea of her power

Samuel reaches down and caresses Eden's beautiful face.

Will she remember?

Kaikare's grip tightens on his shoulder. He turns away from Eden and meets Kaikare's insistent gaze. "Inesa."

He closes his eyes slowly and inhales a deep breath. He nods in understanding. His negative thoughts surfaced during the ceremony allowing the entity an opening to enter his thoughts and cripple his progression. But it didn't have time to attach to Samuel's soul.

"Inesa arukuma," she says. *Inesa stars.*

Samuel nods, acknowledging Inesa's soul is with the stars.

"Inesa, tuna." She moves her hand in a snake-like action like running water, "tuna." *Water.* Kaikare lightly taps her heart. "Turùpo wakü." *Heart good.*

Samuel nods. He has to release his thoughts of Inesa to the river. Let it go so his heart will be good. For as long as he can remember, he has held onto the past and locked it away. He is a better man and has changed his life for Inesa, yet it means nothing if he's not honest with Eden.

Everything in his life has led to being with Eden. Would he have found her if every event of his past didn't exist? His friends' poor treatment of Inesa, him leaving society to live in the jungle, then stumbling across Ulara. Ivy upsetting her family and doing what was considered outrageous for her time—leaving her husband and young son to volunteer in the jungle. Finding Ulara much like he did, maybe.

Had the shaman seen them all coming?

Be it fate or destiny, where's it leading them now that their souls have met?

Eden groans, and her hand wraps under her stomach.

"I'm here," Samuel whispers. He leans down and kisses her cheek. "I'm here, my love. What do you need?"

"Water," she murmurs without opening her eyes. Samuel signals to Kaikare a drinking action, and she scoops water from the bowl and hands Samuel the mug.

"Let me help you." With a hand under her back, he assists her head so it's high enough for her to sip the water.

Her eyes widen. She looks around the room as though awakened by her memory. Rolling onto her side, she pushes up into a seated position with her legs tucked to one side and her other hand pressed to the ground to support her. "Are you okay?"

Samuel smiles. "I'm fine, thanks to you. I'm more concerned about you and your exhaustion. Do you want me to carry you to our hut? You can sleep in the hammock all day."

"Why would I do that? I'm fine."

"Last night was difficult. I understand—"

"I know what to expect now. I'm seriously fine. Though I'm surprised we slept here."

"You don't remember passing out?"

"I passed out," she gasps. "Did I fall?"

Samuel asks Kaikare to tell him what happened step by step. He translates the night to Eden, what happened in his visions and the moments after she passed out.

"I remember seeing the eyes in the forest and..." She clutches her throat.

"Do you need more to drink?"

"No. I mean, yes, but I remembered something, and it spooked me a little."

"About your spirit?"

"No. I have no recollection of myself in another form." Her brow pinches, and there's a hint of doubt in her words. "Kaikare said you were an owl and a macaw."

Samuel stares up at Kaikare. He asks her what happened for her to tell Eden his sacred birth name. Kaikare explains his spirit was scaring her, and she sensed your energy leaving your body. Eden was afraid of losing Samuel, and Kaikare reassured her his spirits were watching over him.

"Wakü Turùpo," he says to Kaikare. *Good heart*. He touches Eden's cheek. "It's time we talked about something I have kept from you." He takes her hand and assists her to stand. "First, you need to eat, and then my day is yours."

🌴

"I'm tired." Eden cradles her head on Samuel's shoulder as they sit on a boulder near the stream. "I think I'll take that nap later."

"And you didn't eat enough. I'll gather more berries for you."

"It's weird as I'm always hungry, but lately, I've lost my appetite. I'm sure after a nap, I'll be fine. You should also rest. Even the shaman slept until late morning."

Samuel stares into the forest while he decides what to tell Eden. "The shaman's visions are complex and multidimensional. He travels to the future and the past while the forest delivers a message."

"Did he receive answers last night?"

"I haven't had a chance to speak with him. It can wait until tomorrow."

Eden kisses his cheek. "I told you I'm having a nap. You don't need to stay with me while I'm sleeping. Go and speak with the shaman."

"He'll summon me."

"Of course, he will," she snaps.

Samuel chuckles and scoops her up in his arms and wades with her into the water.

"Wait! My skirt and beads," she exclaims.

"Will dry quickly." Samuel chuckles. He drops onto his knees with Eden in his arms until the water comes to their necks.

"It's freezing," she shouts.

"Refreshing," he corrects. With wet fingers, he wipes the dirt from her face and then from his own.

"You know..." she swipes her tongue over her teeth, "... I could do with a good toothpaste and a new toothbrush. The plants and my worn brush ain't cutting it at the moment."

"Ain't cutting it," he repeats and laughs at her Aussie accent.

Eden thumps his shoulder.

He chuckles again. "I'll have Asoo bring you some more supplies. Anything else?"

"Yes. What did you want to discuss with me?"

He leans his forehead against hers. "Remember the time I spoke of Inesa?"

Eden nods. Her eyes widen, and in them he senses her compassion and relief that he's finally opening up to her.

"It's time I told you what happened."

Taking his cheeks in her soft palms, she kisses him in a way to remind him she's here for him, always.

27

EDEN

"It's a long story, but I'll keep it brief," Samuel says as he climbs into the hammock beside me. Lying on his back, he lifts an arm for me to lay my head on his shoulder. He stares up to the pointed ceiling, the bamboo angling to the sky.

"I don't mind," I whisper.

"It began in high school. A girl called Inesa took the brunt of our heckling. I later found out Sean had been sleeping with her but never spoke to her outside the bedroom.

"Looking back, I realize Brant secretly liked her, but she was, in his eyes, not at his level. He was top dog of the social status ladder, and Inesa was the girl next door." He rubs the side of his jaw slowly as though he's considering his next words.

"I didn't participate in the bullying, but I didn't stop it either. In time, she developed severe depression, and it took a toll. Years later, she ended her own life.

"Two days before..." he clears his throat, "... I bumped into her at a bar in Santa Monica. I was home on a short break. She'd been drinking and wasn't herself. She told me how much she had loathed me because although I did nothing, she knew I was weak." He taps his chest over his heart. "And for that, she never forgave me for not condemning my friends' behavior. When I told her they wouldn't listen to me, she didn't believe me and then broke down. If only I spoke up just once and made her feel worthy of respect.

"When her tears stopped, she lectured me more, telling me to do something constructive with my life. Do something for the greater good, for the underprivileged. She pointed out studying medicine isn't for the greater good because I gained a monetary reward.

"I had status and an ego and thought I had the power of life and death in my hands. In her words, if I were truly a decent human being, I would give and seek nothing as repayment... a kindness to others without remuneration. I didn't know what she was talking about until dark thoughts consumed me, and realized what society stood for and the part I was playing... power."

"It wasn't your fault," I whisper.

"No? But I wasn't an innocent bystander, and I should've seen between the lines and told her she was worthy. Stopped her..."

I take his hand in mine and squeeze it. His face screws up with the burden he has carried all these years. "You weren't to know."

His Adam's apple bobs as he swallows. "I attended her funeral. None of my friends bothered. Watching her heartbroken family sob at the graveside ripped open my heart. I knew I couldn't continue on the same path, only I didn't know where to turn or start. All I knew was from that day, my life had to change. Standing by her grave, I made a promise to be a better person and do good in a world without relying on compensation. That's when I applied to volunteer in a remote area as far down the socio-economic ladder as possible. The rest is history."

I stroke his beautiful face. "All these years you've been too hard on yourself."

"No. I'm glad I found Ulara. Even more delighted that I found you."

"I'm glad you found me too." I lean up and kiss his cheek. "You'll always be the kindest man I've ever met."

He meets my gaze and stares, really stares.

"I see you," I murmur. "And I'll always love you."

"And I love you," he croaks. "You're now my reason for life." His brow crinkles.

"What is it?"

Lifting his arm from behind my head, he pushes up. "I've just remembered something." Throwing his legs over the edge of the hammock, he springs to the floor. "I'll be back soon."

A moan comes from my throat with him leaving me. Only I'm too tired to object. One thing I'm certain of is now nothing will hold us back from a future with our daughter. He has taken steps to face his past. The next step is to return to society with me.

28

EDEN

Supporting the swell of my abdomen, I roll over in the hammock.

"Bloody hell," I groan. Now I need to pee. How long have I even slept?

I sit for a moment on the edge of the hammock to gather my balance.

With a hand resting under my abdomen, I push up to stand. I wander out to the jungle border to do my business. I check the ground and the tree close to where I choose to relieve myself because it's huge and helps hide me from people and creatures. Checking for creepy crawlies is all second nature now.

I feel better already.

Pushing the palm leaves aside, I head back to the hut. Before I reach the edge of the forest, I stare through the fronds at a woman standing outside Samuel's hut.

Kaikare.

I smile and call out to her.

She comes to me and wraps her arms around my

back with a gentle squeeze. "Waküperö?" she asks gently. *How are you?*

"Wakü." *Good*

She releases me and checks me over. She places both hands on my abdomen and closes her eyes.

I stare at her face, searching for clues. Her eyes remain closed. There's no pinching of her brow in concern or smile of joy dancing on her lips.

Nothing.

She pulls her hand away. "Senneka Awarö."

Senneka is a word the Ularans use for activities like work. Awarö means bad. I rub my stomach. "Wakü?" I repeat in a tone she understands. *Good?*

Kaikare smiles, and I let out a sigh of relief.

Glancing over my shoulder, she peers into Samuel's hut. When her eyes meet mine, I sense torment. Shit, do I need some of his medicine?

"Fff-o-to," she pronounces.

It takes a moment for my thoughts to align and not think her concern is about my unborn child.

"Photo?" I repeat.

Kaikare replies with one curt nod.

I take the lead, and she follows me to the steps of the hut. I point to my hammock. She sits on the edge while I rummage through my backpack to retrieve the tightly wrapped package containing my grandmother's past.

"Here we go." I pull out the brush first and hand it to her while I unwrap the photographs. Kaikare lightly brushes her hair, and I smile, imagining her sitting in front of a mirror doing just that, only with my grandmother standing behind her. Dammit. I swipe a tear that forms quickly. These bloody hormones.

I envision them fifty years ago. My gran's long blonde

hair was cut after returning from Ulara. I imagine her with her newly styled bob cut with a curl at the ends, in a way reminding me of Marilyn Monroe. She smiles down at her daughter, brushing the length of her wavy, long brown hair. The gorgeous girl with brown eyes and ochre skin like her father, although she has her mother's kind heart. I witness the twinkle of compassion and love of my grandmother in Kaikare's eyes every day. Taking every step slowly so as not to break the precious time these two have together, even if it's a figment of my imaginings, I hand the photographs to Kaikare.

I take a few steps back to give Kaikare the space to absorb the memories of her mother, her brother—another life.

A tear cascades down her cheek, and the sight has air catching in my lungs. "Turùpo," she whispers and lifts her hand to her chest. *Heart*

"My heart hurts for you as well," I murmur. I sit and wrap my hand around her waist while she slowly peruses the photographs. "And look, this one is of us in the curiara." I smile at her. "Ina." *We.* I circle my finger between us.

Kaikare's lips curl up, and I'm glad our photo gave her some joy.

A warm feeling sweeps down my neck and spine to my abdomen. Shit, I have to pee again.

I push up and point to the forest.

Something in Kaikare's expression changes, and there's now a seriousness in her eyes that concerns me. She shoves the photographs to me as though the reminiscing session is over. I wrap them in the waterproof packaging and hand them to her. "Amäre." *You.* They are here for her when she's ready.

A few steps before I reach the jungle, water gushes down my legs.

I gasp and spin to Kaikare.

She strides to me and assesses the small area of wet dirt between my feet. I'm mortified at the thought of peeing myself only I know I didn't. "No," I wail. "It can't be. Not yet," I beg to the universe.

Kaikare takes my hand and leads me through the village. My thoughts are in overdrive. I can't have my baby here. In a moment of panic, I assess how to get to the nearest hospital. While my mind unravels, I allow her to guide me, assuming she's taking me to find Samuel.

When we reach the village center, Kaikare speaks to the women cooking over the fires. Three elders stand and gather sticks and leaves in a pile before speaking to Kaikare in calm words. I spin toward the shaman and chief's huts, only they look deserted, and there's an eerie silence descending over the village.

She holds up a hand, and I know I'm to wait. She rushes to her hut and returns without the photographs. Taking my hand, she leads me in the direction of a stream. Not to Samuel. The three women push the wayward branches and fronds aside to make a path for us to follow.

"Kaikare, I need to find Samuel," I blurt. "Väi Uarati Kún-imá," I say his Ularan name. *Sun man with long leg.*

The women ahead of me shout something over their shoulder while Kaikare remains tight-lipped. Oh God, I can't have my baby alone out here and not without Samuel.

"Argh." Wrenching my hand from Kaikare's, I stop and grab my stomach as a contraction rips over my abdomen. Shit, this is real. The practice is over. "Väi

Uarati Kún-imá," I repeat with a sob. *Sun man with long leg.*

Kaikare places a hand on my shoulder. She smiles and moves aside and points to a tree where the women are busying themselves. The tree is enormous with a massive hole cut out of the base, making it appear like a wooden cave.

"I'm not going in there," I tell her.

The women have already created a smoking fire, placing long branches with a mass of leaves around it. Woven twine dangles from a branch as a noose.

What the hell?

"Awarö," I say sternly and bring my hand down in a fast swat. *Bad.*

"Ahh," I cry out again with another contraction. I'm not well-educated on the matter. I thought I had more time. I thought contractions started slowly, like thirty minutes apart. This one is a couple of minutes from the last. I grab my stomach and hobble over toward the ladies because right now, they are my only help.

If ever I have agreed to some stupid things in my life, this has to be the dumbest.

Two of the women disappear while the other has a sheet of bark. She waves the bark over the little fire sending smoky clouds toward me, causing me to splutter and cough.

This can't be good.

"Samuel," I call out, only it's more of a croaky sob. Where is he? I'm so bloody scared something will go wrong, and he's not here to help me. I stare through the smoke with more clarity. These women have aided birth without medical help or assistance from the outside world, but Samuel has told me repeatedly that I'm not like them.

Kaikare cares for me. I have to trust she'd do everything in her power not to allow harm, physical or spiritual, to come to me. She lifts the beads over my head and places them on the ground. Then she unties my skirt and lays it alongside the beads.

Here I am, in the middle of the bloody jungle, butt naked in front of three strange women about to smoke my baby out of me.

My heart is pounding against my ribcage. I can't think straight.

I have gone mad.

Kaikare takes my hand and leads me closer to the fire. She pushes up on her toes and kisses my cheek, left then right. She wipes the tears from my eyes. Reaching up, I grab her hands and give a gentle squeeze.

"I trust you," I whisper. "I'm bloody scared, but I trust *you*."

Kaikare stands with her legs wide apart and points for me to do the same.

Mortified and frightened, I do it. The smoke is wafted closer between my legs, and I close my eyes and pray to my god and the forest gods that I'm doing the right thing.

"Ahhh," I groan and bend in pain. Kaikare rubs my back until the pain eases a short time later. When I straighten, more smoke wafts my way, blurring my vision. The two elder ladies have returned, and one is placing leaves over the fire. The leaves sizzle and produce an aroma that makes me somewhat lightheaded. It could be the desired drug effect. The other *wise-woman* has a residue-like sapling mixed with a fatty substance. She and Kaikare rub it over the leaves in a fast action. I assume the friction and heat from the fire does something to the leaves. At this point, I don't care as long as it helps with the pain and assures a safe delivery.

They spread warm emollient over their hands, then massage my stomach and lower back, and damn, it feels amazing.

My breath catches when two hands go between my thighs and near my private area. I glance down to Kaikare —a little less embarrassing since it's her—rubbing the fatty substance over my inner thigh and groin.

"Argh," I shout out when a contraction is stronger than the last. I lean over to catch my breath. Placing one hand on Kaikare's shoulder, I lean my weight on her. Kaikare places both hands on my stomach and closes her eyes.

Her face is unreadable. I search for a crinkle, a sign to know what she's thinking. "Please tell me she is okay," I whisper.

The women break into a song, one that has them pointing to the heavens and trees.

They prepare paint on a small banana palm, dot my face with white and red paint and then decorate each other's faces.

"Nooo," I scream out when the contraction rips through me again, ceasing all curiosity about the paintwork. What the hell was in that balm? Now the pain is tenfold. With my eyes closed, I pant through the agony of my cervix twisting like a rope.

I can do this.

I can do this.

Nearby, movement has my eyes shooting open. One woman rushes away and returns moments later with more sheets of soft bark.

They take the smoked palm and lay it at my feet. In front of me, Kaikare drops to a squat, encouraging me to do the same. Slowly, I ease my way down in an unladylike manner and cringe when all eyes focus on my vagina.

Even I know the baby's head isn't crowning. I shove two fingers inside of myself to verify and hunch a little in relief when I feel nothing but soft flesh.

"Nooo," I scream out when the contraction has me thrusting forward onto my hands. It feels almost natural to be on all fours. Focusing on a controlled breathing rhythm to get me through the pain, I rock back and forth in a gentle sway. Keeping my eyes closed, I remain like this—rocking and breathing, my thoughts drifting to the beach with calm, clear water where I can visualize the seashells in the sand at my feet. For a few minutes, it calms my mind until the next contraction is so intense, my head could spin like in the *Exorcist* as the pain takes control of my body.

"Samuel," I shout at the top of my lungs. "I'm not having this baby alone with a piece of bloody bark to catch our daughter!"

As one contraction rolls into the other, I pant my way to some sort of sanity, then screech his name again.

"Samuel!" This time my screams are loud enough to silence the monkeys. The birds nesting overhead squawk, then scatter through the trees for cover.

As more pain hurtles through my body, I hope and pray that Samuel comes soon.

Please, Samuel.

Be here for me.

29

SAMUEL

Samuel asks Itariru to repeat her answer.

He understood her words as *Tamu'ne Akare is with Kaikare and the elder ladies, preparing Eden at the birthing tree.*

She says the same words again.

He has only been away a couple of hours.

Maybe Kaikare is teaching her their ways as practice. Even more of a reason why he needs Eden to leave Ulara and be safe in her home country. He can't allow the tribe to have a claim over their child.

A scream from the jungle has him spinning in the direction of the stream. His heartbeat leaps to his throat. He sprints without further question toward the sacred birthing tree.

Samuel lopes through the jungle thrashing the palms and low-lying branches aside with no medical supplies on hand. A week ago, he prepared an emergency pack hoping his worst fear didn't come to fruition.

There's no time. I have to get to Eden now.

In his next breath, he gets a whiff of smoke from the

birthing ritual. If Eden is too far along in her contractions, even he might not be able to save their daughter. What if her lungs are underdeveloped, and she's unable to breathe unaided? The rainforest might be known as the lungs of the world, but it's no oxygen tent.

Another minute passes. The stench of smoke is stronger. He's close. He falls into the clearing, stumbling to gain his balance.

Eden is naked and on all fours. His breath catches. Panic builds in his chest. His thoughts race as he battles to calm himself, calm his heart and mind.

Kaikare crouches beside her and lifts Eden's head to meet Samuel's gaze, a look telling him he doesn't belong here.

"Airö," the eldest woman shouts. *Goodbye.* She tells him to wait until he's summoned.

"Make no mistake, I'm now in control," he tells them in Ularan.

"Hey," he pants, crouching down beside Eden.

Her eyes meet his. "You're here," she sniffles. Tears stream down her cheeks, and it rips at his heart.

Samuel gently places a hand on her shoulder. "Yes, and no matter what, I'm not leaving you. How is your pain?"

"My bloody vagina is on fire. I don't know if there's smoke coming out of it or if it's from the friggin' fire."

"It's not on fire," he assures her. Even without assessing her, he can tell she's closer to dilation than he assumed. The eucalyptus and citrus aromas alert him to the balm already covering her body. "What the women have prepared for you is safe and quickens the birth, so you're not in pain for long."

Blue eyes brimming with tears peer back at him. It

crushes him to see her in pain and trying to brave. "You don't have to do any of this *their* way. I have medication back in my hut. Only some I can't give you. Depending on how far you have dilated will influence what drugs I can administer. Do you mind if I examine your cervix? It will be uncomfortable."

"Do what you have to-oo—" she screams out the last word and pants through the next contraction. "Just hurry."

"You're doing great, Eden," he tells her. "Let's focus on you, okay?"

"What do you mean on me? Jesus mother of all hell," she curses at him when his fingers slide inside of her. She bucks a little. And he quickly whips an arm beneath her to support her weight. His thoughts tick over.

He can feel the baby's head.

There isn't much time.

"Kaikare." He tells her to go to his hut to retrieve his emergency pack.

Kaikare shoots a hand down in a swift axe-like action. She says the other women will fetch it for him as she's not leaving Tamu'ne Akare. He doesn't have time to worry about the women rummaging through his belongings or his private work.

Kaikare asks Týkire to run to his hut, and Samuel explains the special case for her to bring to him.

Týkire's name means yellow—they gave her the name after she was jaundiced at birth. It's a trigger for his brain, and he races over the possible implications of having a premature birth, including the complications Eden could suffer.

Bile rises to the back of his throat. He struggles to think clearly.

Eden is his priority.

His focus has to be on stabilizing her. What if she hemorrhages?

Eden screams out, and it breaks his control.

"I'm sorry," he tells her. "I didn't wish for you to have your baby here like this."

"Too late now," she growls. "Just get our daughter out of me."

"Do you need to push?"

"No. Oh God, did I just pee myself?"

"It happens," Samuel shifts for Kaikare to remove the bark from beneath Eden's legs and flips it to empty the urine onto the ground. She gathers more bark from near the fire and replaces it between her legs.

"Is my baby supposed to land on that? Please tell me you'll catch her," she moans.

Samuel rubs her lower back. "If the women need to lay the baby somewhere to attend to you, that's where they place her. The smokey aroma mixed with the bark can help the process. And don't worry about Arukuma Turùpo," he says for her ears only. "I'll be here for her."

"Promise me you'll do what you can to save her," Eden pleads through a muffled sob.

How can he promise when he doesn't know the extent of their baby's premature birthing complications? "I need you to focus."

"No, Samuel. I'm serious. Promise me," Eden rasps.

He meets her gaze before her eyes clamp shut with another contraction. "Yes," he whispers, hoping his word to be true.

"Argh, I need to move. I think I want to push now."

He assists her to squat, and he asks Chirké to come and sit behind Eden to take her weight.

"I want you," she croaks. "I want you to hold me."

"Then I won't be able to assess you. Give me a moment, and if I'm satisfied, then I'll allow Kaikare to observe your progress."

"I'm scared," she rasps.

He strokes her forehead. "It's okay to be, but Kaikare has assisted in childbirth for many years."

She reaches out and grabs his hand. "Do you think this is how my gran gave birth to her?"

He leans in and kisses her damp cheek. "There's a high chance it was here under this tree. She'd be proud of you. Like her ancestors, Kaikare has learned much of her practice over the years in the same technique used for your Gran." She smiles at him, and her joy in the smallest thing gives him a reprieve.

Eden squeezes his hand. "It hurts so much," she wails and curls in on herself.

"You're doing great, my love. I'm so proud of you." Samuel maintains a serious expression when the baby's head crowns and slides back. "I want you to push on your next contraction," he gently urges.

"Okay." She pants a few times, then groans loudly. Holding her knees, Eden grunts hard while pushing for as long as her breath allows. She falls back into Chirké's arms. "I'm spent. I can't push like this," she sobs.

"Eden. Eden, look at me," he demands. He waits for her bloodshot eyes to meet his. "See that twine hanging in a loop?"

"God, what's it for?"

"To help you push. You squat while hanging onto that and use it to help push. We can carry you over there."

"No, I'm not moving. Please don't make me move. The pain is unbearable."

"It's okay." He offers her his balled hands. "Use me to help bear down."

Curling her back into a C-shape, Eden gives three more pushes. Samuel lets go of her hands to assess her progress. "Pant through the next contraction."

"Why? What's wrong?"

He uses his fingers to help stretch her labia around the head. "I'm giving you time to adjust so you don't tear."

"Tear? Ugh, great."

Kaikare tells Samuel she's preparing the twine and pipe and walks to the fire.

"Okay, push when you're ready."

On the next contraction, Eden pushes with all her energy, groaning until the end of her breath. "Good," he tells her. Pure joy pumps through his body, his head feeling light with excitement and fear. "The baby's head is free. One more push." Eden isn't out of the woods yet.

She clenches her teeth and bears down again. The baby slides out, and Kaikare is beside him with her pipe and twine.

Eden screams in relief as Samuel eases their daughter's feet out. "Let me see her," Eden cries as she slumps back. Only their daughter has not made a sound.

Samuel rubs her back. He tries not to panic. He hopes the quick labor has left their baby a little stunned. She's limp in his arms, and he's suddenly nauseous.

"Samuel, what's wrong with her?" Eden rasps.

"Tamy mïta," Kaikare directs. *Tobacco mouth.*

"Give her to me," Eden wails.

If he does, the baby might not take its first breath. He has no suction equipment, and Týkire hasn't returned with his pack of small instruments. There's a tiny hand pump that could help. He searches the nearby shrubbery. There's no sign of movement.

"Samuel," Eden's voice demands, her arms outstretched.

Samuel nods at Kaikare and holds the baby closer. Kaikare sucks in a breath through the pipe and blows smoke over the baby's face. Their daughter lifts her arms in the startle reflex and cries a beautiful sound. Kaikare meets Samuel's gaze, and her eyes are brimming with joy. She gives him a curt nod.

Their beautiful daughter wiggles, and a tiny scream bursts from her. He lays her on Eden's chest. "She's perfect like her mother."

"You're perfect," Eden whispers to their daughter and kisses her cheek. Her soft cries quiet down as her mother comforts her.

While Eden gushes over their daughter, Kaikare and Samuel use the heated twine to tie off the umbilical cord, and Kaikare cuts the cord with a piranha tooth.

Panting comes from the bushes, then Týkire springs out of the forest. She hands him his box, and he scurries through it searching for his stethoscope and sphygmomanometer.

Kaikare presses lightly on Eden's abdomen.

"Can you hold her with one arm?" Eden holds out her arm for Samuel to apply the cuff. "It's Ularan tradition to gently press and massage your stomach to help pass your placenta. Are you okay with this?"

"Fine." Eden is too preoccupied with their daughter to care what they are doing. As soon as he establishes her health as stable, he'll be right by Eden's side, cuddling them both.

"Your arm will feel tight with the pressure." She

shoots him a look, one telling him it's nothing compared to the pain she has endured.

The reading is low.

Shit.

Emotion comprises his decision-making. His throat is tight, and his heart is racing with the realization of everything that could possibly go wrong. He's unprepared for an emergency in an unsterile environment with limited instruments.

"Look." The joy in Eden's voice brings him back. Their daughter is sucking from her breast.

Their baby doesn't suckle long. "She's beautiful," he purrs.

Eden stares longingly at their tiny bundle curled into a ball. She runs a finger along her spine. "I think I'm going to spend the rest of my life gazing at her." She looks up at him, eyes twinkling. "Do you want to hold her? I know you have already held her, but you didn't cuddle our angel."

His heart still thumps like he's being chased by a leopard. He is afraid to get attached to their daughter. His heart couldn't bear losing the two loves of his life. Until he has them both safely in a hospital, his guard will remain in place.

Eden's eyes flick over his face.

"Of course," he whispers. Samuel lifts their tiny bundle and cradles her to his chest. He closes his eyes as a wave of emotion washes over him. He allows himself to feel the love of being a father, a partner, and having his daughter nestling close to his heart. So, this was what it was like to belong, to have your own family. His demeanor cracks, and with it, a tear of joy cascades down his cheek.

"What do you want to name her?"

Samuel can't take his eyes from their daughter. "Rose," he whispers. "She's my Rose, a rare flower only found high on a tepui determined my belonging and commitment to Ulara. Our little Rose has stolen my heart, and my vision is for her, and..." he meets Eden's gaze, "... her beautiful mother."

Eden's eyes hold the warmth and love that fills his heart. "Rose, it is." Her expression changes and her brows pull tight. "Oh, what's that?" she moans loudly, and Kaikare is there to assist with the placenta.

"Give me a minute." Samuel carefully passes Rose back to Eden and moves so he can assess the organ for tears in its entirety. He passes the organ to Kaikare and moves to trade places with Chirké so Eden is leaning against his chest.

"Where are they going?" she whispers.

"To bury your placenta. They believe we come from the earth, so they give back to the earth. The placenta gives life, and the nutrients will be returned to the soil to sustain more life."

"You know I thought they might ask me to eat it," she says seriously.

"It makes sense. It would help with your iron levels."

"If it meant survival, I would. If you had asked me a year ago, I'd have said no. But I'm not that same girl. I'm braver and wiser and would do anything for the two people I love the most."

Samuel kisses the hair on her crown. With one hand, he holds the love of his life while his left hand strokes the shoulder of their baby asleep on Eden's chest. Neither Eden nor Rose are clear of medical complications, and until both can be assessed, only then will his mind relax.

At the bottom of his medical pack, he pulls out the satellite phone and fires it up. In the past, he'd never have used it in front of the Ularans. The circumstances have changed. He hopes to the gods it has coverage and reception isn't blocked by the towering tepuis encasing them in the jungle.

It beeps, and he lets out a sigh.

He taps in Asoo's number and smiles when he answers.

"I have little time to speak. Eden has had the baby. How soon can you get here?"

30

EDEN

I was more exhausted than I realized as I slept between feeds. Yet, there was awareness of Samuel remaining awake. In the dark of night, he touched my skin and took my pulse. Telling him to rest was pointless. And now he's moving through the hut with the sun's light breaking through the trees.

"Morning, beautiful." A soft kiss lands on my cheek, stirring me from a deep sleep.

"Is it morning already?" I moan, my eyes fluttering open. Samuel stands beside my hammock with our daughter pressed to his chest. "Oh, I didn't hear her cry. Is she hungry?" I adjust myself in the hammock and hold out my arms for Rose.

"She was stirring, and it was an opportunity to cuddle her before her mother does." He gives me a guilty smile. "Once you have her in your arms, you never want to let her go." Samuel kisses her cheek before passing her to me to feed. "And you need to prompt her to suckle."

Caressing her cheek with my nipple, Rose turns her face and opens her tiny mouth. "She's doing fine," I boast.

Samuel smiles, although the concern is still there by the way his forehead wrinkles. "Asoo is on his way. When we arrive in Canaima, your case will be at the reception. We're not stopping." He gives me a pointed look. "We'll take a flight to Ciudad Guayana. I have covered your health insurance, and we'll remain there until your condition has stabilized."

"Well, I feel stabile." I return the pointed look he shot at me. "Although, I feel gross," I mumble. All night I wanted to wash. With only a few pairs of underpants and limited sanitary pads Samuel had in his pack, I'm making do hygiene-wise. Up until now, I've never menstruated in the jungle, and I have a newfound respect for how the ladies deal with discharge naturally.

"I'll wash quickly," I tell him even though the distance I have to walk is something I can't hurry. How the women are back in the fields working a few days after childbirth is damn amazing.

Samuel takes Rose from me. "If Mommy wants to bathe, then we bathe," he says to Rose.

"Don't make it sound like I'm the boss," I mock as I clamber out of the hammock.

He gives me a look, and I can't help giggle. "You bend rules or make your own, and everyone around you allows you to do it."

"You make me sound like I'm a bully."

"No." He takes my hand and leads me out of the hut. "You merely charm those you meet. The moment I first saw you, I was under your spell."

"It's not the way I recall it. You wouldn't speak to me." I bump his hip with mine.

"I was lost for words."

Samuel rubs his nose over Rose's mouth. She opens her mouth ready to suckle.

"Stop teasing her."

"I'm encouraging her suck reflex."

"Stop worrying. We're going to be fine." Only I know he won't relax until we have been checked over in a hospital. "How difficult is the process of applying for a birth certificate?"

"I'll see that it happens quickly."

"Okay." He seems to have contacts everywhere, yet something is bothering him as his expression has tightened, and he's back to his closed thoughts and tight expression like he expects nothing but doom. "We're going to be fine. I know it, so please relax."

"I will tomorrow," he says. "When you get your test results."

Samuel's concern remains with him the entire time I bathe and packed up my belongings. He has been like this since he returned last night after speaking with the chief and shaman. All he told me was they granted us leave, but the shaman thought it unnecessary as we aren't unwell.

Packing the remainder of my belongings gives me a sense of déjà vu. Samuel insisted I bring everything in case I need it, yet it reminds me of my first time here, preparing to go home. I inhale a sharp breath and turn in a full circle, imprinting our *home* into my brain. I have to face the realization it might be one of the last times I stay here.

"I think that's it," Samuel announces as he places his sack on the bench. He lifts Rose from the twine basket where she's swaddled in banana palms.

Kaikare appears at our doorway. "Oh, you're here." I

take each step carefully, and then wrap my arms around her neck and lay my head on her shoulder. "Thank you for yesterday," I whisper.

Samuel translates my words, and both her hands rest on my back. I take an extra second to feel my aunt's love before I release her.

Kaikare sidesteps me when Samuel comes to my side. He leans and positions Rose in his arms for Kaikare to get a better view. A smile stretches his lips from almost ear to ear. Lifting a finger, she trails a path over her forehead and down her nose in one straight line. She whispers strange words as she does. Then she makes an invisible line from her temple to the opposite cheek and repeats it on the opposite side. It's the Ularan's symbol—an 'X' with a straight line through the center.

Was it a blessing?

Samuel lifts Rose and kisses her cheek. His gaze lifts and meets mine. There's a sense of apprehension, and then he closes it down. "Ready?"

I nod and take Kaikare's hand as we all meander the trail toward the river. We reach the sandy beach with no sign of Asoo.

"I'm going to miss you," I say and hug her. "I'll see you soon."

Samuel translates my words.

She takes both of my hands and squeezes affectionately. Her dark eyes flick over my face. There's a sense of sadness and appreciation. "Waküpe-küruman," she whispers. *Thank you.*

I squeeze her hands back and nod my head. "Samuel, I need you to translate for me. Please tell Kaikare I'm grateful to have met her and forever thankful for all she has done for me. And our daughter will know how her aunt loves her." I'm not counting on this being the very last time I'll see her, but I have an overwhelming urge to express my gratitude and love.

We hold each other's gaze while he does. Her eyes brim with tears, and then I can't help it, a sob shoots from my throat. We hug each other again, and her warmth and love seep into my heart. She then releases me and steps to Samuel. She opens her arms, and Samuel hands Rose to her. Kaikare lifts Rose close to her face, and she rubs her nose over her cheek. The sweet moment only lasts seconds as the putt-putt sound of the motor divides our attention.

She hands Rose to him, and in seconds, disappears into the forest before Asoo steers the curiara onto the riverbank. If she's more upset than she was displaying, I hope there's someone in the village to comfort her. I wipe my eyes and steel myself for the journey ahead.

"My friends." Asoo waves out to us. "I happy to see you."

Both Samuel and Asoo assist me in boarding before Samuel steps in gracefully even with Rose in his arms.

Asoo leans closer to see our daughter while maintaining a respectful distance. "A beautiful girl," he says. "I have your packages." He points to the pack wrapped in plastic.

"Please pass it to Eden." Samuel nods at me. "There are diapers and some clothes for Rose."

I can't help but frown. We haven't even left the riverbank of Ulara, and he's wanting to clothe Rose.

He catches my scowl and shakes his head. "She's yet to pass her first stool. I don't think Asoo would appreciate meconium covering the seat of his curiara."

"Me-con-ee-um?" Asoo repeats.

"Poo," Samuel translates. "It has no aroma, but it's thick and sticky, a little like tar."

Without further question, I take the pack and retrieve a nappy, or a diaper, as Samuel calls it.

"Please no tar on seats," Asoo says as he steers us toward Canaima.

Samuel sits beside me in the cut-out area Asoo has created for me. He unwraps the banana palms swaddling Rose's arms, and she gives herself a fright lifting her arms when she's set free. Samuel has the nappy under her rear and secured in seconds. I've had experience with my nephew, but I've forgotten so much from when he was a newborn. I barely saw him until he was a few months old. Rose is so tiny, and neither Samuel nor I were prepared for her sudden entrance to the world.

She's barely made a sound since birth, and I know it concerns him. She has suckled which is a positive sign, although I'm aware my milk won't come in for a few more days.

For the rest of the journey, I settle back with Rose in my arms and enjoy the view of the jungle caging us on the river as we slowly leave the towering tepuis behind us.

🌴

Sitting aboard the small aircraft, I'm more afraid of being up here in the clouds than in the green wilderness below us. Every turbulent bump has me clinging to Rose.

For the short time we were in Canaima, I wasn't allowed to hug Victor or Asoo. Samuel's concern is now on Rose's immunity, and we both need to keep our distance from people. I thanked them for all they did for me and hoped to see them soon.

My rear then leaves the seat, and I let out a little scream.

"Are you okay?" he asks.

"Yes," I say quickly. It's a short flight, and I'm counting the minutes until we're back on the ground.

The small Cessna aircraft touches down, and no sooner are we inside the terminal than Samuel is on his cell, pacing the floor. I remain on a chair nursing Rose with our luggage by my feet. I told him I didn't need my entire case considering we'd only be gone a week, but he told me to bring it for extra packages like diapers and clothing for Rose because his case is small and barely the size of an overnight bag.

Rose pulls a face as though she's unsettled. I don't have a maternity dress and can't breastfeed in public when I'm unsure of the rules or what society accepts here.

"Samuel," I say loud enough to get his attention. He stops pacing and stares at me. "I need to feed Rose. Where should I go?"

He speaks quickly in Spanish and ends the call. "We'll go to a feeding room." He slings his case over his shoulder, then wheels my bag, leading us along a corridor until a baby on a sign indicates we're heading in the right direction. Inside, there's a cubicle, and he locks the door.

"Wait." He pulls antibacterial wipes from his bag and wipes down the vinyl chair and armrests before we sit. The antibacterial wipes are one of many items he ordered and had Asoo store in Canaima. He assists me in pulling my arm out of my dress so I can feed Rose. He waits until

I'm feeding before he speaks. "We have a change of plans. We're heading back to Georgetown in Guyana. You'll need your passport. Dr. Vásquez has verified our passports with the authorities and that Rose is ours. We have a private flight booked in an hour."

"A private flight?"

"There are risks flying with a newborn, and many airlines forbid it. I'm transferring money to a company I have worked with over the years so we can get there hassle-free."

"Hassle-free." I roll my eyes.

He ignores me and continues listing the items we need to purchase. "If Rose requires formula milk, we'll need a bottle sterilizer as well."

"She's feeding from me," I state.

"Your milk hasn't come in. You're thinner, and your diet has been lacking. I'm thinking of Rose and whether she'll need to be topped up with formula milk."

"My God, stop. You're worrying unnecessarily."

His brow pulls tighter. "We have a few days to organize everything. I can do most of it while you're in the hospital."

"Wait. I only need tests. I shouldn't have to stay. I could come back to the hotel with you."

"I'll be staying at the hospital with you since I'm paying extra insurance."

My shoulders slump. Here I am telling him to stop worrying, yet I'm a burden with hospitalization in a foreign country. "I'm sorry. I'm sure my medical insurance will cover it."

"We're not claiming your insurance. It's easier for me to pay and get the best service, and besides, I have contacts."

I release a sigh.

Life in Ulara was simple.

Everyone did what they had to and got on with business working the fields and cooking the meals. Everyone ate what they needed, and the hunt was merely for meat once a month—maybe even less. Money didn't guarantee a better service or divide social classes.

Everyone had a role.

Everyone contributed.

Right now, I feel lost, and I understand why Samuel didn't want to leave.

The ultrasound beeps, and it reminds me of my time here in the same hospital when I was dehydrated and ill. I was afraid of losing Rose and wanted to go *home*. Now she's safe with me, and they are checking my uterus for retained placenta as a precaution. Samuel has ordered every test possible even though Dr. Vásquez has reassured him some are unnecessary. The amount of blood the nurse took from my arm was incredible. I shook my head and gave Samuel a dark look. I know he's going to send me home when ironically, I now want to stay.

Last night, he finally opened up and told me that Asoo had mentioned more drones are flying closer to Ulara, scoping out the land. He assumes illegal mining is to blame, but they can't point blame until they have facts. Samuel's concern is for the Ularans' safety, and I understand that. When I asked him what the solution will be, he merely shrugged.

Samuel doesn't shrug.

Even though he opened up by telling me this, he's still avoiding matters that concern both of us.

Like now—his gaze is fixed to the screen while he's speaking in Spanish.

Dr. Vásquez turns to me. "Everything is clear. There's no evidence of placenta. Are you clotting at all?"

I shake my head.

"We'll take some swabs and make sure there's nothing untoward, and then you're free to leave when your blood results have returned. Over the next day or two, we'll observe Rose for jaundice, keep a check on her feeding and urine output. Has she passed a stool?"

"Yes," Samuel says quickly. "On the flight." He looks at me and grins. It was a moment we both laughed as we tried to remove the revolting sticky stools from her little buttocks. Thank goodness it didn't stink out the cabin of the plane.

Rose cries out, and Samuel brings her to me so I can feed her. Dr. Vásquez leaves us to take my samples to pathology.

Samuel lowers Rose to my lap after I have adjusted my clothes. "The colostrum will help with her immunity, and it's satisfying. Tomorrow she's likely to be unsettled right before your milk comes in."

I raise my brows at him. "Unsettled?"

"I just thought you should know."

"Is this how it's going to be between us?" I ask in a direct voice. "You, always aware of the possible problems and alerting me to what I *should* expect. I mean, motherhood I can handle. Being in the jungle and not knowing what to expect is a time you shouldn't have left me to discover my way. It's one extreme to the other."

"I'm only trying to help."

"Help, yes. Having yourself in a constant state of worry and watching over me like I could be obliterated in seconds isn't comforting. I want you to be with me, Samuel, the man I love. Not Samuel, the doctor."

He lowers his gaze and rubs his thumb over my hand. "I'm sorry. I guess old habits die hard."

"Old habits? Or are you hiding something from me?"

"Hiding?" He raises his hand to rest it on the back of his neck.

"Keeping something from me. It's like you have to be with me every second. I'm not complaining, but we have the rest of our lives to be together."

His lips tighten, and I sense I've hit the nail on the head.

"What? Tell me what you've planned?"

"I don't have a plan." He massages the back of his neck as though ironing out the kinks. "I'm continually changing my course of action, and I don't want to concern you with matters that won't affect you."

"If they don't affect me, then they shouldn't affect you."

"I have charged your cell." He pulls it from his case. "You can call your family and friends to inform them you're safe and announce the birth."

"Don't change the subject." He holds my gaze momentarily, then places my phone on the table beside the bed.

"I also have my own calls to make." He heads to the door and closes it behind him.

Shit. I want to know who he's calling because we both know it's not his parents.

31

SAMUEL

"Samuel?"

"Hi, Mom." Samuel paces the length of the garden outside the hospital. This is a phone call that has taken a hit on his dignity and something he can't do sitting down. "Is Dad with you?" Samuel raises his arm to check his wristwatch—the one his father gave him when he graduated from medical school. It's not something he wears often considering the value, only it keeps exceptional time, and he has used it to track Eden's pulse rate. After giving his other watch to the Watache as a gift of goodwill, when he arrived in Canaima, he retrieved the watch his father had given him that he had locked in a safe. In Guyana, it's lunchtime. In LA, it's morning, and he assumes his father has already commenced work for the day.

"Are you okay?" she blurts.

"Yes, I'm fine."

"And Eden?"

"I need a favor. It concerns Eden."

"Wait, I'll put you on speaker. Christopher..." she says,

"...it's Samuel. Okay, we can both hear you. You may need to repeat yourself as your father isn't well, which is why he's home on a Monday. His ears are blocked from an upper respiratory infection."

Samuel's throat thickens. "Are you okay?"

"Yes, son. It's just not something I can afford to spread to my patients."

Samuel understands the need for caution. He glances up to the third-floor window to Eden's room. "I'll just get to the purpose of my call. Congratulations. You're both grandparents to a little girl."

His mother gasps. "Oh my."

"Rose is well." His voice is filled with pride. "And thankfully, so is Eden. We're in Georgetown, Guyana, having tests for precautionary measures."

"Precautionary. Were there complications with her labor?" his father asks in a stern voice.

Honesty is best. "She delivered in the village where I work—"

"Heavens," his mother says in a breathy sigh. He can visualize her with a hand on her chest.

There's a moment of silence.

"Eden did amazingly well, and I arranged transport immediately to a hospital where I know the physicians who'll give her the best care. Rose is almost seven weeks premature and doing well considering her size."

"Rose?" his father repeats.

"Yes, Rose. We're yet to give her a middle name and will decide tonight for the authorization of the birth certificate."

"This is wonderful news. We're thrilled you called and can't wait to see our granddaughter. Please send some photos."

"I will."

"Now, you mentioned a favor?"

"My work here isn't complete."

"You can terminate the contract with the pharmaceutical company, son. I can call—"

"Dad," Samuel interrupts. "I have another commitment in which I have never expected you to understand or support. I intend to join Eden in Australia soon. *When* I do, I hope you can come to visit. We'd also like to make a trip to LA, but my priority is getting her home as soon as possible. Eden wants to support me and remain by my side. Don't worry yourself as I'll not allow it and prefer if she were home with family and safe in her country."

"At least you're thinking straight regarding your... partner."

Samuel withholds the urge to cuss. Instead, he focuses on the garden bed of red geraniums lining the paved path.

"I intend to marry Eden when we're in Australia. Dad, please don't make this about doing the right thing by Eden in the time-honored way you conceive as respectable. We love each other and plan to spend the rest of our lives together. Eden understands my commitment, and when upheld, I will, in your words, do *what's right*. My phone call isn't to discuss moral obligation. I need Eden home, and I don't have the funds to fly her on a private jet home to Australia without having to first arrange an appointment with a bank in another country. I don't have the time to fly to Colombia."

"You want us to fund the flight?"

"No. Consider it a loan. You know I have the funds since I barely touch my salary given my lifestyle. The protocol in accessing it is difficult. Years ago, I set up steps to prevent theft. Please understand time isn't on my side."

His parents murmur quietly between themselves.

"You understand the risk of a newborn flying?"

"It's why I need a private jet to minimize human contact for Rose's immunity."

"Eden and Rose will require clearances from the hospital."

"It goes without saying. I won't put my family at risk. The arrangement is to safeguard them." He almost added *from me* only he held his words, knowing it could incite an argument. Instead, he offers words of peace. "I'm sending the photos of Rose to your email now. I know Mom will gush. She's truly my little princess."

"Consider it done, son. Just do the *right thing*."

Samuel closes his eyes and slowly opens them with his father's words opening wounds of the past. "It's my intention. I'll email you the details of payment. Thank you. This is generous, especially considering the short notice. I'll be in contact soon."

"I'll email you when the funds are ready."

"Thanks, Dad. Bye."

Holding the phone to his chest, Samuel assesses his next move. He has a mental list to tick off before he can arrange the flight for Eden. With no time to waste, he calls the private jet company to secure flight dates. He glances up to the window where Eden waits and inhales deeply. They promised each other no more secrets. Only he can't share his plan to keep her safe, for without a doubt, she'll fight him on it until her last breath.

Samuel bows his head and prays she understands he's doing it all for her.

The long, white-walled hallways of the hospital ward remind him of where he studied. There are fond memories mixed with bad. In his final years of medical school, he decided he had to be a better person after Inesa asked him to promise not to follow the same path he was on.

He hopes he has made her proud.

Hopes he has fulfilled his obligation.

There's one more matter to uphold before he can move on with his life.

He opens the door to where his future awaits and hears her on the phone. Their eyes meet. She laughs, and a twinkle lights up her blue hues.

"I can't wait for you to meet her, too... I'll send more photos... I know, I know. I'll tell him he has to look after me." She grins at Samuel. "Love you all. Bye."

Pulling the AirPods out of her ears, she says, "My friends say hi."

He nods. "Have you sent photos?"

"I have, and they want more." She giggles lightly as though still high on happiness, and it's a moment of reassurance that sending her home is the right thing to do.

"Have you called your parents?"

"They are next on my list." Her eyes narrow. "Did you call yours?"

"I did. They send their regards to Rose and you and can't wait to meet you both. I also need to send photos, so I'll compose an email now."

"Okay... while you *compose your email*, I'll call my parents."

His phone vibrates before he does so. It's the private jet company. "I'll give you some privacy," he tells her. "I have to take this."

Samuel opens the door and says, "Samuel McMahon," and then closes the door behind him.

I can't believe he called his parents.

I take a moment to absorb the steps he's taking for Rose and me. I wish he had given me the chance to speak with them but given their history, I understand he has to smooth out some personal issues first.

Inserting the AirPods in my ears, I glance to Rose, still sleeping in her crib, and dial my father's number. It's close to midnight in Australia so I disconnect the call. Dad will be sleeping. The only reason my friends called is because they received the photos I sent and were out late at the Shores nightclub celebrating Yasmine's achievements in her new job. I miss them, but if I had a chance to go back in time, I wouldn't change a thing. My future is with Rose and Samuel, wherever they lead me.

I type out separate messages to Mum, Dad, and Faith with images of Rose attached. At least they are aware we're safe and well. Before I place my phone on the table, it sounds with an incoming call from Faith.

"Hey, you're awake?"

She makes an exasperated sound. "I'm nocturnal and

barely sleep, something you'll know about soon enough. It's great to hear your voice. I can't lie and pretend I haven't worried about you."

"I'm fine, I promise. Did you get my message?"

"Yes. It came through in good timing since I'm feeding James. Oh, honey, Rose is just adorable."

"She is," I coo. "I'm sorry my messages were scarce, but you know I had limited internet in the village."

"Yeah, I understood. Bloody hell, you had her seven weeks early. Is she okay? Where are you now?"

"In a hospital in Guyana. I'm not sure for how long. Everything is fine, so I assume we'll be discharged soon. Not to mention beds are scarce, and I don't want to take a bed from someone who needs it more than me."

"Your baby was born premature. There are steps and precautions you need to follow. I guess they can discharge the mother, and you can visit."

"What? I can't leave Rose. If she stays, I stay."

"Does your insurance cover you?"

"Samuel is paying. He won't even tell me how much or anything. He said to just concentrate on Rose. Seriously, he worries more than our father."

Silence.

"Faith, are you there?"

"Yeah. If Samuel is worried about something, then I think you should be as well."

"He's worried about many things and not only for Rose and me. Her sucking reflex is good, and she has no jaundice. Her breathing is fine, and her blood-oxygen level is great. Yet Samuel wants me to fly home soon. He has some loose ends to tie up here before he can join us."

"That's good news. When is your flight?"

A wave of nausea hits me. I shake my head as my

thoughts mesh into a jumble as though I'm blocking out the idea of leaving him. "There are matters to organize first... Rose's birth certificate, and we have to be cleared to fly."

"So... three to four weeks? How quickly can Samuel make it happen?"

I chuckle lightly. "He somehow pulls strings in the medical world, only I presume this is a government department so it may take longer."

"Where will you stay?"

"To be honest, I'm not sure. Wherever Samuel thinks is best. It may be here in Guyana close to the hospital. The next step is to make sure Rose thrives from my breast milk." I hesitate in telling my sister I hope to return to Ulara to say goodbye to my friends one last time. I glance over to my bag and see Gran's diary sitting on top. "I have so much to tell you, even more about Gran."

"Gran?"

"Yeah. While here, I started reading her diary. When I return, I'm going to look up her friend, Brenda, and ask for the diary she gave to her for safekeeping. I think it's an account of her stay in the jungle."

"Whoa, do you think that's a good idea? Seriously, it's all in the past, and people have moved on."

My hand rests on my chest thinking about Gran's life. "She did some wonderful things, and we should be proud of her." Tiny grunts come from Rose's crib. "Sorry, I have to go. Rose is waking. We'll talk soon, okay."

"Eden, keep me up to date with what's happening."

"I will."

"Stay safe, sis."

"I will. Love you."

With an overbearing need to sigh, I allow my

shoulders to drop. There's one more phone call to make, but I'll have to wait until morning to speak to my parents. Shuffling off the bed, I go to Rose and peer down at my daughter. She has the purest pale skin with light hair on her crown, and her eyebrows are barely noticeable. Tiny lips pucker, and she stretches out her back.

Oh my. I could watch her sleep for hours.

"Are you ready to feed?" I whisper. I inhale a sharp breath, and my hand rises to my right breast. Suddenly, a tingling sensation in my breasts is followed by a feeling of fullness. I think my milk just came in. Rose gives a little whimper, so I pick her up and cradle her until I'm in a chair. Adjusting my clothing almost comes naturally, and I position her on my breast. Her little eyes open as she sucks slower and stronger. "That's it, my Rose. Good girl," I whisper.

"That's truly a sight to behold."

I glance up at Samuel standing in the doorway. He comes to us and brushes a long finger over her little head.

"My milk came down," I say proudly as though it's an achievement.

His lips curl into a smile. "A few days of her getting the extra rest to grow and feed without complication, and you'll be on track to going home."

"Home? I thought I'd remain here for at least another month. I mean, you're the one who's over the top about her immune system."

My phone vibrates on the table, and Rose pulls off my breast with a scowl. I help her reattach, and before I can say anything, Samuel has picked up my phone.

"It's your father."

"Right. I sent him a message and thought he'd be asleep."

Samuel swipes the screen. "Evening, Mr. Monteford. This is Samuel."

I hold out my hand, but he walks away from me.

"No," I say firmly. "Let me speak first." My heart pounds in my chest. My father will be concerned, and I wanted to calm him down first. "Samuel, you're so frustrating."

He stops and turns to me. His gaze locks with mine, equally determined. Suddenly, his expression softens. "Eden is feeding our beautiful daughter. She's almost finished and excited to tell you about her. I'll hand her cell to her to speak first."

He gives the phone to me and mouths, "I also want to speak to him."

"Hey, Dad. Congratulations, you're a grandfather again."

"Are you okay, sweet pea?"

"Yes, I'm great. I'm in a hospital in Guyana. We're all well. I'm sorry to wake you, so we can chat tomorrow if you like."

"It's fine. I'm relieved to hear your voice. And now I can't wait to meet my beautiful granddaughter. When are you coming home?"

He has jumped to this subject quickly. Doing my best to ignore Samuel's serious expression, I steel myself to answer calmly. "Oh, you know, whenever the birth certificate arrives, and it's safe for Rose to fly."

Rose pulls off my breast and has a little vomit. "Oh, honey."

"May I speak to him while you care for Rose?" Samuel holds out his hand.

"Dad, I'm handing you over to Samuel for a moment. I need to attend to Rose."

"Okay, love. Mum is also here, and she wants to ask you questions about the birth."

Samuel takes the phone.

I don't fight him because Rose is squirming.

"Can you put it on speaker," I ask.

Only it's too late.

He has closed the door behind him.

33

SAMUEL

"It's a pleasure to finally speak with you. Eden talks highly of you."

"I have to admit I didn't approve of my daughter traveling to a part of the world I considered unsafe while pregnant to be with a man I have never met."

"I understand, and I want to apologize for any worry we have caused you. During her time with me, I have done my utmost to protect her and keep her safe in the village." Samuel rests a hand behind his neck and stares at a spot on the ceiling.

"Thank you for taking care of Eden. Please tell me she didn't give birth in the bloody jungle!"

Samuel swallows hard and closes his eyes at the harshness in Mr. Monteford's tone. "Sir, the baby came early, and we didn't expect—"

"That's the thing about babies. I thought as a physician, you, for one, would understand the spontaneity."

Samuel's eyes flash open. "Yes, sir. I acted swiftly, and

Eden and Rose are now safe in the Georgetown hospital in Guyana."

"Where the hell is that?"

Samuel opens his mouth and closes it again, realizing Eden's father isn't really interested in the answer. His comment is to emphasize his concern at his lack of knowledge of her whereabouts.

"I'm aware you want to speak more to your daughter, but I hoped to have a quick word first." When Mr. Monteford doesn't respond, Samuel continues to speak.

"Eden and Rose are my priority. I love your daughter more than anything and refuse to allow harm to come to her." He blocks out the time the Watache kidnapped her and how many times he has failed her. If her father knew the truth, he'd probably ban Samuel from having anything to do with his daughter. And Samuel would accept it and understand.

"Eden loves me, and she wears her heart on her sleeve more than any woman I know." There's a light chuckle of understanding on the other end. "So, I have had to take extra measures to protect her. There are a few matters that prevent me from returning to Australia with Eden. If given a choice, she would, without a doubt, choose to return to my place of work and be by my side. This isn't something I want for her, and since she's as stubborn as she is, I have gone behind her back and arranged a private jet through my father's company to transport Eden and Rose safely back to Australia. This can happen in the next two weeks, depending on two things. The first is Rose's birth certificate and whether it's processed in time. The second is my daughter's health. We need the doctor to clear both Rose and Eden as being fit to fly. From my end, the private jet will be ready when they are. The biggest hurdle is getting Eden to agree to this. She's not aware, and I'm afraid she'll object. So, I hope to have your support in convincing your daughter this is the right decision for everyone. I promise I'll be with her as soon as I can." Samuel inhales a deep breath and waits for Mr. Monteford to respond.

"You've organized that? For her?" Mr. Monteford's voice is loaded with caution.

"Yes. There's nothing I wouldn't do for your daughter."

"That's... that's very good to hear." Could Eden's father be crying? Something cracks in his voice as he says the words, but he clears his throat and continues, "I certainly agree the best place for Eden is home with her family. What can I do to help?"

34

EDEN

Christmas Day

After leaving the hospital, Samuel and I checked into the Ramada Hotel.

He had his reasons not to leave Georgetown, and he agreed to stay here and celebrate Christmas together.

"Morning," I say and roll over in bed and kiss Samuel. "Merry Christmas."

Samuel lifts an arm, and I snuggle into his side. "Merry Christmas, Eden." He kisses me and then kisses me again.

Rose whimpers. We both turn to the crib, our focus no longer on each other.

"Stay," he says. "I'll get her." He passes Rose to me and sits on the edge, stroking Rose's back while she feeds. "She's so precious."

I smile lovingly. "Our little miracle."

"I'll order in breakfast as the dining room will be busy."

"Sure, but not much. I don't want to spoil our lunch."

I grin at him. Samuel stands and opens his bag and pulls out a box tied with ribbon.

"You said no presents," I blurt.

Samuel smiles and places the box on the bed beside us. "I didn't want you shopping in the crowds. I ordered this and had it delivered."

"And I could've shopped online as well if I'd known you were breaking the rules."

He chuckles and pats my leg. "I'll shower first, and then I'll burp Rose."

Staring at the box, I'm tempted to untie the red ribbon and take a peek. It's a small rectangular box, and it's not as small as one that holds a ring. Besides, we agreed to buy my engagement ring together. And that won't be until Rose can be in public with a stronger immune system.

Rose pulls off my breast, her lips pursing as she makes a contented sound. "Did we drink too much?" I say and giggle at her adorable facial expressions.

The bathroom door swings open, and a freshly showered Samuel emerges. He towel-dries his sexy blond hair. "Is she finished?"

"Yes. I think she overdid it."

He takes Rose from my arms. "Okay, baby girl, no puking on Daddy." He places a hand towel on his shoulder and moves around the room while gently patting her back.

"Can I open this now?" I hold the box in my hands.

"Go ahead." He beams a smile at me.

I untie the ribbon and lift the lid. "Oh, Samuel." My hand rests at the base of my neck. "It's beautiful." I can't take my eyes off the intricate gold heart on a chain. The design is a 3D heart with smaller hearts on vines to make the shape. Inside the cage are three diamond-encrusted hearts.

Samuel sits on the bed beside me. "The vines and hearts represent *love grows*. And the three smaller hearts—"

"Represent the three of us," I say enthusiastically.

Balancing Rose on his lap, he leans in and kisses me. "I love you."

Taking his face in both my hands, I hold his lips to mine and show him how much I adore him.

"I'm sorry I don't have anything for you."

Samuel shakes his head. "I have you and Rose. I don't need anything else."

I kiss him again and then head to the shower. I take my time washing my hair and lathering the fruity-scented soap over my body. Taking the bathrobe from the hook, I wrap it around me before opening the door. Our breakfast platter is on the table. "Oh, did I take a long time?"

Samuel chuckles. Rose is asleep in his arms. "Take all the time you need." He places Rose in the crib and joins me at the table. Besides the usual fruit Samuel insists I eat for my health, there's a plate of scrambled eggs, toast, and fruit juice.

"I'm not sure if this qualifies as a light breakfast."

He hands me a glass of camu camu juice. "No, but you need nourishment."

"We," I add with a smile.

He stands and finds my gift, then he clips the necklace around my neck. I lightly touch the heart hanging between my breasts and close to my heart. "I'll treasure it always."

"Ready?" Samuel asks with Rose secured in a wrap around his shoulder and tied at the waist. He's wearing a white button-up short-sleeved shirt and navy shorts.

Brushing my hair for the last time, I check myself in the mirror, admiring my forest green dress, then take the elevator to the ground floor. Tinsel and sparkly Christmas decorations line the hallway and foyer. I smile, thankful to be sharing this day with Samuel.

A waiter directs us to a table with a red umbrella to protect us from the sun. The sapphire blue pool has floating tables all decked with candles, tinsel, and angel statues.

"It's so pretty," I tell him.

Samuel pulls out a chair for me to sit. I can imagine him as the perfect gentleman in society.

"Thank you." I sit opposite him and Rose, then take in the colorful ornaments surrounding us.

"I love Christmas."

🌴

After our meal, we retreat to our room, and I nap for an hour until Rose wakes me ready to feed.

Samuel is sitting on the balcony. Lifting Rose from her crib, I walk out onto the balcony to feed her in the chair beside him.

Below us, the pool hums with revelers still celebrating.

"Do you think we could take another drive tonight and find more Christmas lights? I'd love to see the huge Christmas tree in Rahaman Park."

"Of course," he says and strokes Rose's crown. "I hope to discuss something with you." His eyebrows pull together, and there's a seriousness in his eyes.

Oh no.

His expression is scaring me, so I glance down and focus on Rose feeding. "What is it?" I murmur.

"You know I love you and Rose and only want what's best for you both," he says in a level voice.

"Just tell me, Samuel."

"I need you to go home and be safe with your family."

I nod, still not looking at him. "And you'll eventually join me?"

I look up when he takes my hand between both of his. "I promise I will. As soon as possible."

I scan his face. "But that's not what you want to discuss with me, is it?"

Samuel holds my gaze before speaking. "Tomorrow, there's a jet flying directly to Adelaide with a stopover in New Zealand. I'd like you on it."

My heart goes to my throat. "And if I say no?" I rasp.

"Please, Eden. I needed to take the extra measures to keep you both safe."

"So, I don't have a choice?" I croak. "Why now? Why not wait until the new year?"

Samuel bows his head.

A sob escapes my throat, and I can't control it. I sniff loudly. "No." I shake my head. "I'm staying here with you!"

35

EDEN

The Following Day...

"We're ready to board," the flight attendant says to me.

"So, this is it." I swipe a tear before it trails down my cheek.

Samuel's bloodshot eyes portray his sadness, but unlike me, he has been stiff-lipped the past twenty-four hours and not shed a tear in front of me. We're the only ones standing in the private hangar with the two pilots already boarded and two other flight attendants.

"Call me when you arrive in New Zealand." His large hand cups Rose's cheek.

I nod quickly. "I will and again when we touch down in Adelaide."

He pulls me close, careful not to smother Rose, who's cuddled into my chest. My bones are weak, the sadness seeps deep, and the littlest pressure could send me to my knees. God, I wanted to drop to my knees several times and beg him not to send us away.

"Ask Asoo to keep me updated. I know time gets away from you, but every minute will feel like days to me," I croak.

"And me. I don't want to go around in circles, but it's for the best. I'll be with you in a month or so." He kisses the side of my cheek, and I grab his arm to stop him from pulling away.

"It's too long. How quickly can you speed up the final documents in Caracas to end your contract?" I reach up with my spare hand and cup his neck, so his lips lower closer to mine. I kiss him through the tears and the burn in my throat, so he knows he's my everything, and I hate being apart from him for a second, let alone weeks.

"Sir," the flight attendant interrupts. "They have given us clearance, and we need to get the plane on the runway."

Our lips break away, and Samuel leans his forehead against mine. "You're the love of my life, Eden." A sob escapes my throat. "My heart will be with you and Rose. Take care of it until I can be with you both again."

I can't stop my face from squishing when an ugly cry threatens to undo every inch of composure I have left. Tears roll down Samuel's cheeks. His demeanor cracks. "Go," he rasps. "Please go." His voice breaks, and like me, his face screws up in pain.

"One month," I say to confirm our separation. "I'll see you in one month."

The flight attendant takes the bags at my feet. Samuel waves to me and turns, then keeps walking. He doesn't look back. Not once. Head down, long strides, he walks out of the hangar and around the back to where a black Audi awaits him. His father ensured Samuel had enough money to cover us for a quick departure, and now Samuel can drive himself back to the international departures section and catch a flight to Venezuela.

"I'm Daryl," the attendant says with a Spanish accent. He walks beside me holding my three carry-on bags filled with what I need for the next twenty hours for Rose.

"Jenna is a nurse and will assist you with any needs on board." Daryl offers a warm smile, only right now, I doubt anything will help with the gaping hole in my chest. The neckband of my shirt is wet from the tears spilling off my chin and onto my chest.

I climb the stairs and take the first step into the luxurious furnishings of the jet. There are white leather lounge chairs wide enough to transform into beds. To the side are lacquered wooden tables. Lush carpet runs the length of the plane. Up front, a glass bar catches my eye with stools strategically placed in an arc for guests. Samuel and his father must have paid a mint for this. The thought makes me angry. Normally, Samuel lives a simplified life and places no value on money. If we'd waited, I could've flown using my return ticket and not wasted a shitload of money unnecessarily just to get me home early. Rose's immunity is the point he emphasized in his reasoning for the private jet. Yet, for the sake of a few weeks, he could've saved himself at least one hundred thousand dollars. The thought of him going behind my back angers me, and right now, I'm using the anger to stop the tears.

Jenna points to a seat that's more like a luxurious lounge suite. I force a smile. "Ms. Monteford, I need you to adjust your seat belt until we're in the air. I'm here if you need anything after take-off, including assisting you with feeding and minding Rose when you use the restroom and to make sure you get adequate sleep. I'll monitor Rose for any signs of distress, including difficulty in breathing. The lower air pressure may be problematic, and the changing cabin pressure may cause her to have some ear pain. As soon as you're settled, I'll get you to feed her, so she's sucking during take-off and again on each descent."

I undo the clip under my right armpit, so my top falls away to reveal my right breast—quite the invention for feeding mothers. I unclip the cup of my maternity bra, which would have to be the ugliest bra I have ever worn, and tease Rose's mouth with my nipple. Apparently, my nipple isn't enticing. "Rose," I whisper. I run my fingers over her cheek so she turns her head. A few more attempts, and she opens her mouth to attach. I nod at Jenna. "She has been slow attaching the last week."

"It's not unusual in premature babies." Her hand rubs my arm. She wraps an additional strap over Rose and attaches it to my belt. "This is just until we're in the air."

Jenna signals to Daryl we are ready, and the plane crawls along a path as we head toward the runway.

When the nose is pointed upward to the sky, I lean my head back and close my eyes, wishing it didn't have to be this way. I swallow the lump in my throat to even out the pressure in my ears. The plane levels, and I look out my window to the city disappearing below. Within minutes, the view turns green with the vast rainforest covering much of the country. A world where I belonged. A world so far from the one where I live.

Tears fill my eyes like wells and fall onto my cheeks. I can't fight the gnawing pain in my chest any longer. But my tears aren't only for Samuel. This was probably my last visit to Ulara—the last time I'll see my friends again. I screw up my eyes, knowing Kaikare will expect me to return with Samuel. What will she think?

Samuel told me they were to migrate soon. If they do, we will never know their whereabouts—only that they were heading closer to the Colombian jungle and then south to the Peruvian jungle. A journey that could take months—even years. Kaikare may never meet my father, nor will she see me or her niece again. In those last weeks together, I'm glad I gave her a photo of us even though Samuel warned me against it. I smile. Kaikare and I are family, and we did secretive things so the men didn't get upset. Her eagerness to know more reflected she had some of my grandmother's blood flowing through her veins.

In Ulara, I was brave and free.

My Gran, Kaikare, and I may be wild at heart, yet we're courageous, strong women. Now Rose will join our legacy. I wonder if she'll have the same drive to return to where she was born to find her jungle spirit?

Wiping away the tears that land on Rose's head, I look back to the window and watch as the vivid green fades and the clouds block out my view.

Through the heartache and frustration, I can't help my concern for Samuel. Not only for his safety. How will the shaman react to him for sending us away?

🌴

"We have begun our descent into New Zealand," Jenna whispers. "Do you want me to take Rose for you?"

I stretch out the kinks in my neck and force my eyes to open. Despite the comfort of a bed on a jet, I barely slept with my thoughts whirling about the future. "No, it's fine," I murmur. Pushing up onto my elbows, I reach for Rose sleeping in a small crib beside me.

"Let me help you." Jenna lifts Rose and waits for me to sit up. After adjusting the pillows behind my back, I then hold out my arms for my daughter.

"Take your time," Jenna says softly. "I don't mind holding her." She gazes down with a contented look in her eyes.

I adjust my top and bra. "Thank you. I can manage now." I lift the window blind to dark skies and the sun peeking over the horizon.

"We should land around six o'clock. It will give us time to refuel. Then when the tower clears us, we'll be in the air and on our way to Adelaide." She gives me a warm smile as though this is reassuring. It only confirms the distance separating Samuel and me is increasing by the hour.

"Thank you," I say quickly and gaze out the window once more. I can't look at her because I'm holding myself together by a mere thread, and the slightest comment could unravel me in seconds.

It's only when the plane jolts as the wheels hit the runway do I notice Rose has detached and is asleep in my arms. She didn't cry. Not once. I shake my head and curse under my breath for not realizing this sooner. I have to snap out this haze of self-pity and focus on my daughter.

Jenna unclips her belt and comes to me. "She's a remarkable little girl." She pushes her dark hair behind her ears, then leans for the antibacterial hand sterilizer and applies it to her hands. God knows how many times she has used it on the flight. I can only imagine Samuel's instruction to the crew.

"Allow me to hold her while you freshen up. There's a private restroom just outside the hangar. You can use it as we all have to disembark while the plane refuels. Unfortunately, we can't venture any further because of our visas. Airport customs staff are waiting, and they'll monitor us even though we're a private company."

"Right. Do you think I could make some phone calls?"

"Yes, you'll have time."

Jenna remains with me while the customs staff asks questions about our travel. "Let me care for her while you make your calls," she says.

God, I must look miserable.

"I'll change Rose first, and then I'll shower. Do you mind taking Rose while I do?"

"Of course. But you go, and I'll change Rose's diaper."

"Thank you."

As much as I want to remain under the water spray, it doesn't relieve the tension the way I had hoped. Eager to call Samuel, I dress quickly and head back to the lounge area.

"I really appreciate your help," I tell Jenna. I bag up my dirty clothes and head to a quiet corner of the room, then bring out my phone.

"Eden." I smile at the affection and relief in Dad's tone. "Are you in New Zealand?"

"Yes, it's a quick stopover to refuel. We should be there in around five hours, but I'll need to go through customs." I gaze down to my new gray sneakers, the ones I bought after throwing out the old ones. "Did you get the list of things we need? I'm sorry it's short notice. I can't believe how unorganized I am."

"It's fine, my girl. James is using a larger car seat now, so we have his smaller seat for the car for you to use for Rose. We have everything you need. We've done it all before. Only I'm not used to seeing so much pink again." He chuckles, and I can't help but smile at the sound of it. I'm looking forward to seeing my family, only I hoped Samuel would be with me to greet them and show them *our* beautiful daughter together.

"It will be good to see you all." I look up in the direction where Jenna is taking slow steps with Rose in her arms. She's not bouncing her, but she sways like the camu camu leaves moving in the breeze.

"I can't wait, love. It's been too long."

I nod to myself. "I better go. I think Rose may be a little unsettled. I'll call you when I land."

"We'll be waiting at the airport for you," he says enthusiastically.

"Bye, Dad." I end the call and rush over to Jenna. Rose isn't crying, and she's still sleeping. "Is everything okay?"

"Yes. She started to pull a face, so I thought if I moved around the room slowly, it would help her to settle."

"She already has us wrapped around her tiny finger," I joke. "I have one more call to make." The hardest of all.

I call Samuel's phone, and it goes to his voicemail. "Dammit." I hope this isn't how it's going to be between us. Samuel was aware of my flight details and what time I'd call him. I pace in the corner of the room thinking of what to text him when the phone vibrates in my hand.

Thank God.

"Samuel, I was beginning to worry."

"How was your flight? How is Rose?"

"Good. We're fine. How could we not be? It's a beautiful plane. Rose has barely cried, which is good, and she has fed regularly."

"The staff has assisted you?"

"Yes. Wonderfully."

"Good."

We pause, and I sense he's hiding something with the formalities. "I miss you," I say, and my throat dries with the pain in my chest.

"I miss you too."

"Did you send your email to Caracas?"

"Eden." He hesitates a moment, and my heart goes to my throat. "Asoo called me. There were more drones flying near Ulara, and this time, he followed a boat. When they realized he was behind them, they didn't take the secret turn down the river. They continued on, and the boat was more powerful than Asoo's curiara."

"They had boats... what are you telling me?" I croak.

"Asoo believes they are scoping the area, and it's putting the village in danger."

"And?" I whisper.

"When I return to Ulara, I'll have a meeting with the chief. I think it's time they considered migrating deeper into the jungle."

"And?" I repeat.

"Eden, please don't read into this. Allow me to return and assess the situation. I'm in Canaima now. I feel obligated to keep them safe."

"They're not your responsibility anymore," I whisper. I glance up as Jenna strolls toward me. Daryl is collecting my bags, and everyone is heading toward the jet. "I have to go. Please don't make any rash decisions. I'll call you when I'm in Adelaide. I love you."

"I love you too. I'll speak to you when you're safely at home. Look after our precious Rose."

I nod and end the call as Jenna reaches me and blink away the tears. "Is it time?" I fake a smile.

"Yes, we're cleared now."

I follow Jenna toward the plane and hope to hell Samuel doesn't leave for Ulara before I have a chance to speak to him again.

On board the jet, I settle back into the seat for the final leg of the journey. I glance down at Rose sleeping in my arms. "We're going home," I whisper. "You're going to meet your grandparents, your aunty and uncles, and your cousins. You'll love your new home."

It's weird to think Ulara was her first home, one she'll never know. Maybe a home she would have loved, like Kaikare, as she'd be ignorant to what lies beyond the jungle, the privileged world that relies on money as power rather than survival skills.

I promise to teach you to respect the land, all creatures, and people just as you would if you lived in Ulara. Money will not rule our egos or happiness.

Leaning forward, I kiss her cheek, and her little lips purse in the sweetest duck face I've ever seen.

Once the plane is in the air, I unclip my belt and the strap over Rose and place her in the crib. Digging into my bag, I pull out Gran's diary, ready to embrace the last of her words before she begins her journey.

Date: 15th November 1962

The journey by boat has been long.
The nausea never leaves me. Most days, I vomit. I intended to

write in the diary every day on the boat, but it's dragging on, and after being surrounded by nothing but blue, it has affected my mood.
So this is my last entry in my diary. I have bought a new leather diary for my volunteering journey, and I can't wait!

Her adventure is about to begin just as mine has come to an end.

36

"Estas seguro?" Samuel asks Asoo. *Are you sure?*

"Sí." *Yes.*

Asoo explains to Samuel the men in the powerful boats were near the riverbend when their drones flew over Ulara. The Ularans are in immediate danger, and Asoo races to get Samuel back to the village. Samuel is a mess of emotion. He has gone from deep sorrow saying goodbye to Eden to a clustered mess of anger and fear, knowing the Ularans safety is at risk. He has raced off to help, yet he has no gun or any weapon if it comes down to fighting these men. He's fast if he needs to run, but he hopes his negotiating skills will be his best defense. Either way, if someone enters the village, their secret is lost and their immunity compromised. Who knows where these men have been and who they have associated with?

In the back of his mind, he has accepted the inevitable. In Canaima, he collected his phone, identity papers, passport, and important belongings that will fit in a backpack. He left everything else with Victor. Most of it is replaceable. He has another two backpacks in Ulara for notebooks, long accounts of his work, and other medication and first-aid.

His phone and charger are wrapped in plastic. He's sent his last message to Eden, and he has no idea when he'll be able to contact her again.

They turn the final bend, and Samuel squints to make out the boat moored on the bank of Ulara.

"Apaga el motor," he says. *Cut the motor.*

They glide into the embankment near Samuel's makeshift campsite. The imposter's boat is thirty yards away. Both men spring from the boat and dash to the thick shrubbery to take cover. Samuel scouts the area, inspecting the ground for footprints or freshly broken twigs or palm leaves. There's no evidence of anyone around his campsite, but he fears the worst. The men could be in the village. It's a ten-minute walk, less if he runs. He tells Asoo to leave now, otherwise they'll discover his curiara.

"Esconde la curiara," Asoo suggests. *Hide the curiara.*

They sprint back to the river and drag the curiara into the bushes, then snap palm leaves to cover it. It's not completely covered, although it's obscured enough not to be obvious.

"Te vas a quedar?" *Stay?*

Asoo shakes his head. Both men take off through the jungle, slapping palm leaves aside, careful to avoid the prickly vines. When they near the village, they slow to a walk. Pushing a low-lying branch aside, Samuel assesses the situation, yet everyone is going about their business. The women are cooking over the fires, the children kick a coconut in a small clearing, and the older men sit cross-legged weaving baskets.

"Quédate." *Stay.* This time, it's an order. Samuel walks past the ladies and holds a finger to his lips. They give him a subtle nod, yet there's an uneasiness in their eyes. Kapeá Tapire is now around six months pregnant herself, and she's not working in the fields today. He squats next to her and observes her cooking a broth in a clay pot. He looks to the chief's hut and then to the shaman's hut. Only now do English words carry in the air. He asks her how many men are in the shaman's hut.

"Oko." *Two.*

"Jopoto?" *Chief.*

Kapeá Tapire nods.

"Pyjai?" *Shaman.*

She nods again.

"Kaikare?"

Kapeá Tapire shakes her head. She points to the other side of the village. Crouched beyond the trees are several figures. From here, he can make out Kaikare and Timenneng.

"Waküpe-küruman," he says. *Thank you.* Samuel instructs her to tell the ladies to remain calm. While monitoring the doorway of the shaman's hut, he darts to the other side of the village and speaks to three warriors and Kaikare.

"Tamusi areku." *Old man angry.* Kaikare points and shows more distress than the others. She explains how the men pushed her father into the hut and demanded his gold.

Samuel asks her to remain calm and says he'll try to negotiate with the men. He doesn't know if it will help, but at least he can communicate in English.

Standing outside the shaman's hut, he signals his

approach. "I'm a physician, and I work in the village. Is there anything I can do to help?"

"C'mon in, doc," a gruff voice demands, a voice sounding raspy as though he has chain-smoked for fifty years. The chesty cough confirms it.

Samuel ducks his head to enter the doorway, and no sooner than he's inside, a gun is shoved near his face.

"Take a seat. Perhaps you can translate what we want because your chief here has no clue." The two Caucasian men have fair hair. This one speaks with an American accent. The odor reeking from their khaki shirts and the dirt smeared over the sweaty arms and shins indicates they haven't showered for days. He assesses their clothing —matching khaki shorts and worn leather boots with the clay mud coating the exterior. No belts carrying knives or ammunition.

Samuel shifts his attention to the chief and then to the shaman to assess their well-being. Both men have fresh bruises on their brow and scratches to their cheeks, shoulders, and arms, as though their faces have been pushed into the ground. The shaman's eyes reflect sorrow and disappointment. The chief has a defiant look, and it concerns Samuel.

"They have something I want." The gun waves between the chief and the shaman. "Tell them to give me the gifts other travelers have left for them."

"I have no clue to what you're referring, but I'll ask," Samuel says. Samuel asks both men if they have something of value from people who visited the village before Samuel. The chief tells Samuel the stone mountains are unhappy that he took Rose without a formal blessing. And now they are being punished.

Ignoring the comment, he asks the shaman again. The shaman meets his gaze and gives a curt nod.

Samuel speaks to the shaman in their native tongue, so the outsiders don't understand their conversation. Samuel asks him what's of value and who gave it to him.

The shaman explains there was a man before Ivy, but since Ivy, there were no visitors until Samuel. He stands and walks to the back wall. He reaches into a twine basket and retrieves a brass vase. Samuel has not had the privilege of seeing this vase. The shaman tips it, and a chain falls into his hand. On it dangles a huge gold nugget. He tips the vase again, and a strand of pearls lands over the nugget. He tells Samuel the pearls were Ivy's.

Samuel explains this is all the shaman has, but the pearls aren't authentic, hoping the travelers disregard them.

The gun fires.

Samuel, the chief, and the shaman drop to their knees in response to the explosion. Samuel uncurls his body and checks the chief beside him who's hunched with his hands over his ears.

"Wakü?" *Good?*

The chief's eyes are wide, and beyond the fear, he gives a curt nod. The shaman moans. Like him, he has fallen to his knees. A hand rests over the left side of his abdomen. He flops backward. His brow pulls tight, then he lowers his gaze and lifts his hand. Dark blood cascades between his fingers and down his stomach toward the band of his skirt.

Fuck. He shot him!

"Don't take me for a fool." He angles the gun at Samuel. "Don't tell me lies."

The other guy pushes the chief, and he falls to the dirt. Samuel's heartbeat thumps behind his ears. He wills his panicked thoughts to calm, but he can't take his eyes off the shaman. Mentally, he's assessing the puncture wound and his blood loss.

"Bring me the box and chain." The man's sinister expression turns into a smirk as though he's enjoying the power. "And no tricks because the next time will be you."

Suddenly the gunman's face turns gray before he falls flat on his face, the gun spinning from his grasp. His eyes are wide with instant death. A small dart in his back is to blame. Samuel and the other low-life turn to the doorway. Another dart hits the accomplice in the chest. Timenneng lowers his poison blowpipe.

It takes a moment for Samuel's thoughts to catch up. "Shit," he shouts and rushes to the shaman. He rips his T-shirt over his head and presses it to the wound. With his free hand, he lifts the shaman's head so he rests on his lap. Behind him, the men's bodies are dragged from the hut by the young warriors, and the chief is rushed away. Terrified screams come from outside the hut and then Kaikare appears in the doorway. Through the silence, there's quiet panic in her eyes.

"Pyjai," Samuel tells her. *Medicine.* He explains he needs her to go to his hut and get *his* medicines. Without question, she does what he asks.

Seconds later, Asoo appears at the doorway, his eyes as round as a full moon.

"Kaikare is getting the first-aid box. I need the women to concoct some heated leaves to stop the bleeding and help with the pain. Can you go to the ladies cooking over the fire and give my request?"

Samuel looks down at the shaman. He hums a

harmonic tune as though he's singing to the forest. He can't give up. It isn't his time. Samuel's chest tightens with panic. The musky rust scent of blood fills his nostrils. Samuel adjusts his T-shirt, and with the pressure, the material soaks up blood faster than Samuel can manage to control it. He needs emergency surgery. Something he can't perform here. Major blood vessels and organs are damaged, and without medical equipment to scan the shaman's wound, the extent of the damage is unknown. Managing blood loss, shock, blood pressure, and infection are his priority, and one T-shirt will not be effective in saving his friend's life.

Samuel tells the shaman he's getting his white man's medicine.

The shaman lightly shakes his head. He explains to Samuel the forest calls him.

Samuel keeps the conversation positive, telling the shaman his medicine will act quickly. Samuel looks to the door wishing for Kaikare to appear.

"Come on, Kaikare. Please hurry," he murmurs.

The shaman's breathing becomes heavy, labored, and sweat beads over his forehead and face. Blood streams from beneath the material and pools on the dirt. He's suffering, and yet the shaman's expression remains stoic. With one hand, he reaches up, and a rough skinned palm cups Samuel's cheek.

"Airö, upetoy." *Goodbye, friend.* "Wewe pyjai," he rasps. *Trees call the shaman.*

Samuel shakes his head in a desperate attempt to remain positive.

"Mosìpe nono oma." *Long earth path.* The shaman lifts a weak finger and points to Samuel. "Urekon." *We.* "Aina," he murmurs. *Hand.*

Samuel takes his hand and squeezes it. Is it his way of giving his word in the Western world in the form of a handshake? Samuel stares into the shaman's eyes. His lifeforce is fading. Samuel's chest tightens knowing there is nothing he can do. The realization is a dagger to his heart.

He has the knowledge of both world's medicine and yet he feels helpless, a failure again.

Panting in the doorway diverts his attention. Kaikare is out of breath as she runs toward them.

"Thank God," he rasps.

She bends down and places the case beside Samuel. He asks her to unclip the lid. He points to the dressings and tape, and he swaps places with her so she's cradling her father's head in her lap and hands. Her sad eyes hold his gaze as he peers up to her apologetically. They whisper to each other while Samuel washes the wound and presses clean dressings to the area. The shaman doesn't flinch—not once. Instantly, bright blood soaks the white bandages, and Samuel catches the fear in Kaikare's eyes before turning her focus back to her father. He tells her it's her time. She lets out a quiet sob. He asks her to be strong, no tears, as his journey is complete.

Samuel works as fast as he can. His hands freeze hearing Ivy and Dawn's words, and Samuel realizes the shaman is talking about Kaikare's mother and their time together. The shaman's eyes shutter closed and slowly open again. He's losing consciousness and soon will not be alert enough to know what's happening around him.

Samuel tells the shaman coming to Ulara was the highlight of his life. Through him he found a father figure, a mentor, and a friend. Samuel sniffs and wipes his nose with his forearm. The shaman has taught him many things about life and himself, and he's proud to call Ulara home.

The shaman mutters, "Areku," he asks them not to be *angry*. He closes his eyes and asks for Samuel to help him. Samuel assumes he means with his treatment, only he mumbles. "Mosìpe nono oma." *Long earth path.* He opens his eyes long enough for Samuel to nod. Then his hand softens in Kaikare's palm, his eyes closing in peace.

Samuel removes the dressing. The blood loss has slowed. Taking Kaikare's hand, he closes his eyes. He doesn't need to touch his neck to know the shaman's heart has stopped beating.

Kaikare curls over her father's limp body and whimpers. Gently, Samuel rests a hand on her back. Her whimpers turn to wails as she mourns her father. His heart aches feeling her loss. She is now alone without family and he has sent Eden, her blood relative away.

"I'm sorry," he murmurs and rubs her back. "So, so sorry." He understands the need to grieve before Kaikare steps up to be their leader. She squeezes Samuel's hand, her bloodshot eyes begging for support.

"I'll stay with you as long as you need me," he tells her in their native tongue. He then quietly stands and leaves her to have the final time with her father, alone.

As soon as he exits the hut, he's hit with chaos. The men run and shout, shock etched into their expression. Asoo rushes to him.

"The men throw bodies into boat," he says in a shaky voice.

"We need to dispose of it now. Remove all the evidence they were here."

"How?" Asoo covers his eyes with his hands. "This will end bad."

"Can you retrieve my bags from the curiara?"

"Si." Asoo scampers toward the river.

"Timenneng," Samuel shouts. When Samuel catches up, he asks him to dispose of the boat. Timenneng nods and then gathers the warriors.

Samuel finds Chirké, one of the elder ladies, crouched by the fire. He asks for her help to calm the women. The younger women sob, not yet controlling their emotions like the elders, and it's scaring the children. Samuel doesn't want to deny the Ularans a sense of mourning. His heart has splintered into a million pieces, but now isn't the time. They need to support one another and keep noise to a minimum in case other intruders are sailing nearby, searching for their friends. He places a hand on the back of a young lady and tells her it will be fine. He then heads to the chief, ready to inform him of the shaman's wishes and his insight.

It's time to move on. Take the great earth path and find another home.

Kaikare will become the shaman, and Samuel will be by her side until they settle deep in the jungle where no man ventures.

He has made promises to the people he loves.

Eden.

The shaman.

But a promise to a dying man's wish to save his Ularan family when Samuel's family is safe in Australia is important to him. Samuel has the paper maps that only he can read and Western medication and knowledge to assist the Ularans in their voyage. He'll help with replanting vines and other medicinal herbs until more can be discovered. In the coming weeks and months, they'll need him more than Eden. In fact, the entire civilization depends on him for their safety.

His gut twists in pain. How will he survive without her? Will she forgive him? Without her by his side, the journey ahead will be torturous, but he *will* return to her again, only much later than he promised.

Asoo returns carrying Samuel's packs. "Two more I not manage."

"It's fine, my friend. It's time for you to go. The Ularans will move on from this site as it has become too dangerous for everyone. I need you to leave now before anyone recognizes you and associates you to what went down here today."

Asoo tilts his head. "Samuel come with Asoo?"

"No, my friend." He lays a hand on his shoulder. "I'll travel with the Ularans until they find peace and safety deeper in the jungle. Their migration was inevitable... the timing, unfortunate. I made a promise to the shaman to remain with Kaikare and assist her on a safe journey. I need your phone to send a message to Eden. Please let her know I'm safe, and I'll be with her soon. I'll type out a message for you to send in Canaima. She'll call you, so please just reinforce I'm safe so she doesn't worry."

"Where you go?" he asks, his voice thick.

Samuel exhales loudly. His words will not be reassuring. "Southwest toward Colombia and Brazil. Preferably closer to Peru."

Asoo groans. "No, friend. Brazilian Garimpeiros and Colombian Guerrilla control much of the land."

Samuel bows his head momentarily before meeting Asoo's wary gaze. "I'll keep away from towns and stay close to the river. My map will guide us."

Asoo shakes his head as he reaches down to his pocket, pulls out his phone, and hands it to Samuel.

Samuel types a message to Eden. With every word typed, he endeavors to remain positive as he knows she'll consider his journey a death wish.

He can't help thinking she's right.

He hands the phone back to Asoo. "Send it when you're in Canaima."

"Miss Eden will be sad."

"And I'll need you to reassure her I'll be fine." Before Asoo replies, Samuel hugs him and pats his back several times. "Thank you, my friend. You have helped me more than I can ever repay. One day we will meet again."

When they break, Asoo wipes his eyes filled with fear. "I'll tell Miss Eden you a good man."

Samuel smiles and bows his head, hoping she sees it that way.

Asoo and Samuel strain to push the curiara from the riverbank into the water. Asoo turns and gives his friend one final salute before revving the motor and guiding his curiara to safety.

Samuel drops to one knee as the sound of the motor fades as it reaches the bend in the river. He bows his head when Asoo disappears behind the thick, overgrowth overhanging into the murky water.

Samuel's demeanor cracks. Asoo will not return here for weeks. Realization sets in. His chest burns as though a knife has ripped down his sternum and someone has pried his ribs apart.

Alone, the tears come and blot the sand beneath his feet. He allows himself this moment until he can breathe again without pain.

A roar of a motor in the opposite direction catches his

attention. The intruder's boat is alight as it sails across the river. It explodes into a fireball before reaching the trees on the opposite side. Smoke billows toward the sky, a tell-tale sign to anyone searching for the men.

Samuel pushes to his feet.

He'll stress the urgency to move on to the chief before more men come searching. He sprints in the direction of the village for possibly the last time. The next path Samuel treads is toward the stream and deeper into the jungle.

Deeper and away from any form of civilization.

And.

Eden.

37

EDEN

Wheeling my case behind me and holding Rose in my other arm, I exit through the customs gate in Adelaide with the other passengers. Peering through the glass barrier, I spot Mum and Dad chatting to each other. To Dad's left is Faith. She is holding James in her arms, and she's distracted by Seb running around.

"Eden," Mum screams as I exit through customs. She pushes past a young couple in front of her and rushes toward the arrival gate. "Oh, darling." She wraps one arm around me despite the grumbling of those travelers behind us trying to exit and meet their families.

"It's great to be home," I tell her and move aside so people can pass us.

"My girl." Dad hugs me.

"Hi, Dad." We exchange brief smiles before their focus switches to Rose.

"Oh, Eden," Mum coos. "She's just delightful."

"Hey," Faith says, pushing past Mum. "Let me give her a hug." With her free hand, she embraces me.

I kiss her cheek and then kiss James. "Where's the rascal?"

Faith stops James from poking a finger at Rose's cheek, and while holding his tiny hand, she swivels and calls out to her son.

A moment later, Seb is pulling at my skirt. "Let me see."

"Where are your manners, Seb?" Faith rouses. Dad lifts him so he can see Rose. "What about a kiss for your favorite aunty?"

Faith chuckles as he leans in and gives me a sloppy kiss.

"Do you want to meet your new cousin?" Faith asks. He stares at Rose as though she's made of china, and he knows he's not allowed to touch.

"Give Rose to me, darling. You must be tired." Mum takes Rose from my arms and stares down at her admiringly. A pang of sadness rises inside me in a weird way with Rose being taken from my arms.

This is it.

The start of our new life outside of Ulara.

"Let's get home, so we can all hear about your adventure," Dad says. In the months I've been gone, he must have had time to digest my reasons for traveling into the jungle. He takes my case from my hand and then grabs hold of Seb's hand.

Faith and I fall in behind them.

"You look exhausted," she says.

I give her a sideways glance and smirk. "So do you."

Faith rolls her eyes. "I've barely slept the last two years. Rose is only three weeks old. I want to know *everything*."

"And I'll tell you. But what's with Dad showing interest in the jungle?"

She smiles warmly. "He has done a complete circle while you've been away. He didn't want to lose you, so he'd rather support you. I may have mentioned his secret sister."

"What? He knows?" I whisper.

She nods. "Pick your words. He's still fragile."

"Understandably." Though I doubt us all sitting around and bonding over a cup of tea and cake will be enough to prepare him for what I'm about to say.

While away, Faith has updated to an SUV with more seats, so we all file into her new car fitted with two car seats and a baby carrier for Rose.

"This is nice," I tell her as I buckle my belt. I wiggle Rose's belt to ensure she's safe. Her little eyes are wide open as if she's listening to the unfamiliar noises surrounding her.

During the drive home, I check my phone for a message from Samuel.

When none register, I drop it into my bag. The last thing I want is for my parents to see me pining for Samuel. It might alert them that something isn't right, and I don't want anyone to assume anything.

When we reach the esplanade, I'm distracted by the blue ocean, a beautiful azure color that I love this time of year. I've missed celebrating Christmas by a few days, but the decorations still twinkle all around us.

We pull up in the driveway of our apartment complex. The white façade looks different, and yet it's the same. I guess it's what time away does to your memory.

"Walk, don't run," Faith says to Seb as he dashes

toward the stairwell. "You would think he doesn't know how to walk."

He holds up his foot to show me his sneaker. "I got new shoes, and they make me run fast."

I laugh at my nephew. "I bet they can make you superfast."

Inside my parents' penthouse, Dad follows me to my room. I haven't decided where I intend to live with Rose, but for now, home with my parents is best. "We have Rose's crib set up beside your bed. I assumed you would want her in with you for a while."

I open the door and admire the new set of pale pink water-colored paintings donning the wall near the crib and a mobile fixed to the side of the crib.

"Thank you. This is great, and I appreciate what you have done for me on such short notice."

"Anything for my girl." Dad places a gentle hand on my shoulder. "Now, are you tired? Do you want to rest, or do you want something to eat or drink?"

"I think I'll eat first and then feed Rose before I take a nap."

"Okay, then." Dad parks my case in the corner of the room. Then we head out to the kitchen to Mum still cradling Rose and Faith chastising Seb.

"May I?" Dad takes Rose from Mum's arms. "Eden is hungry, so we'll sit for a while before she takes a nap."

"Great. Mum has baked you a cake that has sustenance for when you're feeding. It's loaded with carbs, and I'm not sure *I* should have any, but damn, it looks delicious." Faith closes the refrigerator door with her foot as she balances the cake with both hands.

"Gosh, it will take me a month to eat it."

"Not with your father and sister around." Mum

giggles. "It's a carrot and banana cake mixed with walnuts, raisins, cashews, and almond meal."

"Topped with the best cream cheese icing you'll ever taste," Faith adds. She slides her finger over the edge and sucks the tip of her pointer finger. "Yep. I'm not denying myself this pleasure."

"I can't remember the last time I've eaten cake. Well, any sugar, actually," I say. My family all turn and stare at me as though I've arrived from another planet. I'm unsure whether it was my tone or my choice of words.

"Yeah, about that," Faith finally breaks the silence. "Do you want to tell us more about where you've been the past few months?"

I smile warily. "Where do you want me to start?"

"The beginning." Dad gives me a firm look and then nods. "I want to know everything."

"You mightn't like all I have to say," I murmur.

"It's fine, Eden. We need to hear the truth. You have arrived home safely, and I want to hear about your journey and what you have learned about…" Dad's voice cracks on the last words.

"Your half-sister?" I ask gently.

He bows his head as though ashamed. "Yes. I'm sorry I didn't trust your instinct before. I'm not going to lie and say I wasn't worried, as there were days I was beside myself and cursed you for not being in contact. But you've arrived home safely, God willing, and achieved more in finding out about Mum's life than I cared to know. But I respect what you did, and I'd like to hear about it."

"Okay. But I'm going to need a cup of tea, weak maybe, but something to moisten my mouth as it's a long story."

For an entire hour, I speak about the shaman, Kaikare, my life in the jungle, and, of course, Samuel and how amazing he is doing the work he does. I'm careful to omit the kidnapping story as I'm not sure any of them are ready to hear it.

"Well, I think you're amazing," Mum says quickly. "Having your baby in the jungle with minimal help—"

"I had help. The women were skilled. They supported me and knew what to do. They were like any midwife here and had decades of experience delivering babies in the village."

"That may be so, but you were far from any hospital or medical service if you needed emergency surgery." Faith raises one brow, challenging me.

"Yes, but I had to be positive and hope everything would go well. Other mothers have done this for hundreds of years. To panic wouldn't have benefitted Rose or me."

"It was wise to leave the worrying to us." Dad stares down into his cup of tea.

"Yes, you told me several times how you worried." I reach over and pat his hand. "But it's all okay. I'm home and not going anywhere."

"Which brings us to Samuel. When does he arrive?"

It takes an effort to keep a poker face and not think about what's currently happening in Ulara with illegal mines threatening the Ularans' quiet existence and the safety of the people I love.

"He has resigned from his contract. He has a few things to tie up before he can join me. I assume he needs to sort out his visas, etcetera, before he can apply for work here." I stall as not once did we discuss him working here and if he'd continue as a physician.

Shit.

He hasn't worked in society for six years. Is this even what he wants? My bottom lip quivers, and I take a mouthful of lukewarm tea to disguise my stress.

"We're looking forward to meeting him," Dad reassures me.

"Yes, I hoped the circumstances had changed so he could make the journey with you." Mum tilts her head, and her eyes fail to hide the disappointment behind them.

Maybe my stoic expression needs work because Faith is out of her chair, arms outstretched to take Rose from Mum. "Eden is looking tired. I think she should feed Rose and then take a nap."

Faith holds Rose close to her chest and waits for me to stand.

"If I'm still asleep in two hours, please wake me. Otherwise, I won't be able to sleep tonight."

"Honey, you might sleep through."

"Mum, she has to feed Rose."

"Oh, of course. Well, if you need help, just wake me."

Faith chuckles low.

The moment we get to my room, she closes the door behind us. "What's Mum going to do? Help Rose attach to your breast?" She rolls her eyes. "She never offered to help me during the night. Not even with James."

"I guess she thought you had Jake to help you," I murmur with fatigue setting into every crevice of my body.

"And you should have Samuel here to help you." She raises one eyebrow. "So when—"

"Not now, Faith." I shake my head. "I'll tell you about it tomorrow."

Faith sits quietly on my bed while I settle into the pale-pink faux-leather armchair in the corner of the room.

"You have both made a beautiful baby," she tells me genuinely.

"Thank you." I stroke the fine layer of fair hair on Rose's crown. "We think so too."

"Which is why I don't get why he didn't return with you."

I close my eyes momentarily and inhale a deep breath. "I'm struggling." I meet her gaze, and the moment her understanding sets in, it triggers tears to my eyes. "I begged him to come with me. But he promised he'd come as soon as he ties up a few things. And one of those things..." I say before she interrupts, "... is eating away at my ability to stay strong. If Dad knew, then he'd have reason to worry."

"What? Tell me," she demands with her serious gaze. The one I'm sure she uses in a court of law.

"It has to do with the illegal mines. Some groups are seeking new sites close to the Ularan community. Samuel is doing all he can so their safety isn't threatened."

"Bloody hell." Her face pales. "Eden. I have been reading up on these mines because I was tracking what was happening in Venezuela.

Of course, she was.

"I never filled Dad in, but I knew it wasn't good. What's happening to the land and the Amazon rainforest is shocking. The damage they are doing is just heartbreaking. They are destroying not only the flora and fauna but poisoning the waters with gold and mercury.

The Ularans' future and that of many tribes in the Amazon looks bleak."

"I know." I pull a face to stop myself from bursting into tears.

"Oh, honey. Here, let me take Rose and burp her."

"Thank you." Wiping my eyes, I try to pull myself together so I don't fall into a blubbering heap. "Samuel thinks the Ularans are his responsibility, so he'll do anything to keep them safe."

"But they've survived hundreds of years before he began living with them."

"Ugh. Yes, but he's a loyalist, and the reason he remained there stems back to honoring someone he knew in school and college after she died."

"Honor? How is living primitively honoring someone?"

I focus on how Faith rolls the cup of her hand in small circles over Rose's back. Her tiny face falls to the side with her chin supported in Faith's other hand. She makes motherhood look easy while I'm still fumbling my way through the first few weeks of Rose's life.

"She asked him to be a better person and to do something worthwhile in the world where he didn't achieve the accolades. To do something purely for the good and not for the benefit."

"But there are many—"

"I know. Can we talk about this tomorrow? I do need to take that nap."

Faith places Rose in the crib and then comes to kiss my cheek. "Rest up, sis. I'll see you tomorrow."

The moment my head hits the pillow, my eyes flutter closed.

The sound of my phone vibrating with a message alert on the table beside me is enough for me to open my eyes. The time on the screen shows I have been asleep for two hours. At least with daylight savings, the room is still light. And I have woken covered in sweat with the late afternoon sun beating down on my bedroom window. I groan loudly and rub my eyes, then reach for the air conditioning remote. I switch it on to cool the room at a comfortable temperature. After months in the stifling humidity of the jungle, I'm not going to deny myself modern-day comforts. I thought I'd be mentally tougher and not bothered by the dry heat. I need more sleep, that's all.

Assuming the message to be from my friends asking when they can see me, I casually raise my phone to read the text.

Asoo:

Eden, it's Samuel.

Three words, and it's enough for me to sit straight up in the bed. Mentally, I prepare myself for the words to follow as Samuel's track record with messages and notes usually brings heartbreak.

There was an incident. Drones located Ulara, and two men who worked at a nearby illegal mine assumed treasure was hidden in the village. They expected previous travelers would have left gifts for the shaman to assist them on their travels. A gesture by explorers from earlier days if lost and then taken sick. Some indigenous communities helped these explorers until well enough to travel again. At first, I thought someone had given them false information. But it seems there was someone before your grandmother, as the shaman had a gold chain with a massive nugget hidden in a brass vase. The vase was disguised easily as a clay sculpture, the tarnished metal so old.

With my hand on my chest, I close my eyes and remember Kaikare's tarnished mirror from Gran.

These American men were looking to get rich quick. The shaman was shot and killed.

I gasp. My stomach flips, and my eyes burn as the sadness engulfs me.

The men are no longer a concern. Their boat exploded on the river, and the billowing smoke was a tell-tale for the village location. We expect more men will come, and it will jeopardize the Ularans' safety. There's no other choice than to migrate deeper into the jungle. The shaman foresaw the migration in his last ceremony. The timing is now imminent with increasing danger.

I'm so, so sorry.

"Please no," I murmur.

I promised the shaman I'd guide them with paper maps and head southwest toward the Colombian and Brazilian border, away from those areas controlled by Guerrillas and Garimpeiros. When they are safe, I'll come home to you. I will come home to you. In the meantime, please message Asoo if you need to speak with someone. I'll not be in contact with him, but there may be a way for me to get a message to Canaima.

"How? With smoke signals?"

Please don't worry about me. I'll find my way out as you are home, the beacon to my heart. Think of it as a minor setback —our future together delayed by a few months. In the big picture, we will look back with only a memory of our short time apart. I love you. Please kiss Rose and tell her I love and miss her like I do you. I'll come back to you. I promise. Samuel xx

"Don't worry. You have got to be bloody kidding me." My bottom lip quivers all too easily, fragile emotion like a pendulum swinging from fear for the safety of Samuel and my friends to relief at being safe at home with my family. As much as I want to be with him, this journey isn't something Rose and I could endure.

Reality sinks in.

Covering my face with both hands, I sob and sob,

releasing the fear of never seeing him again. "Why?" I croak through the tears. "Why would you do this?"

The shaman was shot and killed.

Clamping my eyes shut, the sadness turns to pain and it seeps bone-deep. The emotional weight fills my legs with what feels like lead, and I sink into the bed. Now paralyzed with overwhelming grief, I don't want to open my eyes and see the world as it truly is. I fail, and my thoughts fill with the possibility of Samuel dying in the jungle. If not from hunger and dehydration along with exhaustion, from a bullet like the shaman as they head into an unknown country.

Poor Kaikare. She has lost her father, her mentor, and best friend. The village has lost its healer and the man who decides its future. The future is dire for all of us, and I can't help it—I fall apart, one tear at a time.

When I can breathe again, I swipe the screen to send my sister a message.

> What do you know about the Colombian Guerrilla and the Brazilian Garimpeiros working near the borders?

Seconds later, my phone vibrates in my hand.

"Hi. I just received a message from Samuel," I say before she fires the first question. "He's not coming here until he finds the Ularan people a new place to live and build a new village."

"Um, what? And you're telling me this is going to be in the heart of where F.A.R.C and Guerrilla Garimpeiros own the land, and by own, I mean control?"

"To be honest, I have no clue exactly where he's going, but he said he'd avoid those areas."

Faith snorts. "Yeah, like he'll even know if they have recently gained control of a new community."

"You're not helping," I rasp. Closing my eyes, I will the tears to stop rolling down my cheeks. "How will I ever get a message to him or know if something bad has happened to him?"

For a moment, Faith remains silent.

Then she rallies, her voice calm and confident as always. "Eden, you need to remain optimistic. Your positive attitude has gotten you this far when we thought you'd gone mad. You're home. Samuel *will* come back to you."

I smile even though I know she truly doesn't believe it. But she's right—it's all I have—the belief that he'll do whatever it takes to get out alive. If I convince myself it will happen, then hopefully, the universe will continue to look out for me.

"At least I know Gran's spirit will protect him in the jungle."

"What?"

I let out a sigh. "Another story for tomorrow..."

38

EDEN

My thoughts home in on the ticktock of the kitchen clock on the wall before me, a grandfather clock handed down by my grandfather. The swinging time-keeping element is hypnotic in the silence.

Seb calls out to Faith to help him go to the bathroom, and like dominoes, our shoulders fall in relief to the ending silence.

"No wonder you didn't sleep well," Mum says gently. "I thought you must have been awake because of Rose."

"No." I shake my head. "Rose was great. Fed and went back to sleep. But I do need to make an appointment to see a pediatrician to check she's on par with her development. I don't want to assume her quiet behavior is that of a good baby."

Dad nods, but his expression is blank, and I assume his thoughts are fixed on the news I just relayed to them all. "Part of me despises the man..." he says in a low voice, "... although it also saddens me knowing the shaman was part of Mum's life." Dad dips his chin and rubs a hand over his jaw. "Questions about Mum's life in the jungle is now lost."

"Your sister is out there." Mum rubs his shoulder. "Answers may be lost, but she's alive."

"Mum," Faith interjects as she returns to the table. She hands her phone to Seb to watch a child's program.

"*Bluey*," he sings and jumps up and down to the theme song.

"Apart from the sadness of the shaman and the whole new sister thing for Dad, Eden's main concern is Samuel. He may never get out alive. She just told us that she doesn't know how to contact him, and if something tragic happens, she may never know about it," Faith says.

A whimper sounds from James in the playpen set up in the corner. He throws a toy train aside. Faith pushes up from her chair and lifts him over the barrier. She places him on her lap and raises her top to feed him.

Dad rubs his hands over his face. "How long did he give you? How many weeks did he calculate it would take him to find a new home for them?"

"Months." I bow my head, unable to look at them with a wave of dread washing over me. "He then has to find his way out of wherever they are hiding, *alone*. If he does, then I assume he'll need to return to LA and organize his visas to come to Australia." Every time I weigh it up, I find it more difficult to remain optimistic.

Faith's serious expression conveys her concern. "And he's heading into areas controlled by the Colombian Guerrilla or the Brazilian Garimpeiros." She pushes dark locks away from her face before gazing down at her son.

"Can we do anything to help? Anything at all?" Dad's gaze meets mine, and his eyes brim with fear.

"Distract me." I force a smile.

"All these years, I had a sister, and now I may never meet her," he mutters. "I barely know anything about her."

"I'll tell you about her." I smile. "I'll remember more when I'm not so emotional. I intend to find Brenda and ask for the diary Gran kept while she was in the jungle. I know Grandpa forbade her to keep it, but it might help us understand some things."

Dad nods once, and it's in slow motion, as though he's absorbing what I'm telling him. "Can you print off those photos you have of Dawn... I mean Kaikare? I can't get her face out of my head. I can see a little of Mum in her."

"I know. From the moment I arrived, I sensed there was something about Kaikare. And the way we connected was different to everybody else." I shrug. "I'm going to miss her." My voice is hoarse, and I stop myself from saying more. "I'll send the photos I have on my phone to you."

Dad peers up at me and smiles. "What's done is done," he says, putting on a brave face. "We have to get on with our lives. Let me know how you do finding Brenda. If you meet a dead end, I might be able to help."

"Thank you. I'm heading out to see Yasmine and Amy tonight. So I won't need any dinner."

"Before I leave, I can help you fit the baby seat from my car to yours," Faith says and stands. "Mum, can you watch the boys for me?"

"Sure." Mum takes James into the lounge where Seb is lying with Faith's phone.

"I can help Faith," Dad says.

"It's fine. If you could watch Rose, I'll go since I need to learn how to do these things."

Dad takes Rose from my arms. "Hello, my princess," he whispers.

I wait a few seconds to absorb the moment, the loving relationship between my dad and daughter to help heal my pain before I follow Faith down the stairs.

As soon as the door opens, I'm hit with the salty clean air. I inhale a deep breath. "I've missed the scent of the sea. I've missed the vista, everything about the beach. Only when I was with him, I didn't care. I could've been living in a dark hole and loved every minute because we were together."

Faith wraps an arm around me as we take the last step before the parking lot. She squeezes my side and says nothing. Right now, her support is enough.

🌴

By the time dinner time comes around, I can barely control the anxiety consuming me. The one thing keeping me from losing my mind is Rose. Babies can pick up on emotions, so I'm doing my best to control the fear. The thirteen-hour time difference between Adelaide and Canaima has been frustrating, as I wait for a reasonable time to call Asoo. I'm due at Yasmine's at six thirty, so I hope he's awake.

I call his number and pray he answers.

Just when I'm about to give up, a voice answers the call.

"Hello? Asoo?"

A woman speaks in Spanish.

"Si."

A moment passes, and then my shoulders relax on hearing Asoo's voice in the background.

"Hola."

"Asoo, it's Eden," I blurt.

"Oh, Miss Eden. You home now? You safe?"

"Yes." I close my eyes and exhale. "I'm in Australia. I received your message. My heart breaks."

"Si. It sad. My heart break too. The shaman..." He makes a tsk sound. "Bad men still come, Miss Eden. We afraid. We can't go near Ulara as they have men in the area."

I swallow the lump in my throat. The one that has grown to the size of a small apple and refuses to go away, a lump that burns every time I think of Samuel and try not to burst into tears. "And Samuel?" I rasp. "When did you last see him?"

"After those men shot shaman, Samuel told me to leave and not come back. He tell me they are walking into the jungle when the moon rises."

"They're walking at night? That's insane. It's the most dangerous time."

"Men won't find them. They follow maps and walk night, then day. Rest on the second night. Samuel took men's guns. Bad. Bad. I know nothing more."

"I understand." He has to be careful as someone may be listening to our conversation. "If you hear anything, please message me," I plead. "I'll then call for you to tell me any news."

"Si."

"I'm scared." My lip quivers. "Scared he'll never make it out of the jungle, never make it home to me."

"Samuel have maps. Samuel good man."

A sob escapes my lips. I want to say his merit will not save him. Instead, I say, "He is. I hope he knows what he's doing."

"Samuel loves you, Miss Eden. He'll come to you."

"Thanks, Asoo. Stay in touch, please. You're the only person I can contact."

The line goes silent. Holding the phone to my chest, I take a moment to compose myself, willing all the tears cascading over my cheeks to stop.

I'm none the wiser about Samuel's safety—I only know that people believe in him. With no other choice, I pray for him to be safe and get out of the jungle alive.

I strap Rose into her baby seat and drive the ten minutes it takes to reach Yasmine's apartment.

Before I reach the front door, it swings open, and both girls scream with excitement. I giggle and check they haven't startled Rose. Yasmine gives me a quick hug, then takes Rose from my arms.

"She's just gorgeous," she coos and heads inside. "Let's get you out of this heat."

"She was born in the jungle. It's the winter months I'm worried about." I hug Amy and almost have to pry her arms from my neck.

"I missed you," she whispers. "So damn much. I can't say I'm sorry you're home even though I know you wanted to stay with him."

"Before."

She steps back and gives me a quizzical look. "What happened?"

"Shit went down." We both follow Yasmine inside and sit on the couch beside her. For the next ten minutes, I give them a rundown of my last days, the latest shitstorm, and how Samuel is now wandering the rainforest with a bloody paper map. The more I repeat the story, the more frustrated I become. "So now I just wait and hope he comes out alive."

Both girls' eyes bulge.

"You're kidding me." Amy shakes her head. "Does he want to die a fucking hero?"

I shrug one shoulder. "His loyalty is something else. I haven't told you the story yet of how he ended up there."

"We're eating first," Yasmine quips. "You need your sustenance for this little princess." She stares down at Rose as though she's the most beautiful thing she has ever seen.

"I do. And I have several appointments in the next few days for us both to be checked over."

"Well, she's perfect." Yasmine smiles at Rose. "I can't wait for you to move in with Aunty Yas."

"We can discuss that when I'm back at work and earning money again."

"Which is why you're not paying for dinner." Yasmine eyeballs me.

"Thank you."

Amy sits sideways on the couch, so she's facing me. "Surely, you don't have to go back to work for a while. I mean, *Ethan* is still there. You could look for something else now like you originally planned."

"I haven't thought about anything. The paperwork is being processed, and then I have to apply for maternity leave. It's on my long list for this week, although I'll probably work one day here and there to get back in the swing of things and as they need me. As for changing careers, being a new mum is challenging enough for now. Until life calms down, I'm not considering anything else. I want things to be easy and to do what I know, so it doesn't take time away from Rose."

"Absolutely." Yas runs her nose over Rose's cheek. "I

love how Rose just stares as though she knows who we are. Already knows her *aunties*."

We all chuckle.

It feels good to be home with my girls.

39

EDEN

One Week Later...

On Saturday morning, I bathe Rose then dress her in a cute little summer dress before placing her in the stroller to wander along the esplanade on my way to meet Yasmine and Amy at our favorite café in Glenelg.

I'm grateful I didn't have to rush off for clothes suitable for feeding in since Faith gave me most of the clothes she wore after Seb's birth. She gained more weight with James and bought freer-flowing styles. My family has thought of everything, and I'll only need to buy more clothes for Rose when she grows into the next size.

I pull the stroller cover down to protect Rose from the sun's rays as I head outside. A slight breeze with a hint of jasmine mixed in the salty air hits my senses, and I smile.

Home.

My thoughts shift straight to Samuel. I hope he loves it here as much as I do.

The optimism remains, and yet there's always

underlying doubt. After all the effort it would take for him to come to me, it could all go pear-shaped if he hates living not only in a strange country and knowing a handful of people but living in society in general.

I stop walking the esplanade path. A man behind me grumbles as he walks around the stroller.

"Sorry," I murmur.

It hit me why Samuel's gone into the jungle.

Is it his intention to get lost and never come out so he doesn't have to return to society?

I shake my head to dispel the thought.

No.

No, he wouldn't do that to us. He'd *try*.

My own bloody thoughts are going to be my undoing.

Instead, I smile at everyone sitting on the grass enjoying the morning sunshine. Yet it's hot enough that I'm eager to get Rose and me inside the café and out of the heat.

A woman greets me at the door. "Welcome. I'm Deanne. Do you have a booking for a table?" She has short brown hair and the kindest eyes, maybe because they are the same color as Kaikare's.

"My friends should be here." In the corner of the café by a window, Yasmine is chatting with Amy. "There they are."

"Yas and Amy. Oh, you must be Eden. I feel like I know you already."

"I hate to think what they have said about me."

Deanne laughs once. "All good, I promise. They are here at least once a week. Today they requested a larger area to fit the stroller by the table." I follow Deanne, and I'm surprised when she introduces me like she's part of our little group. "Eden is here."

Yasmine's expression tells me I've interrupted a serious conversation, but a smile soon grows on her lips when she acknowledges me.

"We thought Rose might be napping." She stands and peers into the stroller before hugging me.

"I'll come back in five and grab your order," Deanne says, leaving us alone.

"Thanks, babe," Yasmine shoots over her shoulder.

Babe.

"Deanne is new here," I say.

"She started working the week you left," Amy says. "We were both upset one day, and she sat down and comforted us."

"By giving us brownies and extra caffeine on the house," Yasmine adds. "We became friends, and she meets us at the Shores if we're in the mood for cocktails."

"Is that code for she enjoys getting wasted with you?" I take a seat beside Amy.

"Pretty much." She chuckles. "She's one of the most interesting people I've met. Besides helping us out when we were missing you, she reassured us you would be okay."

I frown at Amy. "How could she when she knows nothing about me?"

"Dee has been to Brazil and then did a week in Venezuela, including time at Angel Falls." Amy lifts her brow to emphasize her trust in Deanne.

"Right. I'm curious to know what tour she did and her take on what's happening to the ecosystem."

"You'll have time to ask her as she's meeting us on the weekend... if you're up to it?"

Yasmine rolls her eyes. "Don't, Amy. Eden has Rose to consider."

"It's fine. I can pop down for an hour but count me out for any big nights for at least the next few months."

Amy wraps her arm around my shoulder. "To be honest, I'm getting sick of going out all the time."

Yasmine laughs. "Whatever. I'll remind you of that tonight."

"We know it's too early for you to come out with us. But in a few months..." Amy smiles. "Everything will settle down for you."

In a few months, I hope Samuel has found his way back to me.

Yasmine peers down at Rose sleeping in the stroller. "We'll have our own special days just for you and Rose."

"She still looks so tiny." Amy looks adoringly at my daughter.

"She does, but we've had several appointments this week, and she's on track in her development."

"Is that your sister?" Amy nods to the doorway.

"Yeah," Yasmine confirms. "Cleo is the physiotherapist for The Thunder football team. They've commenced pre-season training. They just had a beach recovery session."

Amy twists to check out the shirtless men filing through the café. "Does she need any volunteers to help?"

Yasmine rolls her eyes. "She gets that a lot." Her expression changes. "Actually, she's also just started working at Lombardi's Restaurant in the city on weekends, and I want to celebrate my birthday there. The owner, Oliver, has turned the front section into a cocktail bar at night, and Cleo said it's attracting some famous people."

It takes a moment for my mind to catch up. "In two

weeks. Are you celebrating on your actual birthday or the weekend?"

"The Saturday night. Is Rose okay?"

Leaning forward, I check on Rose. It's unusual for her brow to be pinched.

Oh no. She only pulls that face when she—

"Oh wow." Yasmine's eyes widen.

"Rose," I say, pretending to chastise her for passing gas loud enough for the people on the table next to us to stop mid-conversation. "I think that's my cue to leave. If she follows through, then she'll also be hungry, and I'll need to change her nappy."

"Yeah, I'm not ready to help with that," Amy apologizes and shrugs.

"Is anyone ever ready for poopy nappies?"

"No, except when you don't have a choice." I push up from the table. "It's the first time I'm leaving without coffee, and I have a feeling it won't be my last."

In one short week, I've realized my life here will not be the same as it was before I left. I have come home a different person, and I need to adapt to my new life.

🌴

On Monday, with Rose in my arms, I slowly pad the stairs of our apartment complex to the office located on the ground floor. It's time for me to show Dana my daughter. I'm filled with guilt because I didn't take her last week. I know Dana has been waiting for me to visit the office. Only Ethan will be there, and I didn't want to be emotionally vulnerable around him after everything that's happened.

I hate that I need to be strong around Ethan, prove to

myself I'm the bigger person and forgive him for treating me like shit.

Pushing the door open, I find Dana alone in the office. She gives a little squeal and rushes around her desk toward me. "Finally," she says, smiling, her arms outstretched toward me.

I give Rose to her for a cuddle and turn toward my father's empty office. "Dad's out?"

"Yeah, he and Ethan are in the city for an appointment with a construction company."

"About the pool renos?"

"Yeah."

Damn, now I want to know what they are planning as this was my project—the Bali-inspired resort pool.

"When are you coming back to work?" Dana's eyes remain on Rose, although her tone is a little desperate.

"I have four months leave, although I could pop down and help when you need me."

Her eyes lift to meet mine. "Between you and me, Ethan isn't covering your work. He's paving his way to assist your father and leaving me to pick up his slack."

"Help Dad? In what way?"

Rose whimpers, so Dana places her on her shoulder and pats her back. "No idea. Your father thinks rainbows shoot out of his ass."

I chuckle. "I can come in for a couple of hours when Rose takes a nap during the day."

"Thank you. And seeing both of your faces here will help to cheer me up." Dana smiles. "What else have you been doing to keep busy?"

"Just trying to be a mum." I shrug. "And I'm trying to get in touch with Brenda, a friend of Gran's. But I'm not having much luck."

"I remember Brenda. Was she the one at your Gran's funeral that wore the—"

"Red shoes. Yes."

"Good luck with that." She hands Rose to me, then reaches for a tissue to wipe her forehead. "I can't wait to hear about your adventure. Your dad has already announced Samuel might not return."

"He said that to Ethan?"

Dana nods.

"That's not entirely true. He's just going to take longer to come here."

"The sooner he arrives, the better."

I smile at Dana. I need to be around her more. "I have a story to tell you about Gran too. I'll feed Rose in here while Dad and Ethan are out, and I'll fill you in."

"Let me make a coffee since it's my lunch break. I want you to tell me everything."

40

EDEN

Two Weeks Later...

Shutting my laptop, I close my eyes and hope I've done the right thing. Emailing Samuel's parents with an update as to his whereabouts was a precursor in case things go pear-shaped. At least they know now, and if they want to alert any authorities, they have more power than me to do so. I also attached photos of Rose as they wanted to be updated on her progress. It's the least I can do for them.

It's mid-morning, and I promised Dana I'd assist her for a couple of hours. After feeding Rose, I place her in the stroller and walk along the esplanade until she falls asleep. It doesn't take long, so we turn back and head to the office. The moment the door opens, Ethan is on his feet and walking around the table to greet us.

"Eden," he says affectionately. "It's good to see you again." He leans to get a closer look at Rose. "She's beautiful. The image of her mother."

"Thank you. I think she's beautiful, but I'm biased." I look around the office. "Where's Dana and Dad?"

"Dana is in the restroom, and your father is in the city meeting with some lawyers."

"Right."

Brown eyes meet mine, the ones that used to turn my legs to jelly. God, his eyes are still beautiful, but he no longer affects me that way. "I've missed you." He takes a step closer and rests a hand on my back. "Come and take a seat. I'd love to hear your stories?"

His comment throws me off-kilter because I find it hard to believe he wants to hear about Samuel. Maybe he's trying at being a friend. "I can't right now. I'm here to help Dana."

Dana strolls into the room. "You're early."

"Yeah. Rose settled quickly, so I came here while she was sleeping. What do you need me to do?"

Dragging over another chair to her table, I take a seat while she runs through a list that I could complete in an hour—if Rose remains asleep. If I get more time, then it's a bonus.

Ten minutes later, Rose wakes and screams at top volume. "Sorry, she started screaming like this two days ago. It's only after she feeds." Scooping her into my arms, I lay her on my shoulder, patting her back as I walk around the room. "If she doesn't settle, then I'll get you to email anything you need me to complete, and I'll do it from my room."

"I can help," Ethan says. He watches me closely as I pad around the room. "Give Rose to me so you and Dana can work together."

"Are you sure? Do you even know how to hold a baby?"

"I'm an uncle now. Know all the tricks." He winks at me.

"What? Harry has children?"

"No, Myles." He grins.

"No way," I say. "When did he get a girlfriend?"

"This time last year. They keep to themselves. There were a few surprise pregnancies last year." He holds my gaze for a moment, and there's a touch of sadness behind those chocolate eyes. "Anton is two months old."

"Okay, here you are." I hold up Rose, and he lifts her over his shoulder and then paces the room. Within minutes, she stops crying, opens her beautiful eyes, and watches us as Ethan circles the office.

"You're a natural," I tell him.

"Yeah, yeah. Now get busy as I don't know how long my magic touch will hold out."

I laugh and head back to Dana's table. She's eyeing him, and from where I stand, it's obvious she still doesn't trust him.

🌴

"Is Rose okay?" Mum asks me as I pace behind the kitchen table with Rose over my shoulder. "What age do they develop colic?"

"James had reflux, and he was so much harder to settle than Seb. After endless sleepless nights, I had him checked, and they diagnosed him at around one month old. It might be worth getting her checked out." Faith stands and comes behind me to assess Rose. "She appears happy enough now."

"I know. After every feed, I have to do this until she calms. Some nights it's two hours of pacing the room."

313

"She looks tired, dear." Mum stands and pours herself another wine. "If you need me, just come and wake me up." After a glass full of wine, she won't feel like getting up at two in the morning to help me.

"I wish Samuel was here." On my next lap around the table, I sense everyone's eyes on me. Shit, did I say that aloud?

"Still nothing?" Dad sits back in his chair and folds his arms.

I'm only days away from being home for a month. It's too short a time to have heard anything from Samuel. The early days will be the hardest for the tribe to remain hidden and reach the jungle beyond the tepui. A journey many of the Ularans will struggle to complete, especially with the pace having to suit the women, the children, the elders and the men.

"I don't expect to hear anything for at least another month." I close my eyes, determined not to get upset because Dad isn't convinced Samuel will do the right thing by us. He hasn't said it in so many words, but his eyes and demeanor tell me the truth.

"Do you expect him at my sixtieth birthday celebrations?" His brows arch before he reaches for the red wine and half fills his glass.

Dad's birthday is this weekend, but he has postponed the party to the end of March when Will returns from college, and his friends in Sydney, who are tied up with business, can get away. They have planned not only the party but a men's weekend including an AFL football game and five days holidaying at Victor Harbour, fishing, and then touring the McLaren Vale wineries.

"I hope so, but..."

"So do we," Faith says. "I'm looking forward to

meeting him. As for Rose, book an appointment with the doctor, and I'll come with you."

"Thank you. I appreciate it." With Jake working all day and late into the night, I'm grateful to spend more time with Faith.

"See if you can get it on a Thursday when the kids are in daycare."

"So where are we going for dinner?" I ask.

"Lombardi's. It serves the best Italian food in the city," Mum says.

"Yasmine's sister, Cleo, works there."

"The physiotherapist?" Faith asks.

"Yes. She's saving to travel, so she is working two jobs."

"I saw Yasmine at the health shop on Jetty Road," Mum says. "How long has she worked there?"

"A while now. She's studying naturopathy and is an influencer on Instagram. She uploads videos of her special shakes and herbal snacks and now has two hundred thousand followers."

"Is that impressive?" Dad says, obviously clueless.

"If you checked our hotel's Instagram profile at all, then you would know it is. I have to say Ethan has done a great job marketing Monte Hotels while I've been away."

"He has. I hope he stays with us, but I think our HR role isn't the challenge Ethan wants."

"But he's also doing the marketing, and he's involved in the recent development." I'm not sure if Dad was hinting at something else.

"Yes. I think Ethan is ready to take on an assistant managerial position."

The room falls quiet.

I stop walking, and Faith's eyes meet mine. In the silence, there's an understanding passing between us.

"Don't you think it's premature to be promoting him in our *family* company?" Faith says seriously.

"Ethan's been working with us for a year now. He has demonstrated his capabilities, and I see his potential through his commitment. And he works late almost every night."

"What about Dana?" I interrupt. "She has been with us for decades. I think it's an insult not to promote her first."

"These are two different roles. Besides, I think Dana's husband is looking to transfer interstate. I really don't know how long she'll continue working with us. I hope a while longer. Otherwise, I'll need to find more admin staff to assist you when you return to work."

"Me?" I look at Faith to get a gauge if she knew about any of this. She rolls her eyes. "I can help for now, but I don't know what my future holds. I haven't ruled out studying nursing either. It will depend on Samuel when he returns and on his work as well. I mean, we may need to move to the country for him to get a job."

Dad huffs. "Every damn hospital is crying out for doctors. He'll get work here. Besides, you don't know when and if this will happen. In the meantime, you need to work and secure a future for you and Rose."

"For one, Eden will have maternity payments from the government for a few more months," Faith argues. "And I think it's up to her to decide what her future holds." She holds up a hand when Dad attempts to interrupt. "And don't speak like she's going to be alone for the rest of her life."

Standing behind Dad where he can't see me, I mouth to Faith, "Thank you."

"Thank you for a lovely dinner, Mum. I'll try to settle Rose in her crib while she's quiet." I walk around the table and kiss Faith goodnight. Then I meet Dad's gaze. "I understand what you're saying about Monte Hotels, and it concerns you how Faith and I aren't there to work, especially when it's our family business. Please be careful, that's all. Will hasn't even finished college yet. Give him a chance to decide. What I'm saying is, I don't want you to hand it over to someone who isn't family." His expression changes, and I know exactly what he's thinking—what he hopes for Ethan and me. "When you meet Samuel, I think you'll understand why I'm holding out with every drop of hope I have inside of me that he'll return to me safely. He truly is the best man for me and the best father to Rose. I just have to be patient."

I head to bed thinking about what Dad said. The notion of Samuel not returning sticks in my head.

Alone.

A life without him.

Until this point, I believed I was strong and had grown into a confident woman. Without Samuel by my side, I'm not sure she exists. All I can envision is an empty shell of the person I had become, even less of my former self, and I can't and won't go back to being her.

As I'm laying Rose in her crib, she opens her eyes and stares at me before closing them again. My heart melts. She was created from love, and I see Samuel in her every day. I have to be strong for her. For us.

"Daddy will come home soon," I whisper.

I lean in and kiss her cheek before flopping onto my bed.

Beside me, the phone screen lights up with an alert. One new email from Christopher McMahon.

Dear Eden,

Thank you for your email concerning Samuel's safety. Despite the alarming reference to him finding a new location, we appreciated you reaching out and keeping us updated. We especially appreciated you taking the time to send photos of beautiful Rose.

She has grown at just six weeks old.

Rose reminds Caroline of Samuel when he was a baby. It has cheered us somewhat to see the photos. Please keep in touch, and one day we hope to meet you and Rose.

As for Samuel, I'm disappointed in his decision not to return home and be with you as soon as he could. His place is with you, not with some primitive tribe that doesn't need his help as much as you do.

Please don't worry. This is nothing new to us. For years, we suffered with the fear of losing our son and not knowing what he's doing or where he is. In previous years, he had disappeared for eighteen months at a time with no contact. For some reason, he loves his work and is smart enough to find his way out of trouble. He'll do it again.

We know how much he loves you, and he'll do what it takes to come find you.

Please stay in touch.

Yours sincerely,
Christopher and Caroline McMahon.

Without responding, I set my phone aside and close my eyes. His parents have no idea how dangerous this journey is, how it's nothing like Ulara. When I think about it, Ulara is the people, and wherever they settle, Ulara will be. It's not a place or a river, it's a state of heart and people being as one to form a close community.

But if anything happens to Samuel, they'll not notify his parents or me. As time passes, we will just have to assume the worst. I can't imagine the gut-wrenching pain that will consume me if he fails.

He can't.

He has to do this.

It's been years since I prayed, but tonight I close my palms together, bow my head, and ask for Samuel to be guided through the jungle and then return safely to me.

41

EDEN

Two Months Later...

"The decorations are fabulous," I tell Cleo.

Yasmine's dusky pink lips stretch into an admiring smile. "I didn't think you had a creative flair. Honestly, I always believed you were science, science, science, but your artistic skill is next level. Seems like we have similar genes."

Cleo beams a proud smile at her sister. Her skin is makeup-free. She's every bit as beautiful as her sister with dark skin and eyes and high cheekbones. I envy their model-like appearance. "The colors are of the Thunder Football Club, at your father's request. Teal and white and black with balloons and other decorations. The silver makes the teal pop."

"Even the dried flower arrangement on the wall with ribbons and balloons looks every bit as masculine as it does feminine and perfect for your dad," Yasmine says as she continues to peruse the room.

My father's hearty laughter breaks through our

conversation, even from the far corner of the restaurant where he stands in a circle with his mates. "It's going to be a big night for him. I don't think Mum will see much of him after tonight." I tell my friends about his plans for a celebratory week with his mates. "More than likely, it will take another week for him to recover, and I don't think we'll see much of him in the office. He'll probably work from home," I joke since the office building is part of our home. "Walking three levels of stairs might be a bit much for him."

"Why is Ethan with them?" Amy asks. "Surely, he's not staying with the men the entire week?"

I shake my head. Ethan's youth stands out among them yet equally distinguished with his dark hair slicked back and Gatsby-like. "I really don't know."

"Has he hit on you yet?" Amy's brows pull tight as though she expects me to admit to it.

"No. He's been supportive while I'm working. He takes Rose for strolls in the stroller and holds her as he reads through emails while I'm caught up in meetings with Dana."

Amy makes a humph sound. "I still don't trust him."

"He's trying... we're friends. That's all."

"Are you defending him?" she asks in a higher voice.

"I'm giving him a chance at being nice. Being supportive as a friend. And he hasn't tried to get me between the sheets."

"Anyway," Yasmine says. "There's a glass of champagne with my name on it." She takes one from the tray as the server walks by.

We all do the same.

"Cheers," we say in unison and clink the crystal.

"To forever friends," Yasmine chimes.

We all turn and agree, watching my father belly laugh and almost spill his glass of beer.

Cleo's dark spiral curls bounce as she rushes away, leaving Amy, Yasmine, and me alone.

"This is the first time since Rio that we're dressed in ballgowns and drinking champagne." Yasmine looks up to the starry lights dotting the ceiling, and the memory of the night I first spoke to Samuel has me smiling.

"Please take me back," Amy says. "It feels like a lifetime ago."

"Over a year." Yasmine makes a sad face.

"The white gown I wore to the ball at the Copacabana Palace Hotel will never be repeated until Rose is at school," I say and run my finger over the navy material of my long, snug-fitting dress. I wouldn't be wearing a strapless dress a month ago with the feeding bra limiting my daily attire. Unfortunately, my breast milk didn't last, and Rose has settled on baby formula. I'm not sure what I'd have done if we were in the jungle. Eight weeks old and no breast milk... would other mothers feed her? Filled with guilt, I wondered what Samuel would say, yet I blamed it on the stress of worrying constantly about him. At least tonight, I can have a few drinks and not wear a bra.

"Hi, ladies." Ava, Cleo's friend and part-owner of Lombardi's, joins our group. Her long brown hair is swept off her face and pinned in curls around her crown. A long black gown hugs her petite figure.

"Hi," we all say in unison.

"It's been years since I've seen you," I say and smile.

"Right. I hear congratulations are in order."

"Thank you," I say proudly.

"Jardine and I are trying for another baby, though I'm not keen for those sleepless nights again."

I laugh. "Yeah, some nights are tougher than others." I admire Ava as she is two years younger than us, and running a business with children must be tough. And her husband is a famous cricket player.

"How is Jardine?" I ask. Cleo supported Ava through their messy breakup after she had their first child, and now that she has her happily ever after, it gives me some hope.

"Good. He's in Sydney playing in the World Cup finals."

"So, he's away a lot?"

She nods. "It's okay, though. It's not forever, and I have support here with Louis." She smiles as though she understands. "Enjoy the night, ladies. If you need anything, let me know. I'm overseeing to make sure everything runs smoothly tonight and hope it's a fabulous celebration for your father," she says before striding toward the kitchen.

Lifting my chest and pulling my shoulders back, I inhale a deep breath.

Stop feeling sorry for yourself.

Faith waltzes through the door with Jake fashionably late and looking like a million dollars in a red ball gown.

"Hey," she says, joining our circle. "What have I missed?"

"Ladies," Jake says and gives us a nod. "You all look beautiful tonight."

"I've always liked your brother-in-law," Amy says and smiles at Jake.

"Nothing. Although Will still hasn't arrived."

Faith checks her cell for the time. "He should be here soon."

Will's flight was canceled last night, and the next available flight was six o'clock from Melbourne.

We both turn to the entrance, and instead of seeing Will, a group of tall men donning stylish tuxes enter the doors.

"Why is Rhett Williams here?" I say aloud.

Cleo spins toward the entrance. "Good, they've arrived. I asked them to pop in and surprise your father. The majority are players from The Thunder, but I also asked Rhett and a few players from the Blackbirds to come along to spur him on." She stares at me. "Do you know him?"

"Yes, we spent some time together when I had a short stint at university after school. I had to do a subject as part of business studies. Most of it was online, but some required attendance. It was only six months, but he made an impression."

"Sounds like Rhett." Cleo smiles. "I better send them toward your dad. Hope he's ready for a surprise." She gives us a wave. "I'll come say goodbye before I leave."

"Why didn't I know about this?" I ask Yasmine.

"Because I didn't know about it. Cleo takes her work seriously, and the players are part of her work circle. She has a clique, and I'm sure all the girls want to be friends with her just to get inside information. She never reveals confidential player information, and I guess she classified your father's surprise as being confidential."

Laughter erupts from the other side of the room, where Dad is the center of attention.

"Shall we see what's going on?" We all head over until

we're standing close enough to hear the conversation between the players and Dad.

Rhett turns around, and when he recognizes me, he comes over. "Cleo tells me it's *your* dad's birthday."

I smile at him, his blue eyes reminding me of Samuel's. "Yes. And I didn't expect to see you here."

He grins and straightens his bowtie. "Did it brighten your evening?"

"Knowing the effort you went to for him? Well, yes."

He picks up my hand and kisses it. "How are you really?"

I shrug. "I have a baby daughter and a partner who remains in South America."

His eyes widen. "Stuck because of his visa?"

I smile and bow my head. "Something like that."

"Hey." He gently lifts my chin until I'm looking him in the eye. "Dance with me. It will cheer you up."

"God, you're still full of confidence."

I'm suddenly whisked away with Rhett, twirling and swaying as though we're professional dancers. He's right. Within minutes, I'm laughing and enjoying myself.

When the song ends, we're still laughing until Ethan comes to join us.

"Excuse me, do you mind if I cut in? I'd like to dance with Eden."

What's happening? I have two handsome men vying to dance with me. And Ethan rarely danced with me when we were together, so his gesture surprises me even more.

"Of course," Rhett says politely and leaves Ethan and me alone on the dance floor.

Ethan's feet slide in a slower rhythm, and it's more sensual than fun. I keep my gaze fixed over his shoulder with a quick check now and then to read his expression. When I do catch him staring at me, our eyes meet, connecting, before I look away.

"Did I tell you how beautiful you look tonight?" he whispers close to my ear.

"No. This is the first time we've spoken."

He leans back and grins. "That's because you're far more stunning than just beautiful. I can barely take my eyes off you."

"Ethan," I whisper and bow my head. "I can't—"

"I know. I just want to compliment a beautiful woman because compliments are good for the soul."

"They are," I admit. "Is this the part where I tell you that you also look handsome?"

"I think it is." He smirks.

He spins me, and when I land closer to him, I steady myself by gripping his shoulder and waist tightly, so I don't overbalance. After months in the jungle, it's taken me a while to get used to wearing heels again. I glance up to the footballers talking to Cleo, Yasmine, and Amy. Only Amy isn't listening. She's glaring at me. Or is it Ethan? I'm not sure Amy will ever let go of the animosity she has for Ethan.

"Thank you for the dance," I tell him when the music stops. "And for the compliment."

"The pleasure is all mine." Ethan grips my elbow and leads me back to my friends.

Before I say anything to Amy, I'm overcome with déjà vu. And how life is panning out.

The server walks by, and Amy takes a champagne glass from the tray in a swift action, downing half of it in one go. "You two were looking cozy."

"I just realized how easily I have slipped back to my old life, my old ways," I tell her.

"Too easily," she says and takes another sip without looking at me.

"It's not what I want. I don't want to be complimented on my fake dress and makeup that has transformed me to look desirable. I don't want this. I want Samuel… wherever he is. Until he's out of the jungle and can contact me, I need you to stop me from falling further down the rabbit hole of normality."

Amy looks me straight in the eye. "Challenge accepted."

"Will is here," Faith announces.

We turn to the doorway, where Will rushes in and makes a beeline for our father. With champagne in hand, both Faith and I walk over to my father.

"Happy birthday, Dad," Will says in a deep voice and holds out his hand.

Dad spins and ignores his hand, instead taking his son and hugging him in a warm embrace. They both pat each other's back before breaking apart. Dad holds Will by his shoulders and looks him up and down. "You look well, s-son." His voice cracks on the last word.

My dad is turning into a big softie.

And I couldn't be happier about it.

"Hey, bro, what about a hug for your sisters," I say.

Will turns to Faith and me and waggles his eyebrows. "Don't you both scrub up well, especially you, jungle girl," he says and winks.

42

EDEN

Four Months Later...

I'm sitting at home on a Saturday afternoon, a scarf wrapped around my neck and a blanket hugging my shoulders.

Rose lies on the carpet, a safe distance from the fire. "C'mon," I prompt her. "You can do it." I crawl to her right, and she rolls onto her belly. She slowly pushes up on all fours and takes the first few movements to crawl. "Yay." I clap my hands, and she beams her cheeky smile with the cutest two front teeth. "Daddy is going to be so proud of you."

Daddy.

It's now mid-July, and I haven't received any messages from Samuel. And my birthday is one month away, and I hoped he'd be here to celebrate with me. My heart aches for him.

Rose makes a cute sound, saving me from my dark thoughts. She rocks back and forth on all fours—something she has been doing for weeks—but today is the first time she has attempted to move her chubby limbs.

I wipe the drool from the corner of her mouth and assume at seven months old, more teeth will appear soon, especially since her cheeks have a red glow. As I take her hands, she pushes up onto her feet while holding my fingers for support. A giggle erupts from her as she bobs up and down. "You're too cute," I tell her and kiss her cheek.

Letting go of my finger, she balances with only one hand for support while I reach for my phone and pull up a photo of Samuel. I hold the image in front of her face. "Dada," I repeat. She giggles, and I say the word like a mantra. "He'll come to us soon," I tell her. But with every passing day, hope fades a little more, and I face the reality that we may never see him again.

My throat dries and burns. I do my best to shut the emotion down. "Dammit." I open my phone and send Asoo a message.

> Hi Asoo. I know it's a long shot, but have you heard anything from Samuel?

> Every day I worry. Every day I watch Rose grow, and I hate he's not here to see how beautiful she is. Is he dead or alive? Sick or healthy? Does he even want to leave and come find us?

Nausea hits me.

> I don't want to think the worst, but if something were to happen, I doubt I'd ever find out. If they died of starvation in the middle of the jungle, then no one would know. If they ran into trouble with mafia-type gangs and were held hostage or shot, would we ever find out? I'm lost and have no one to turn to for help because everything about the Ularans is secretive.

I swipe my cheek. I have shed so many for Samuel. I can't believe I have tears left to cry for him. In my heart, I want to believe he's alive and trying to get home to us. Only so many months have passed without a single word.

I have to face the truth that he may never come. I don't want a future without him, but the universe has set him on a dangerous journey, and all I can do is hope and pray he's still alive.

Even his parents don't act concerned, and they remind me he has done this before. They won't file a missing person report and told me to wait as he sometimes remains silent for eighteen months.

> I hope everything is good with you, and I miss you all. I miss Canaima. Below is a picture of Rose. Love to all xxx

I attach a photo of Rose in a pretty pink dress with a big smile on her face.

"Darling," Mum says as she enters the room. "Would you like to go out for dinner with me? Dad said he'd look after Rose."

I glance up from my phone and wipe my eyes.

"Honey, what is it?"

"Samuel." I shrug. "I just wish he'd send a message somehow so I know he's okay."

She lowers herself to the carpet and crosses her legs with ease, thanks to years of yoga. "It was around this time last year that I told you about Ivy." I nod. "Look how far you have come. We're so proud of you. You're a wonderful mother, and you work full-time." She gives me a serious look, and I'm unsure what her point is. "Last year you told me you wanted to study nursing."

"My circumstances have changed."

"They did, but I can see you have your life on hold, working a convenient job you're not completely happy doing to support you and Rose. You are waiting and hoping for the love of your life to return to you and *save* you."

Everything Mum has said is true, and every day it's easier to continue along the same path. I close my eyes slowly and open them to give myself a moment.

"Don't settle for second best." She rests her hand on mine. "You deserve more, and you don't need saving. You found yourself in the jungle. You can do it here too. Maybe you have to reinvent yourself or simply embrace the new you... the person you discovered hidden inside." She pushes strands of hair behind my ear. "You're beautiful and strong. Talented and passionate. You have learned so much from Ivy. Don't let it go to waste."

Chocolate brown eyes meet mine, showing me the warmth of an adoring mother. "I want you to promise me starting tomorrow, you'll focus on you. Take steps forward to secure a happy future for both your daughter and yourself. And before you say anything, I hope as much as you do that Samuel is safe and will come home to you. But whatever fate delivers, make sure you're prepared because Rose needs you more than ever."

I glance at my daughter as the words of advice sink in. "Yeah, she does."

"Those first days on arriving home, you said you were going to look for Brenda to find Gran's diary. Did you find her?"

"I hit some dead ends. And life became busy, so I stopped." I bow my head, realizing the promises I made to myself have slipped by.

"I might be able to help. Her husband's brother came into the esplanade café this morning where I meet Kate. Even though I haven't seen him for around ten years, I recognized him immediately. I asked about Brenda's health, and he said she's in a new care facility as her dementia has progressed. It's only ten minutes away. If you want to visit, I'll give you the name of the facility. If you'd rather let it go, then that's okay."

I need to act now in case something happens to Brenda.

"I want to see her," I say enthusiastically. After everything I read in Gran's diary, I now feel closer to Brenda.

Mum smiles as though I responded correctly. "Good. I can come with you for support."

Scooping Rose onto my shoulder, I hug Mum with my other arm. Rose coos with the delight of being in a group hug with her mother and grandmother. "This is for your great grandmother," I tell her. But I have a feeling their spirits have already met.

🌴

After arriving home from a dinner date with my mother, we hang our coats on the wall hooks before heading into the lounge to stand by the fire. Dad is sitting by the fire, his legs raised on a footstool with an empty red wine glass beside him.

"Is Rose asleep?"

"She fell asleep only half an hour ago. We had a fun night. Did you know she can now say, Pa?'"

"No way," I tease as I unwrap the woolen scarf from my neck.

Dad chuckles. "I knew she'd say it before Nan."

Mum rolls her eyes, and I can't help but giggle. "It's not a competition."

"Ah, but it is," he jokes.

"I'm going to join her because I'm beat. Night."

"Night, sweetheart. We're in for a storm, so I hope the thunder doesn't upset her."

"Me too. More the reason to get some sleep now."

After closing the bedroom door, I place my phone on the side table and then settle into bed. Minutes later, the screen lights up with a notification. A message from Asoo.

> Hello Miss Eden. Thank you for photo of Rose. Very beautiful. We not hear from Samuel. I sorry. We hear nothing. There is now a mine in Ulara. They knock down huts. Burn trees. So sad. We stay away. I know nothing more. I sorry I no help. I hope to see you one day. Not this day. This day not good. I hope you hear from Samuel soon. Your friend, Asoo.

Holding my phone to my chest, I'm lost for what to

think. Is no news good news? Not in my mind when I need hope to keep going.

I send a message to Amy and Yasmine, although I expect Amy to be asleep since she has an early start teaching tomorrow morning.

The phone vibrates with an incoming call from Yasmine.

"I've been speaking to Michael. I asked him by chance if he has heard anything from Samuel. He hasn't."

I let out a sigh. "Thank you for asking. I know you care."

"I do. And wish I could help more."

"It's okay. I'll be fine," I murmur. "I just hate not knowing."

"I know, babe. But I need to tell you something. Tonight, I decided I'm going to meet Michael in Peru to do the ceremony like I've always wanted."

Now upright in bed, I blurt out, "What?"

"I'm wiser and smarter, and he knows he's on his last chance. We've been talking regularly, and in my mind, I need to do it."

"Yasmine," I croak. "I don't want you to go alone."

"You're not coming with me," she stresses. "You need to stay here with Rose. Besides, someone might know something of Samuel. Michael speaks Spanish, so we can let you know if we hear anything."

"Thank you," I whisper and close my eyes. "That's kind of you, but I'm still not convinced you should travel alone. Group rules."

She chuckles. "Cute. You know I love you, right?"

"Yes. And I love you too."

"I have to go. We'll talk soon, Edes."

Placing my phone on the bedside table, I consider the

possibility of traveling with her. Only I'm not prepared to take Rose with me or leave her alone.

The best solution is to remain here patiently and hope every day I'm doing the right thing by not searching for the man I love.

Only my patience is measured equally by my stubbornness. Opening my laptop, I type out an email to the USA embassy in Colombia and explain my fiancé, Samuel McMahon, is in the Colombian jungle, and I'm afraid for his safety. I provide dates he was last in Canaima and how he's trekking through the jungle.

I'm sure they would be thinking, *WTF*?

I comment further, explaining I don't expect to hear from him, but I'm concerned he could be unwell or injured. Then I ask if they could check if he has been hospitalized or arrested as I can't communicate with him.

Being I'm in Australia and his parents are in the USA, I expect they'll be notified first of any news. I'm okay with that, but my point is the embassy needs to be alerted that he's a possible missing person.

43

Four Weeks Later...

The unopened email in my inbox from Samuel's parents offers hope. They are my closest link to Samuel since every place and person we know has led to nothing.

Dearest Eden,
Thank you for the photos of Rose. We'd like to Skype so we can see Rose, and she may come to recognize our faces until we can meet her in person.
One particular photo of you and Rose concerned us. You look exhausted. If there's anything we can do to help until Samuel comes to Australia, please let us know. If you need any finance for Rose's needs, please don't be embarrassed to ask for our help. Samuel would want us to offer support.

Regards,
Christopher and Caroline McMahon

. . .

For a moment, I don't respond. Why are they not concerned when their son's life is at risk? And *Samuel would want them to offer support.* Seriously? Wouldn't they want to offer support to their only grandchild?

I type out a reply.

Hello from Downunder,
I'm glad you enjoyed the photos of Rose.
Please don't be concerned. I assure you we're fine and don't
need any financial aid.
Regards,
Eden and Rose

No photo is attached because their email has left me disgruntled.

Maybe it's why Samuel lost contact with them over the years.

Pulling on my coat, I head out to the lounge room to where Mum and Dad are playing with Rose. She's walking sideways around the room, holding onto the furniture and periodically plopping onto her rear until she pulls herself up again.

"It won't be long before she's walking," Dad boasts.

Mum wraps a scarf around her neck. "I hope it's not soon because you'll be chasing her from room to room."

"I know, right." I watch her crawl to the barrier across the stairway and peer down. "No, Rose," I say gently like I do every other time, hoping she understands it's an out-of-bounds area.

"Good luck," Dad says and then scoops Rose into his arms. "I'll distract her while you two make a getaway."

Placing a hand on Dad's arm, I give it a gentle squeeze. "I love you."

His eyes meet mine with an understanding and appreciation of what Mum and I are about to do.

"We'll be back after lunch," Mum tells him and kisses him on the cheek.

We dash down the stairs to her navy Mercedes parked in the basement and crank the heating too high. Mum gives me one last look before reversing the car. "Are you ready?"

"Yes, so ready." Then I pull up the directions to the care facility to visit Gran's friend, Brenda.

The drive is mostly in silence until I direct Mum through a gated driveway and into a parking lot designated for visitors.

I pull my taupe woolen coat around my chest. We sign in and wait for someone to assist us.

After explaining the reason for our visit, the receptionist almost sent us away until she located a note from Thomas, Brenda's brother-in-law, alerting the staff we'd be visiting.

After assigning us sticky visitor badges, she leads us through two sets of glass doors and punches a code into the facility's locked doors.

We walk along a hallway and turn into another until we come across a large lounge area where families and friends are spread out on a dozen sets of lounges.

"If you head outside, you'll find Thomas sitting with

Brenda under a shaded tree. She loves the garden, so we take her outside every day."

"Her friend also loved the garden," Mum replies, and the receptionist nods even though she's clueless as to who Mum is referring.

We make our way across the freshly mowed grass to a garden brimming with colorful flowers lined with lavender. The aroma is delightful as is the rainbow of color. No wonder Brenda likes to come outside.

A bald man makes eye contact and then smiles. "Brenda, you have visitors. Remember Ivy's daughter-in-law and granddaughter?"

Brenda's gaze meets Mum's, and even from here, I can tell she doesn't recognize her. A lap blanket covers her legs, and a navy cardigan hanging loose over her shoulders and arms outlines her thin limbs. In a steady rhythm, Brenda picks at a loose thread in the blanket, her gaze fixed in the distance.

Thomas stands to greet us. "Ladies." He nods.

Mum hugs Thomas. "I'm not sure if you remember my daughter, Eden."

"Nice to meet you, Thomas. Thank you for allowing us to see Brenda," I say.

Thomas smiles. "Last time I saw you was when I was visiting Brenda and my brother, and Ivy called in with you and your sister. You were both under ten years old," he says affectionately.

"It's been a long time," Mum says and rubs my shoulder.

"Take a seat," he says and pulls two more plastic chairs into the circle. "Thanks for visiting Bren. There are days where she sees nobody. Both her children are interstate and visit once, maybe twice a year. She barely recognizes them, and her grandchildren are strangers to her."

"That's sad for her." Instead of sitting, Mum squats in front of her covered knees. "Hi, Brenda. Do you remember Ivy? I'm her daughter-in-law." Brenda hums a tune, seeming unaware Mum is even speaking to her. "We know how close you both were. You had some grand adventures nursing together."

Brenda's eyes flick over Mum's face before focusing on the blanket.

"I'm sorry. I thought there was a slight chance she might remember, but her dementia has progressed. She doesn't recognize anyone." Thomas pats Brenda's hand. "I try to visit once or twice a week. I can't handle that no one is here for her. But when you reached out, I wanted to see if she'd recognize you. For so many years, Ivy and Mum caught up. Mum would tell Ivy stories of her time nursing after Ivy had stopped."

"Yes, Ivy never continued nursing after returning from volunteering overseas. She focused on her husband and her son," Mum says.

I look at Mum, knowing it not to be entirely true since Grandpa forbade her from nursing when she came home from Ulara.

"Brenda," Mum says gently. "Ivy gave you a little notepad. Do you remember? It was a diary of her travels."

Brenda continues to hum, and I doubt she even knows we're visiting. A magpie's fluty song catches her attention. She stares at the branches of the gum tree and then fixes her gaze on me. For a moment, she stares at me, and then something crosses her expression, and she blinks slowly.

"Where have you been?" she asks me.

I hesitate before answering. "Umm, I've been shopping."

"Not to buy him more beer, I hope."

I give Mum a quick look, and she nods for me to continue. Is she talking about my grandfather? "No beer. Just some milk and bread." I shrug my shoulder at Mum.

"Talk about the diary," Mum prompts.

"I needed to buy more pens as I ran out of ink to write in the diary." I bend down so we're at eye level. "Did I give you a diary about the jungle?"

"You gave it to me the other day, remember?" She smiles at me. "Told me never to show anyone."

Shit.

I sneak a glance at Thomas and Mum, and they nod for me to continue prompting her.

"Yes, but I need to write some more. I have remembered what happened in Ulara when I had Dawn."

She reaches out for my hand. She squeezes it and gives me an empathetic glance. "My heart hurts for you. I'm sorry I wasn't there to help you through it."

With my other hand, I pat her arm. "I know. You're a good friend. Can you remember where you hid my diary?"

"Of course. In the bottom of my jewelry box is a secret compartment. Turn it over and push the two buttons together. The base will fling open. No one ever found it. Your secret is safe with me."

Air stills in my chest.

Double shit.

"Thank you. I'm going to borrow it, okay?"

She nods, and then her focus is back on the wayward thread of the blanket.

"Well done," Mum whispers.

"Guess we should see if it is really there," Thomas says.

"I'll stay here with Brenda," I say. Thomas and Mum stroll across the grass and disappear behind the double doors.

"I'm Eden," I tell her. "Ivy's granddaughter. Do you remember me?" Her eyes glaze over. "I loved hearing about your adventures when you and Ivy used to climb out of windows and sneak off to meet Albert and Jonathon." Pretending I'm Gran didn't feel right, and I don't want to confuse her. At the very least, I hope my words trigger fond memories.

"Ivy loved you," I tell her. "You were a great friend." I pat her hand again. "I saw Ivy's spirit in the jungle and got to meet Dawn, her daughter, although her name is now Kaikare. You would like her," I whisper.

The double doors open, and Mum steps out with Thomas. They scamper across the grass until they join us.

"Got it." Mum holds up an old tan leather-covered diary. The writing etched on the front is faint.

"Thank you," I tell Brenda. "I'll come and visit again soon and share stories of the jungle."

"Thank you again," Mum says to Thomas. "We appreciate it."

"If you don't mind, I'd like to come back and visit Brenda and perhaps remind her of the good times she and Ivy had together." I smile at Thomas.

"I think I'd like to hear those stories myself," Thomas says and laughs. "You know she saved my life. I had a heart attack at fifty-five, and she performed CPR until the ambulance arrived. It's why I visit regularly. After all she did for so many people, she doesn't deserve to be alone at the end of her life."

"Perhaps we can all meet here once a month," Mum suggests. "It will give Eden some time to read and absorb what Ivy wrote."

"And since I have read her other diary, I can remind Brenda of all the fun times they had together," I say affectionately.

Mum and I say our goodbyes and head back to the car.

Holding the diary in my hands, I flick the tainted pages like a deck of cards and close it again. "Now I have it, I'm not sure I'm ready to read it."

"It's there for you whenever you are ready." Mum turns her head and gives a quick smile before focusing on the road ahead. "You need to be first to read it even before your father. If some details need screening, then I'll leave it to your discretion whether to tell him."

"I think he's ready to know everything. He has to, for Gran's sake. I need Dad to be proud of the work she did and not think of her stay in the jungle as time lost with him as a toddler. There were many positives of her going to Ulara, and I hope Dad can also come to understand the importance of her journey."

44

EDEN

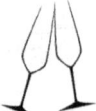

Most people loathe working on their birthday.

I'm no exception.

"Have a good day," Mum says and kisses me on the cheek. Rose whimpers. She's aware I'm leaving for the day, and I'm thankful today is a day she gets to spend with Mum. Mum lifts her onto her hip and leans in so Rose can kiss me.

"Mwa," I emphasize the sound. "Have fun with Nanna, gorgeous girl."

"We'll leave here around six and walk to The Shores. I've booked ahead to ensure your favorite seafood dish is available," Mum says. Rose holds her hands out for me, and I pretend to kiss each one. She giggles, and it's the best sound to warm my heart.

"Have you done something different with your hair? You look different today."

I shrug my shoulders. "Spent a little more time on my makeup trying to make myself feel special."

"My darling, you are special. I like it and think it

makes you look..." Mum hesitates. "You always look beautiful, but there's a glow about you today."

"Ha. That's because I was running around after missy here between finishing my makeup."

We both chuckle, knowing how Rose likes to have us chasing after her.

"It's your birthday. Accept compliments without blushing and feeling you don't deserve them." Mum smiles. "I know you, Eden. Say thank you and smile."

"Thank you and smile," I repeat, mocking her because we both know it will not happen. I laugh when she shakes her head and heads down the stairs.

I open the office door and, "Happy birthday to you," is playing from the computer's speaker.

"Seriously?" I laugh and can't wipe the smile from my face at the dozen pink helium balloons floating from the ceiling.

"Happy birthday," Dana sings and wraps her arms around me. "We have cake for morning tea so bring on ten o'clock."

"Ha, you're always thinking about food." My arms tighten around her back. "Thank you for cheering me up."

"You're welcome." She kisses my cheek. "I think we need to order in lunch for a proper celebration and have a bottle of bubbles."

"You sound like my friends."

"Happy birthday, honey." Dad squeezes me in an almost bear hug. "Your mum has everything under control for tonight."

The second he releases me, Ethan is hugging me tightly. "Happy birthday, Eden. Now you have caught up to me. I can verify twenty-six isn't so bad."

I groan loudly.

"Oh, please." Dana rolls her eyes. "Listen to you spring chickens." She claps her hands and almost stands between Ethan and me. "Let's get this work done so we can celebrate."

Picking up my coat, I place it on the back of my chair and fire up the computer for the day. I set my phone on silent and then scroll through my emails. My heart jumps at an email from Christopher McMahon, and attached is a response from the Colombian Embassy. "Finally," I breathe out the word, my hand touching the heart necklace on my chest, the one Samuel gave me. Only it's the shortest email stating that Samuel's visa is registered in Venezuela, and he hasn't left the country as far as they know.

It was dated only days after their last email.

I wonder why they waited to send it?

Below the attachment is a short response from his parents.

Please don't worry about Samuel. He's fine.

Is it polite to reply with *FFS, listen to me!*

Ugh. I move on to the next email.

Today is a stress-free day. I'll not spend it worrying about Samuel and whether he's alive or freaking dead because I need a day of peace. Head down, I focus on work and not the future.

Dana comes out of the kitchen area and leans her hands on my desk. "It's time."

"What?" I gape at her.

"C'mon, birthday girl, it's cake time." She runs her fingers over the material of her navy skirt as she stands and looks around.

Ethan strolls in with an oversized chocolate glazed birthday cake. The top is alight with as many candles as could fit. The office door swings open, and along with a gust of air, Yasmine and Amy stumble in as though they're blown in by the wind.

"What the?" I say and laugh.

"Dana said to bring bubbles." Amy holds up two bottles and grins at me.

"Dad is allowing this?"

As if summoned, Dad comes out of his office and checks his wristwatch. "Your mum, Faith, and Rose should be here any minute."

"Faith is just parking the car," Yasmine tells us.

I shake my head in surprise at my family and friends who are like family. "Thank you. I feel so special to have you take time out of your day to celebrate with me. I really didn't expect it."

"We know." Amy places a hand around my waist. "But we wanted to."

I lower my gaze. "I'm sorry I've been no fun for a while. But..." I meet all their gazes, "... it will change from today. It's not your job to cheer me up, but I'm so grateful because I can't keep going on like this." I convey an apology with my eyes. "Today is special, so thank you, and from now, my misery ends. I mean, I've been drearier than the damn weather."

Yasmine chuckles.

Everyone is smiling except Ethan. He is staring as though he's hanging off my every word, and my every word holds a silver lining. I'm not sure what to think, but I can feel his eyes beyond my skin to where he once owned a piece of my heart.

The door swings open, and everyone spins and laughs at how my sister and Mum, holding Rose, are swept inside by the wintery August wind. "What did I miss?" Mum asks.

"Eden's speech that she's going to be cheerier than the weather," Dana replies.

"Well, that's easy. It's mad out there."

"Is that a bad omen on my birthday?" I ask Mum. She looks at me blankly.

"Is it bad luck?" I question Dad.

"You have Gran's diary," Faith says, finger-combing her hair away from her face. "Start reading it because I'm sure she'd reference her superstition." She hugs me. "Happy birthday, sis."

"Thank you." I lean my head on her shoulder. "Thank you for coming."

"It was all Dana," she whispers. "She's one of a kind."

Dana comes to me and hands me a knife. "Time to cut the cake."

I make my way to the table, and before I slice the chocolate, she calls out, "Make a wish."

My first instinct is to wish for Samuel's safe voyage home. Only I stop myself and find my daughter now in my father's arms. I close my eyes as I slice through the cake.

I wish to have a long and happy life with my daughter.

Pop. One champagne bottle.

Pop. Another bottle and then laughter.

I turn to my father. "Have we clocked off for the day?"

"Yes." He raises his arm in the air.

"Happy birthday to me," I cheer.

After three hours of sitting around the office and celebrating my birthday, Mum and Faith leave. Yasmine and Amy had left only moments before them.

"Well, I'm heading off," Dana says and wraps her scarf around her neck. "Your father rarely does this, so I'm taking advantage of his generosity." She winks at me and then kisses my cheek. "See you tomorrow. Enjoy the rest of your day."

Dad's office door is closed.

Ethan is packing up his desk, so I do the same, hitting the buttons and closing the drawers a little too hard because the bubbles have gone straight to my head.

I lean down to get my bag and freeze when Ethan is beside my desk.

"Hey," he says and smiles.

"Hey."

"I bought you something but didn't want to give it to you in front of everyone."

"Oh. Okay." I sit then stand again when he doesn't move.

"I want you to trust me." He takes my hand and holds it like it's made of porcelain. He strokes my fingers, and even though I know I should yank my hand away, I don't.

"I do trust you." I mightn't want to, but I do.

"I like you, Eden."

I pull a face probably more dramatically than I should because of said bubbles. "I like you too."

"No. I *really* like you. Haven't stopped. I want you to give me a chance." His chocolate eyes filled with emotion

349

meet mine. I'm vaguely aware I'm gaping. "I'm not trying to spook you. If we could start with… say a dinner date, a picnic. Get to know each other again. I know we could make it work."

"It's too soon," I mumble. I go to pull away, only he grips my hand and turns it over. With his other hand, he places a box in my palm.

"Open it." He lets go and adjusts his tie, undoing the top button of his shirt.

Pulling at the ribbon, I flip open the box to reveal a sparkling diamond ring. Seven to be exact in the gold band.

"It's a friendship ring." He shoves both hands in his trouser pockets.

"With diamonds? I can't accept this." I close the box and hold it out for him to take.

Both his hands remain in his pockets, and he rocks gently back on his heels. Ethan shakes his head. "It's yours. Take it and leave it in the box. Think about it. You don't have to wear it. It's just a gesture of our friendship to show how much you mean to me. If you feel the time is right, then wear it. Then I'll know and might get the guts to ask you out on a date."

I gawk at him.

He's afraid to ask me out.

Since when?

"Happy birthday, Eden." He kisses my cheek and scoops up his suit jacket with his fingers, holds it over his shoulder for it to drape down his back.

He gives me a nod before stepping outside.

The door clangs shut with a gust of wind.

I flop back in my chair and flip open the box.

Do I say no because I'm still praying for Samuel to come to me?

No. I promised myself I'd stop.

I pick up the ring, turn it side to side. The diamonds sparkle under the light.

How does something so tiny cause my chest to tighten like I'm wearing a corset?

45

EDEN

It is not a commitment.

The following morning I'm holding the ring between my fingers, afraid to slide it on in fear, like *Frodo,* I'll disappear. Not my physical self but the person I've become—the person I'm finally content to be because of Samuel. I'll never forget him, but I can't hold out for a man who wants to live in another world. One that doesn't include me.

"It's not a commitment," I murmur for the tenth time.

A symbol of friendship, but the moment I slide the diamonds on my finger, it's a green light for Ethan to ask me on a date.

Is it what I want?

No.

But I'm refusing to dwell any longer.

For months, I have waited and waited and hoped and prayed Samuel would come out of this alive and then be so overjoyed he'd head straight back to LA and sort out his visas to come to me.

What fairy tale am I living in?

There are many scenarios, and as much as I want to think of him alive, my hope is fading every day. In one of the last honest conversations we shared, he told me he didn't want to return to society. He's miserable living a privileged life, and by my own foolishness, I believed that would change, and he'd be happy if Rose and I were with him.

Every day my vision clears and shows me Rose and I aren't enough. He loves us, but to do so, *he* forfeits happiness. Then there's that loyalty to the Ularans he can't let go of. Only now do I realize giving up all that he worked for, all that he believed in, could break him and send him into a depression like he was in years ago.

For a year, I have compromised my happiness to do what's right by Samuel. I have changed for the better. I'm a better person for knowing him, learning from him, and being with him. Now the anxiety from fear of hearing they can't find him is destroying me. I can't continue to beat myself around any longer.

I need to be prepared mentally for any news.

Gran's leather diary is by my bedside table, and yet, I haven't opened it in fear it will completely undo me when I'm already hanging on by a thread. I expect the truth about Kaikare will be revealed. Already I can picture Gran in our jungle home—Rose's first home.

I thought I'd run out of tears by now.

We'll never see Ulara again.

Never see our friends.

Samuel.

Squeezing my eyes shut, I try to stop the tears believing Rose will never see her father again.

The real possibility I'll never see the love of my life again.

Stop.

I have to focus on new beginnings.

Keeping my eyes closed, I hold my breath and take a giant leap and pray to the universe that, like Froddo, I don't disappear.

🌴

Grabbing my coat and scarf, I head into the kitchen and say goodbye to my mother, then head down the stairs without waking Rose.

Inside our office, I fire up my computer and wait.

Ethan should arrive any minute.

Reaching for the glass of water, I knock over the container of pens and groan when they scatter across the floor.

What's wrong with me?

The door closes with a thud, and I jump. On my hands and knees, I peer up at Ethan grinning at me. In a brief second, I'm admiring the blue printed shirt and navy tie with his beige pants. His hair is styled, and those big brown eyes find me.

He raises his hands, and he's still wearing that damn smirk. "I'm not saying anything."

"Good." I gather the pens one by one.

He chuckles loudly. "Why?"

"Why what?" I stand and adjust my pencil skirt and white shirt that has come a little untucked.

"Were you on all fours? I'm not complaining. You looked bloody hot down there." His brown hues bore into me, telling me exactly what he's thinking.

"I was picking up the pens I knocked off the desk," I blurt out.

"What has spooked you?" His expression changes, and his gaze lowers to my hand. When his eyes meet mine, recognition settles in. We stand in silence, considering each other, and I'm aware of my heart thumping against my chest.

So, this is it.

My new beginning.

Not knowing what to say next, I say, "Hi."

In two quick seconds, he's beside me, lifting my hand and bringing it to his lips. "Hi, you."

I smile. "Little steps." It's all I can manage for now.

He nods, his eyes not wavering from mine. Keeping hold of my hand, he says, "To friendship."

"Well, we better get back to work before Dad walks in." I pull out my chair and scroll through my emails, doing my best to concentrate on the screen in front of me.

The moment Ethan logs onto his computer, the door swings open, and Dad closes it behind him with a little extra force. "Damn wind," he grumbles. He glances at Ethan and then at me. "Morning."

"Morning," we both chime together.

Ugh, could we make it any more awkward?

His brow raises enough for me to notice before he turns his back, and then his office door closes behind him.

I let out a breath as though I am a kid hiding a chocolate bar under the table. Unclasping my fingers, I lift them from my lap and continue to type.

"I cc'd you in an email to the city council," Ethan says without looking at me. "And I have three quotes from three construction companies I'll forward to you."

Glad it's business as usual.

Dad's door squeaks as it opens. He stands so the door

conceals half his body. "Dana has called in sick. She said to check your email."

"Right. Thanks."

Dad begins to close his door until a noise has his head jerking toward the office entrance door. The wind blasts it open along with my mother hanging onto the handle and stumbling inside.

"Grace?" Dad's eyes widen as Mum swipes hair out of her eyes.

"Eden," she says out of breath.

I jump up out of my chair and freeze, seeing Mum's frazzled face.

"Is it Rose?" I snap. Every second feels like minutes anticipating her answer.

She shakes her head.

"Close the damn door, Grace," Dad grunts just as the wind blows loose sheets of paper over my desk. "There's a damn storm brewing over the ocean."

Mum spins toward the door but doesn't close it. A man with a buzz cut is bent over as he stumbles inside. He straightens, and I realize he was protecting a bundle in his arms.

Rose.

He looks down, admiring her. Rose has her arms out for me. My legs become weak, and I lean on the desk, unable to take another breath.

"He knocked on the apartment door looking for you," Mum blurts out and pushes the door closed.

Blue eyes meet mine. Even more beautiful without the blond hair framing his face. A face gaunter than the last time I saw him, and yet still as handsome as it was the day we met.

My legs find the strength to move, and he opens one

arm for me to collapse into his side. Burrowing my face into his chest, I sob uncontrollably. "I'm so mad at you. I didn't think I'd see you again." I lightly thump his chest without lifting my head from the wet patch I've created against his tailored black suit jacket.

Then my arm is around his back, squeezing him so I know I'm not dreaming, and he really is alive.

"Mumma," Rose babbles and taps on my head.

I manage a single laugh and lift my face.

Samuel wipes tears from my eyes, then taking my chin, he lifts my face so he can lean in and kiss me. "I promised I'd come find you," he says against my lips. Then he kisses me again.

He smells woody as though the scent of the forest is ingrained into his skin. His minty breath mingles with the salt from the tears that have streamed down my face and onto my lips.

"I've missed you so much," I whimper.

Leaning my head against his chest, I hug him again. Realizing we have an audience, I straighten and lightly dab my cheeks.

I focus on my father. "In case you don't realize... this is Samuel," I rasp.

"I met your mother when I went upstairs," he tells me. He nods at Mum, and she has the goofiest expression as though Samuel's charm has already bewitched her.

Dad strides over to Samuel. "I'm Winston Monteford. Glad you finally found your way here."

Samuel unravels his arm from my waist and takes my father's hand to shake. "Samuel McMahon, and it's good to finally meet you."

Samuel turns to Ethan with his hand outstretched.

Ethan's gaze flicks to mine, and I smile through happy

tears. He gives the slightest nod, and I take it as an understanding between us. "Ethan. I'm a friend of Eden's."

Thankfully, I can't see Samuel's face.

From my position, there's a quick handshake before the men step apart.

Samuel turns to my father. "Sir, I'm exhausted after flying over twenty hours to get here. Do you mind if I whisk my fiancée away for a couple of hours before I fall asleep?"

Dad's eyes widen, and then he clears his throat. "Certainly."

I'm tucked under Samuel's arm. He guides me to the door, where Mum has a permanent smile etched into her expression like she's the joker. She pulls open the door.

"Ready to face the storm?" Samuel asks.

In here or outside, I don't care because right now, my body is warmed as though it's the middle of summer.

"Yes. Always yes, as long as it's with you."

Thank you so much for reading Samuel and Eden's story. Their story continues in Perfectly Wild.

PERFECTLY WILD
Blurb:

My experience in the jungle taught me how fate tested the balance of life and to never become complacent.

I thought returning to modern civilisation would be okay because we have each other.
That our love would be enough.
That our family would be enough.

A perfect love.

Only Samuel is no ordinary man.
And the jungle calls to him.

In my heart, I sense I'm losing the battle.
I have to find another place for us to belong that doesn't threaten our lives.
Because a love like ours is worth fighting for.

Fate has no idea what I will do or how far I will go for love.

Next book in the series
<u>Perfectly Wild</u>

Keep reading for other books by Leesa Bow.

To find about about new books, and sales, please sign up to my newsletter.

ALSO BY LEESA BOW

www.leesabow.com

ACKNOWLEDGMENTS

First and foremost, to my husband, Lynden. Thank you for your encouragement, love, and support of my writing journey.

To my four beautiful daughters, Jamie-Lee, Shauni, Ashleigh, and Demi, for providing constant inspiration. To my wonderful parents, Pam and Vic, and my sister, Vickie, and her family for believing in me and helping in any way possible. Cam, Charlie, and Cruise, I'm grateful that you all are now part of our family and supporting me.

A big shout-out to my friends and biggest fans. Mum, Deanne, and Helen, Dayna, and Alison for believing in me from the day I decided to give authoring a shot. Your love for my story gave me the confidence to take a giant step forward.

To all my friends, and readers who have have been with me from the beginning while I wrote from my heart, I'm thankful every day for your support. To Aunty Brenda for her nursing expertise, and helping with the diary notes, and nursing in the 1950-1960's. To my cousin Jodie, an awesome midwife, thank you for your advice.

To Kim, at Blogging for the Love of Authors, and to Kellie J, thank you both for your encouragement, and words of wisdom, and for reading my story in its raw stages.

To Kaylene Osborn at Swish Design and Editing. Thank you for all your expertise, for answering endless questions, and for making my book shine. Most of all, for calming me when I message or call in a state of panic. You are my rock! And a big thank you to Nicki!

To Lauren Clarke at Creating Ink. You moulded my story into a piece of art, and I'm truly thankful.

To Letitia Hasser at RBA Designs, thank you for my beautiful cover. You nailed Samuel!

My appreciation extends to my Facebook reader group, Leesa Bow's Lovelies, and all the blogging community for helping to get my book out to the world. You all make the book world a much better place. A special thank you to Ena and Amanda at Enticing Journey Book Promotions and all the blogs and bookstagrammers for promoting Beautifully Wild.

To my author friends, who I've chatted with while writing this book. You have been with me from the day I decided I wanted to publish my story. I can't express enough gratitude for all your advice and inspiration. To Nina, Maggie, Jen, Beth, KE, and Jodi you always have my back, and I appreciate you all! To RWA and Yon author group, and all the authors whom I've met at signings, you are my writing family.

To Carol, Kellie, Robyn, Jen, and Megan, thank you for beta reading my story and helping me refine it. You are awesome. And to Carla M for all the information about Venezuela.

To my readers. Thank you for your endless support, and most of all, for loving my stories. Some of you have been with me from the start of my author journey, and to others, I'm a new author. What I love most is you all embrace my characters and stories and love them as much as I do. Thank you for reading, reviewing, and talking about my books to your families and friends in book clubs and blogs.

I appreciate everything you do for me!

ABOUT THE AUTHOR

Best selling Australian author, Leesa Bow writes alphas with a fierce determination to win, and the women who will push for them to fight harder. She is known for her steamy sports romance and her latest adventure romance.

Leesa lives in sunny Queensland, Australia. She spends her spare time with her family, and catching up with girlfriends for coffee or a wine.

Leesa loves to keep fit with pilates, and yoga, and keeping the fun with laughter in her life.

She loves nothing more than to curl up with a good book, and a glass of South Australian wine.